Life Unexpected

Book Two of the "Unexpected" Series

Jodie Lemmert

Copyright © 2021 Jodie Lemmert All rights reserved

The characters and events portrayed in this book are fictitious. Any similarity to real persons, living or dead, is coincidental and not intended by the author.

No part of this book may be reproduced, or stored in a retrieval system, or transmitted in any form or by any means, electronic, mechanical, photocopying, recording, or otherwise, without express written permission of the publisher.

ISBN - 979-8-9853490-2-3
ISBN- 979-8-9853490-3-0

Cover design by: Jodie Lemmert
Printed in the United States of America

Life Unexpected

Chapter 1

"Hey Karla, what are you doing awake?" Owen whispered in my ear after he stepped in my room. "It's almost four in the morning. I went to get some coffee and found it had already been made and then looked down the hall and saw your light on."

"I have to finish some client files. What are you doing up, Owen?"

"I just got called out, there's a group of kids that went rock climbing out at Hallett's Peak and didn't make it back, I shouldn't be gone too long."

"Owen, you realize we're getting married in a few days."

"I know, can't wait." Owen said, chuckling as he kissed the top of my head. "I gotta go. There are kids out there. Love you."

"Love you more. Be careful, Owen." I called out to him as he rushed down the hall.

I heard Owen shut the back door and drive off as I sat looking at our engagement picture I had sitting on my desk. I met Owen just over a year ago. At Eide's insistence, we got coffee one morning after church, and aside from Garratt deciding to rent my house out it has been a momentous year.

Garratt was renting my house out on a home share site when I traveled for work, which created quite a bit of stress, to say the least but as they say, God sends his best angels, and that he did. Owen showed up and has been here ever since.

As I sat here looking at our engagement picture, I noticed how the photographer captured Owen and me in the morning light nearly a month after Owen proposed. Owen woke me up early on the morning of the Fourth of July, which was also my birthday, and arranged for our family and friends to meet us at sunrise to go to a favorite little spot of ours up in the mountains. When I said yes, they all came out, surrounding us in giant sparklers. It was so awesome. But enough musing for now, I decided. I could sit staring at this picture all day. I had to get my butt in gear or there would not be a wedding this weekend; plus, Owen and I still had to find a place to live. Ty wants Owen to move back to his hometown and be more active in their Flight School business, which just so happens to be about five hours away, in West Creek. Owen and I agreed we would not move until after the wedding. We have been looking for a place to live and have not found one, yet.

I felt my phone buzz, indicating an incoming text message, I figured it was Owen texting me they were ready for takeoff; me not so much. I was never ready for Owen to head off into parts unknown for the Rescue Center; today was not exception.

"Hey Karla, you awake?" It was Eide, I realized, picking my phone up.

"Yes. Is Toby keeping you awake?"

"Yea, but what's your deal?"

"I was working on client files and then Owen came in; he got called out and I've been sitting here trying to get my butt in gear."

"Should Owen really be going out this close to the wedding?"

"No, but he can't say no. Some kids went out rock climbing and did not make it back last night. He can't say no to that."

"That guy, he'll get back just in time to leave, if that."

"I know, I'm trying not to think about it."

"I can't believe he's quitting that job and you guys are moving, leaving us lowlifes back in the hood. Okay, I'll leave you to it, talk later."

"Give my nephew a kiss, talk later."

I always like texting Eide during her early morning feeds with Toby, who was born about a month ago. In true Grainer fashion, Toby came early and has had something to say ever since.

Eide always seems to know when I am awake and thinking. I finished the client files I was working on and sent them off later that morning. I used to work for a large firm in Denver and traveled almost weekly to client firms all over, providing marketing assistance, which was a convenient opportunity for Garratt to rent my house out. I had made several major changes recently; and taken on some local clients since opening my own online firm. It was working out well and I liked it a whole lot more than flying off to some client's office every Sunday or Monday, and I sure enjoy spending the extra time with Owen.

After I finished with the client files, I sent emails out to my clients letting them know that I would not be available until after the wedding. Eide, Mom, Molly and I planned to go down to Owen's parents on Thursday to decorate and set up the barn. Owen's parents have this magnificent barn out back of their house that opens to a hayfield with a large corral setup. The barn is truly a sight to see. Owen's dad has been working on planes in there for many years, so the center of the barn makes for a perfect gathering spot. Owen took me to his parents' home last Thanksgiving, and I went out there a few times, Owen showed me around. *I fell in love with it almost as much as Owen.* I thought, chuckling to myself. There may have also been a few moonlight walks or, as Joe proclaims, "I didn't need the exercise and Owen just wanted to kiss me," but hey, I wasn't complaining.

I decided I would get a jump start on packing while I continued to wait for Owen's return. Owen had already been gone a good five hours this morning. I had never gotten completely used to him being gone with the Mountain Rescue team when he flew out, but it's what he does. He's always gone a varying amount of time, so I never know when to expect him back. I just pray for his safe return and try to keep myself busy and my mind occupied. The first time he flew out on a rescue while I was in town, Owen and I were up in the mountains having lunch when he got the call. He wanted to take me home first, but I convinced him to take me to the hangar and I would call for a ride; I watched for a little bit while Owen and his team prepared to fly out. I didn't see Owen for over twenty-four hours. Things really sunk in, and I started to worry about him even more. Arnold, Owen's spunky dog and I had a stressful night waiting for him.

That afternoon I had our luggage packed, the wedding décor organized, yet again and I checked my list to make sure I had not missed anything and decided to clean up the house a bit.

Once I had finished cleaning up the house, I noticed Owen had been out just over twelve hours and still no sign of his return. This was not the longest he had been gone; but still makes me worry about him and his team all the same, especially since this morning Owen thought he would not be gone long. Owen usually never talks about the time he spends out in the field. He usually just reassures me upon his returns that he is okay. Many times, he would just go to bed. I had decided long ago it wasn't so much to recharge his batteries, but his heart.

Putting my worried thoughts aside; I text Eide to see what the rest of the Grainer clan was up to and see if we could meet up; I could stand for a little Toby time.

Everyone else must have had the same idea cause when I texted her, she said Granny and Grandpa Grainer were in the house! Lane and Molly were on the way with pizza; and she wanted to know why the Kasters hadn't sniffed out the party.

Lane and Molly pulled up outside Levi and Eide's house the same time I did. Lane picked up several boxes of pizza from the backseat of his pickup.

"Hey Kar, how are ya?" Lane asked as turned from the back seat, closing the door.

"I'm good. How are you guys?"

"We're good." Molly said.

"Where's Owen?" Lane asked.

"He got called out early this morning and I haven't heard from him since—such is life, engaged to a hunky pilot." I chuckled.

"He'll be back anytime." Lane said as he half-hugged me, nearly dropping the pizza boxes.

"Yea, I know." I said as we walked through Levi and Eide's front door.

"Where's Owen?" Dad asked watching us all file into Levi and Eide's living room.

"He got called out early this morning—I thought it would be a quick trip but guessing that's not the case anymore. So, where's the little guy?" I asked. "He's really the only reason I came."

"Ah well, you're gonna have to fight Granny Grainer over there for him." Eide said, nodding her head in Mom's direction. "She snatched him up practically before I had a diaper on him the minute she got here."

"Mom!" I exclaimed. "You baby thief, my turn, the favorite aunt is here."

"Oh, I suppose I can share, but only for a little bit. You ready for the wedding?" Mom asked as I took Toby out of her arms and sat back on the couch snuggling in, taking in the sweet-smelling baby. "You've got the cutest little dimples, don't you?" I asked Toby, smiling at him.

"Eide, it sure is a good thing this baby takes after you." Lane joked as he sat down with his plate of pizza next to Toby and me on the couch. "Who would want an ugly mug like Levi?"

"Ah, you bro." Levi said. "You forget, you and I look quite a bit alike?"

"I'm definitely the better-looking brother." Lane joked.

"I don't know." Mom said. "I think Toby looks cute in his own way."

"Ah Mom, you're just a little biased." Lane joked.

"You're good with things for the wedding then, Karla?" Eide asked.

"Yep, as good as it gets. We'll decorate Thursday afternoon with Rosie and Elaine and maybe Rachel if she's available."

"Rosie and I don't plan to join in the decorating events." Mom mentioned casually.

"Oh, okay. You're still coming with us, right?"

"Yes." Mom said. "Rosie and I've decided we're taking on grandkid detail. You girls get the hard work."

"All right, all right. I get it." I said, chuckling. "You two good with that?" I asked, looking in Molly and Eide's direction.

"I don't really think we have much choice." Molly said, laughing.

"Yeah, your mom's already practically kidnapped Toby more than once since he was born, so why should this time matter." Eide joked. "Besides, I have some fantastic ideas for decorating this barn."

"Great, I was counting on it, Eide. You're the best at these things."

"How's plans for your wedding coming, Molly?" I asked.

"Oh, great. My mom already has plenty of white lights ordered for the church. She just keeps ordering them and then orders some more." Molly said, holding her hands in the air, looking annoyed. "I think she has enough lights to land planes at DIA."

"I'm telling ya, hon, we should elope." Lane joked. Lane has forever joked with Molly about eloping. I think he thinks if he says it enough, it'll stick. Molly, on the other hand, has always handed it right back to him.

"That would be a hard no, Lane Grainer. I keep telling you, honey. I'm only here for your money and this wedding is going to be the highlight of your Christmas, sweety." Molly joked back with Lane.

"Don't worry about your mom." Eide told Molly. "We'll just hide the lights; we'll make sure that church is beautiful. Your mom has some ordered now?"

Yes, way too many." Molly said annoyed.

"Good, go grab 'em. We'll string them in the barn rafters for Karla and Owen's wedding."

"Oh, nice." I told Eide. "I like how you think."

"Ah, no. I don't think you gals should be hanging lights from the rafters." Dad said, sounding concerned, creasing his eyebrows.

"Not a chance." Levi concurred giving Eide a concerned look. "No rafters, you want lights up there, you need help."

"Good, I think you just volunteered." Eide told Levi, chuckling.

"Yea, Levi, I think you just volunteered for the job." I said, joining in Eide's chuckling.

"Don't look at me, I'm no electrician." Levi said.

"Looks like they're going to make you one." Lane chimed in.

"Why don't you both help them?" Mom suggested. "Darren, you can help, too."

"Huh, what?" Dad asked, nearly taking a bite of pizza but held off. "What do you mean, 'help them?' We're not even leaving until Friday."

"Well, now you're all leaving Thursday, like the rest of us." Mom announced.

"Uh, well. I don't know about that." Levi said, stuttering.

"I do." Eide said. "Thanks for helping out, guys."

"Yea, thanks for helping out." I said, smiling at Levi and Eide's banter.

"What did you just get us wrapped up in brother?" Lane commented snidely.

"This is great, thanks guys," I said, picking up my buzzing phone.

"Hey Karla, just got in, need to put some equipment away and clean up, be home soon. Hope you haven't worried too much. See you soon. Love ya!."

"Good to hear from you, love you, too." I replied to Owen's text as a flood of relief evaporated from me.

"Okay, y'all. I just got a text from Owen. They made it back, so I'm going to go home and get him something to eat before he goes to bed."

"Why don't you just take him a pizza." Lane offered. "There's plenty."

"Actually, that'd be great, thanks Lane."

"Ah, that's good to hear honey, glad he's back." Mom said. "Now give me that baby back."

"Mom, you need to share, maybe Molly would like to hold him or even Lane." I said, laughing.

"Don't look at me." Lane said. "I break those things. I just look from a distance, and they still cry."

"Oh, come on." Molly said, nudging Lane. "He's so cute and cuddly. Yes, I will take him."

"Lane's right, we should just let him look from a distance." Levi said. "I don't want him corrupting my son at such an early age."

"Don't worry, bro, he was corrupted the moment you set eyes on him—poor little guy doesn't stand a chance." Lane said, laughing in Levi's direction.

"All right, everyone. Thanks for the laughs, I gotta go." I said picking up a pizza box. "See you Thursday. Meet up at Owen's at seven a.m." I said hesitantly, waiting for someone to complain.

"Uh well, that's a little early for me." Lane whined.

"You'll survive." Molly said as she knocked him playfully in the arm.

"Thanks guys, love ya." I said, going out the door.

By the time I got home, Owen was already there and showering. I set his pizza on the counter and started a pot of coffee.

I peeked in the bathroom door. "Hey Owen, you, okay?"

"Yea, how are you?"

"I'm fine, brought ya some pizza."

"I'll be out shortly."

I went back to the kitchen and checked the coffee and grabbed a couple cups from the cupboard to pour us each one.

Owen came up behind me as I was pouring coffee and wrapped his arms around me, gently kissing my neck. "Hmm, thank you, you read my mind."

"So, how was your flight? I didn't think you'd be out this long the way you talked this morning."

"Well neither did I. The family thought they knew where the kids were; but they must have tried to get out and that didn't help things. It was a little harder to find them."

"Did anybody get hurt?" I asked Owen, thinking he might tell me little more about his time away.

"A little, but everybody will be fine."

"Are you hurt?"

"No, I'm all good. Ty called me while I was out and left a message. I'm going to the couch and send him a text while I drink this coffee and then I'm going to bed, is that okay?"

"Of course, do you want some pizza?"

"No thanks, I'm good. I wouldn't say no to you joining me on the couch." Owen said smiling before taking a drink of his coffee.

"I'd love to."

"Where were you at tonight when I got in?" Owen asked as I followed him to the living room. "Did you get any sleep last night? You had me a little worried when I got ready to leave and you were already up this morning." Owen asked me before I had a chance to answer where I had been.

"No, I didn't sleep well last night and so I decided to get up and finish my client files, so they were done for the week. After you left, I finished them up and looked for a place for us to live."

"Oh, yea? Any prospects?"

"Yea right, about an hour away and not exactly anything I'd consider a home. There just doesn't seem to be anything available."

"Don't worry, Karla. Gods in control." Owen assured me, yawning, and patting my leg.

"I know, we'll figure it out.

"This afternoon, I texted my family about going to see Toby. So, we all met up and had pizza and talked about the weekend. Owen, you're falling asleep; why don't you go to bed? Did you text Ty back?"

"I wanted to hear about your day."

"We can talk tomorrow; you should go to bed."

"Yea, I suppose. Thanks for the coffee. Karla. Love you." Owen said, getting up from the couch and walking toward the bedroom.

"Love you more." I told Owen just as he slipped into the bedroom. I was grateful Owen was home and could get a good night's sleep.

Early the next morning, I was lying in bed contemplating what I needed to do that day. I was also thinking a cup of coffee sounded great. I'd checked my list yesterday but still felt I was missing something; perhaps I'm overlooking something. I should check it again; I should not have everything ready this close to the wedding. I didn't figure Owen would be up for a while; he was out on that rescue for over eighteen hours. I gathered that one or some of the kids they went after got hurt. I finally decided to get up, flipping the blankets off. I grabbed my robe and went to the kitchen to get some coffee and check over my list. I was surprised to see the kitchen light on when I went down the hallway. Owen was sitting at the table staring at a cup of coffee when I reached the kitchen.

"Hey, Owen, good morning. Are you okay?"

"Good morning, hon. I'm good, how are you?" Owen said, yawning.

I could see he had clearly not slept enough. His hair disheveled and the circles around his eyes were darker this morning than they were last night. "I'm surprised you're up this early."

"Well, I probably wouldn't be. I intended to text Ty last night and then I didn't, and he called me back this morning."

"Oh, what's up with him?"

"He's working on a new insurance policy for the Flight School and wanted to talk it over with me. He wants me to come down and sign some papers this afternoon. What do you have planned today?"

"I was actually coming out to check over my list now, but there's no worries, you can head out today. I'll just catch a ride with Mom and Dad and meet up with you tomorrow."

"No, I want you to go with me." Owen said, taking a hold of my hand as we were sitting at the table. "I told Ty to put your name on the forms, too."

"Owen, that's you and Ty's partnership."

"Don't question this, Karla, this is what I want. So, will it work for you to leave today?"

I grabbed my list and looked it over. "I'm not really sure what needs done today. I packed for us yesterday. Eide and Molly are coming to help decorate and set up tomorrow—we had a whole big discussion about that last night, I'll tell you about that on the way. So, yea, after we load, I say let's go."

"Thanks, Karla, you're the best." Owen said, finally smiling a little.

"Yeah, yeah, don't mention it. You're just getting coffee and breakfast burritos on the way out, you know."

"Absolutely!" Owen said. "Anything for you. I am going to see what you packed for me. And then I'll load the pickup."

Chapter 2

"Hey, Owe. Hey, Karla. How was the drive down?" Ty asked Karla and me when we got out of my pickup after Karla parked in front of the bank. "Glad you could make it this afternoon. Hope I didn't totally mess up your schedule for today, Karla." Ty said, looking over at Karla kind of hesitantly.

"We're good, this is important for you guys."

"Well, Owe wants you involved, too. Did you guys discuss this on the way down?"

"No, not really. I was still asleep when you called this morning, Ty. I'd just gotten in from getting a few kids who tried to go rock climbing and didn't make it back the night before."

"Oh geez, I'm sorry, you should have said so, we could have figured this all out another time."

"It's okay," I told Ty as I thought about all this walking into the bank. I wanted to add Karla to my share of the Flight School partnership, and we were starting with this new insurance that Ty and Rachel found plus a few other things that had recently come up.

"Okay, well, we can hurry. Rach can explain this to both of you way better than I could."

"Hey, Rach." Ty said, walking into her office.

"Hello, how's it going?" Rachel said, standing up from her desk. "Please, have a seat. How was your trip?"

"Ah boring, we got a ridiculous amount of coffee before we left town to keep us awake; only this one didn't stay awake for much of the drive." Karla said, chuckling and pointing at me. "It's the only time I've ever seen a cup of coffee turn cold on him."

"How are things coming for the wedding?" Rachel asked, chuckling at Karla's coffee comment. "Sorry we had to do this today."

"No worries." Karla said.

"Well, I'll be there to help you and your friend's tomorrow afternoon." Rachel said, sounding excited. "I'm looking forward to it. Ty and I were out there a couple weekends ago when Ty picked up some plane parts from Joe. This is going to be a great wedding, that barn is fabulous."

"The guys are coming to help now, too, Eide wants to string lights in the rafters and Mom sort of volun*told* my brothers they'd be helping us." Karla said, chuckling.

"Ah yea, you gals don't need to be swinging from the rafters in the barn." I told Karla.

"Funny you should mention that—Levi and Lane had the same reaction and shortly thereafter Mom wrangled them into helping."

"That's good, we'll get 'em hung for you."

"Well, let's get down to business so you guys can get out to the farm and see your folks." Ty said, breaking into all the wedding talk.

"Yea, that'd be great. Thanks, Ty."

"Okay, so here's the new policy I found for you guys." Rachel said, displaying a few documents across her desk.

"It's an all-encompassing policy: it covers hangar/property, aviation, aircraft. Your flight training facilities, some aircraft maintenance. Ty doesn't really like this component; I guess there has been some trouble. But the policy doesn't expand on what maintenance is needed."

"What kind of trouble, Ty?" I asked, interrupting Rachel.

"A few students have been careless—mostly cosmetic damage, and your dad's been taking care of it, but I think the policy should cover it. Rachel says probably not."

"We can try it, Ty. I'm not the underwriter so I'm not sure." Rachel said.

"Perhaps we should start with a policy change for the students." I said, looking at Ty for verification. "Some sort of class fee when they start, damage deposit, that sort of thing. If everything is good when they're done with the classes, they get it back."

"It's sure something to think about." Rachel said, referencing back to her paperwork. "The rest of the policy has to do with medical coverage."

"What kind of medical coverage?" Karla asked.

"This is actually pretty decent coverage." Rachel said. "It's medical coverage for students and Flight School staff in the event of an injury. There is a small stipend in the event of a death during an accident, but there's better coverage in the life insurance policy that's associated."

"Well, let's not get ahead of ourselves." I said, chuckling. "This isn't the Rescue Center."

"Oh, you guys will be fine." Rachel said. "Just take care of the rowdy ones and keep the aircrafts maintained and you're all set."

"You good with all this, Ty?" I asked, glancing up at Ty who was standing beside Rachel on her side of the desk. Ty looked way too comfortable next to Rachel in her office; he must stop by a lot.

"I am if you are. I think Rach did an excellent job with this. I trust her on it, and our policy needed renewed the first of the month, so I know it's bad timing with your wedding and all."

"No, it's all good. Business is business."

"Thanks, man." Ty said, slapping my shoulder. "How about you, Karla?"

"We're good, Ty, I'm excited for this, too." Karla said. "You just can't monopolize all his time."

Karla was truly an amazing woman; Ty talked to me the night before I proposed to Karla about coming back and being a more active partner at the Flight School. After I proposed to Karla, I talked to her about moving back down here. She never once hesitated; she practically jumped at the idea—she said, "let's do it."

"Do you guys need a plane for your honeymoon?" Ty asked smirking.

"Um, yea." I said, holding back the smirk that was surely slipping onto my face. "If you could spare one for a few days, that'd be great, thanks."

"No problem, you guys know they're at your disposal anytime. And hey when you get back, I'll help you with the move."

"Well, that sounds like an offer we can't refuse. Thanks, Ty. Thanks for all this, too. Rachel, thanks for getting it organized." I said, motioning a hand across the paperwork.

"Yes, thank you, Rachel, we appreciate it. Everything you guys have done." Karla said. "We'll see you both tomorrow?"

"Yep, we'll be there." Ty said.

"Well, that wasn't so bad," I said as we got back in the pickup. "I'm not really good with this side of the business."

"It wasn't so bad for ya, and plus, sounds like it should save you guys some money." Karla said.

"Ready to go to the farm?" I asked Arnold, backing away from the bank. Arnold picked his head up off the seat and barked, then stood and put his front paws on the console and stretched out.

"All right, I'll take that as a yes. Let's go, buddy."

"How's the music coming?" Karla asked me as I drove down the highway out of town.

"Music? What music?" I asked, smirking. "I can turn the radio on if you'd like."

Quite some time ago, Karla was stuck on what to do for music for our wedding. She already had a lot on her plate; and I thought *hmm, how hard could it be to pick out a few songs for a wedding?* I think that was an underthought; no wonder she was stuck, I had a tough time trying to find songs that fit us, but I finally got there.

"Owen, seriously? Stop teasing me."

"Oh, but it's so fun. Your ears get bright red."

"Owen."

"Yes, that's my name, let it shine!" I said, flashing a smile.

"So, what are we having for music?"

"Tupac, NSYNC, Cowboy Troy: how's that work for ya?" I said glancing over at Karla.

"Nope, better rethink your plan."

"Don't worry, I've got good plans. Just you wait and see." I said, driving down Ma and Dad's driveway.

"I don't even get a little preview?"

"Hmm, nope."

"Hey, you two." Dad said as he stepped out of the barn. "We didn't expect to see you until tomorrow."

"Yea, we took off a day early. Ty had some paperwork he wanted me to sign for the Flight School."

"Oh good, getting back into things already. When are you guys going to be down here full-time?"

"Probably in a few weeks. Ty's anxious, he'd have me here next week if he could."

"You guys find a place to live yet?" Dad asked.

"No, we keep looking but there's not much available. I keep telling Karla that God's got this, we just have to let him do his thing."

"That's absolutely right!" Dad said, patting me on the back. "In the meantime, you can stay here with your mother and me."

"We know, Dad, Karla and I talked about that."

"How are you, Karla?" Dad asked.

"Great, Joe! How are you? You ready for us to take over everything this weekend?"

"For sure, for sure. I got the barn all cleaned, took most everything over to Erving the last few days. May need to take a few more things tomorrow depending on what you need for space to set everything up, but we'll see."

"That is so nice, thank you, Joe. I'm sorry we weren't here to help you sooner." Karla told Dad.

"It's no big deal. It was a good thing; it got me in gear to go through everything in there. I found things from nearly forty years ago. I got rid of all my calving stuff; some plane parts that I haven't used in umpteen years."

"That's nice of Erving to let you store everything over there, Owen's told me about him. Would you be sure and introduce him to me sometime? I'd like to meet the man that Owen terrorized as a teenager." Karla said, laughing.

"Hey, come on, I'm right here. I did not terrorize him. Ty and I just ran a few go-karts through his hayfield."

"I think he lost a few hairs over your and Ty's teenage years." Dad said, smiling.

"You told me he liked it when Ty and I rode out there."

"He did and don't you tell him I told you that." Dad said, his smile turning into a chuckle.

"Hey, Dad, where's Ma? I thought she'd be out here by now."

"Bible study—she abandons me every Wednesday night, remember. Makes me cook, even makes me do my own dishes and never leaves me any pie."

"Oh, you poor baby. I forgot Ma has that. How about Karla and I take you into town for supper tonight and save you from your own cooking."

"Anything so I don't have to do the dishes." Dad muttered. You kids don't have other plans tonight, though?"

"No, Dad, we didn't even plan on getting here until tomorrow. So, come on, let's go."

"Well, Karla, you might just be in luck," Dad said as he parked at the Burger Barn. "Looks like Erving came into town for supper tonight, too; that's his pickup parked over yonder. You can meet him tonight." We stepped into the door and Erving was standing at the window ordering his food and Dad walked up behind him.

"Hey, Erving, I got a young woman that would like to meet you."

"Oh, geez, Dad."

"Hey, Kaster, what are you up to tonight? You got more stuff you want to hide at my place?" Erving asked, laughing.

"Yeah, maybe in the morning. My kid's back in town for his wedding, remember. His wife wants to meet you."

"Who could forget about this wedding, Kaster, seems that's all you've talked about for weeks."

"Erving, this is Karla." Dad said, ignoring Erving's comment about the wedding. "The young gal brave enough to marry Owen."

"Thanks, Dad." I said, shaking my head. *I should not be surprised at the things that come out of his mouth*, I thought. "Did you get your meal ordered, Erving?"

"Yea, I just placed it."

"Let's go take a seat, the kids will finish up here," Dad said.

"Ah well, I haven't paid yet," Erving said, looking into the window, prepared to give someone his money but there wasn't anyone standing there.

"That's okay." Karla said. "We'll take care of it—apparently, we owe you, for hiding all Joe's things."

"Yea, Dad. What's he hiding for you?" I asked, laughing when Dad and Erving moved away from the counter. Shortly thereafter the clerk returned to the window. We told her to add Erving's meal to our order.

Karla and I grabbed the burgers and fries and went to join Dad and Erving. Karla passed out the burgers and fries from the tray.

"Thanks, Karla." Dad said.

"Yea, thanks, Karla." Erving said.

"So, Owen, your dad tells me you're moving back here after the wedding."

"Yea, in a few weeks, as soon as we find a place to live. Ty wants me to come back full-time at the Flight School."

"Oh my, you and Ty together again." Erving said, shaking his head. "I thought he got rid of you."

"More like I got rid of him." I said, joking. "I've been living up north doing mountain rescue; but Ty went and beefed up the Flight School."

"Yea, that's what your dad said; you moved to the big city. Well, it'll be good to have you back." I just shook my head and chuckled. I could about imagine the discussions these two have shared since I have been gone.

"What about you, Karla, how'd Owen convince you to quit your job and to come back down here?"

"Oh, I didn't quit my job—well, I did, months ago. I started an online marketing firm. I'm growing my client base in the area, so I'm good with this move."

"Sounds like you kids got everything planned out."

"Well, I hope so. What about you, Erving, what have you been up to?" I asked.

"Oh, nothing much for an old man, getting older by the day. Still got a few cows, and some horses. I don't know why I haven't gotten smart like your old man over here and taken them to market. Sometimes I think they're more trouble than they're worth. But they give me something to do."

"How's Ann and Katy?"

"Oh, they're so good they don't even come home anymore. Katy's up in Denver and Ann's over in Durango; both nearly married like yourself."

"Oh yea, that's nice. Tell them I said hello."

"You going to be over in the morning with any more loads, Kaster?" Erving asked Dad while he crumpled up the wrappers from his burger and fries.

"Ah, not sure. Might get Owen to help me with a few things. There are somethings I was debating about and was going to wait and see what the womenfolk were thinking with the wedding plans. But since Owen's here early, we might just knock it out anyways."

"I don't mind helping—that is, if Erving doesn't mind hiding some more things at his place." I said, laughing,

"No, no. You guys come over anytime you need." Erving said, getting up from the table.

"Thanks again, Erving." I told him as he was about to walk away.

"Yes, thank you." Karla said. "Are we going to see you at the wedding?"

"Oh, yes. I'll be there. Too bad Ty couldn't be here tonight, would have been nice to give him a little grief, too."

"He'll be at the wedding—he's cooking all the meat, so you'll know where to find him." I said looking up at Erving as he stood by the table.

"We'll see you kids later. Talk to you later, Kaster."

"All right, Erving." Dad said.

"What are you hiding over at his place. Dad? Seems Ole Man Erving is pretty interested in all the things you've been trucking over to his place."

"Huh, just you wait, Owen, when you've had a place for forty years, you'll accumulate a massive amount of junk, too. I got rid of some stuff, but I had to have a place to go with quite a few things at least until next week. You guys ready? Your mom should be about home, and she'll wonder what happened to me."

The next morning Dad and I loaded up his pickup and my pickup with things to haul over to Ole Man Erving's barn. When Dad and I backed up to Erving's barn and started unloading things, Erving came walking across from the shop looking our pickups over.

"Morning, you two." Erving said gruffly.

"Hey Erving." Dad said.

"Morning, Erving."

Erving helped Dad and me finish unloading the pickups and then we stood at the back of Dad's pickup visiting.

"Say, Owen, you said last night you and Karla are moving down here after the wedding?" Erving asked.

"Yea, probably in a few weeks."

"Hmm, I thought that's what your dad told me. Where ya gonna live?"

"Good question." I said, shaking my head. *This conversation seems to be running on repeat. I thought.* "Karla and I've been looking but haven't figured that out yet. Might be camping out in the folks' backyard for a while." I said, laughing and slapping Dad on the back.

"Hmm, well, that's quite the conundrum you got going there, don't ya?" Erving said, looking at Dad.

"Oh, we'll be fine." I told them.

"No, I was talking to your ole man." Erving said, laughing.

"Yea, he'll be fine, too. I'm going to head back to the farm. Thanks, Erving."

"Yea, see ya later, Owen."

Chapter 3

Owen and his dad had been cleaning up in the barn that morning and Rosie and I started working on some flowers. Rosie had some great ideas for corsages and boutonnieres, so we quickly assembled them. We were able to finish them up just before lunch and got some sandwich fixings ready before my family got here. Owen and Joe came in just as we had finished.

"Apparently, we're all done carting things over to hide in Ole Man Erving's barn." Owen told me, laughing.

"What makes Erving think you're hiding all that stuff over at his place?" Owen asked his dad.

"Oh, your dad probably told him something along those lines." Rosie said. "They're always bantering back and forth, ya know."

"Have you heard from your family—are they about here?" Owen asked.

"Yea, Lane's texted three times. Claims he's lost since we ditched him yesterday and one text mentions they've crossed over into Mexico."

"Ah, well, that's entirely possible," Owen said. "I'm not even sure GPS can assist getting anyone out here."

"He'll be fine, he's a big boy. I'm sure Eide's directing them. We'll give them another hour and then we'll send the posse out after them."

"Karla, come on, I'll call them."

As soon as Owen started dialing his phone, I looked out the kitchen window. Mom and Dad were pulling into Joe and Rosie's yard.

"Hmm, I do believe Lane Grainer might have been exaggerating a bit, don't ya think? Told ya, Owen." I said, as we all walked out onto the porch.

"Hello." Joe and Rosie said in unison as Mom and Dad started getting out of Dad's pickup.

Joe went over to my dad's side of the pickup and shook his hand. "How was your trip?" Joe asked.

"It was a nice drive." Dad said. "Been years since I've been down in this part of the state."

"Any problems?" I asked. "Where's Lane?"

"He and Molly rode with Levi and Eide; he just hasn't got out yet, why?" I looked over and Levi was sitting in the driver's seat of their Suburban, wearing aviator sunglasses looking like he was some sort of professional driver. I half-expected him to get out and peel off a faded leather jacket.

"Oh, he sent me three text messages; claims you all got lost since Owen and I ditched you guys yesterday."

"Oh please, Owen gave us great directions." Eide assured me. "Lane just got bored coming down; I tried to get him to change Toby's diaper once; he just whined about it and claimed he's allergic to diapers."

"It's a wonder he didn't proclaim he'd break Toby." I said, laughing.

"He did." Eide said, taking her sunglasses off and looking over towards the barn. "Oh wow, Karla, you weren't kidding about that barn. The pictures you and Owen showed us do not do that barn justice. It really is magnificent. This is a great venue for your wedding; even if we had to drive into uninhabited land to get to it."

"Are we ready for a wedding?" Rosie asked Mom as Eide, and I continued talking about the barn and wedding details.

"Thank you for having us, Rosie; I told Karla before she left, we were on grandkid detail, we were going to leave the hard work to them."

"I know, I like that idea, Laurel. Let's go inside, we've got lunch all ready for us."

We all migrated into Joe and Rosie's house. Rosie directed everyone through the sandwich line we had set up earlier and then took a seat at the tables after everyone made themselves a sandwich.

As we sat down to eat, Joe asked everyone to join him as he offered a blessing over the meal. "Bless us, Lord, for bringing our families together this weekend. May we shine in your light as we become a united family between your children, Karla and Owen. Watch over all of us as we walk in your faith to carry out their wedding vows. Bless the meal we are about to share together as a steppingstone, Amen."

And with that Toby must have decided he was going to say the first Amen, because he let out one shockingly loud wail.

"I guess somebody didn't like the three-day car ride, either." Lane joked.

"Ba ha ha, three-days, please." I heckled back at Lane.

"I'm pretty sure we've ended up somewhere south of the border." Lane said, laughing at me again.

"So, Owen, Karla, what's the plan for this afternoon?" Dad asked between bites of his sandwich.

"String lights from the rafters!" Eide joyously chimed in.

"Are you sure you're going to get away from the choir member long enough to direct traffic?" Lane asked jokingly.

"Yes, he'll be fine. Granny Grainer's on deck." Eide said, gently tapping Toby's nose.

"Yes, I got a bunch of white lights that were intended for our wedding." Molly said. "I'm thinking we may just forget to take them down on Sunday."

"Elope!" Lane said slyly in a fake cough.

"You better watch it, Lane Grainer!" Molly fired back just as quickly. Molly knew just when he was about to pull his eloping joke and always had a comeback.

We all finished lunch and headed out to the barn just as Ty and Rachel parked by the barn with the trailer of tables and chairs, we had borrowed from the civic center.

Owen and Ty, and Darren and Joe started unloading the trailer and setting up tables and chairs.

I don't know how Eide managed to direct two events at once but by late afternoon the barn had been totally transformed under Eide's direction. I was very thankful for her vision: round tables set up symmetrically around the barn, and a dance floor erected at the back of the barn that would spill outside into the moonlight. My favorite part was where Owen and I would stand with the minister and exchange our vows, the space that divided the dance floor and dinner tables. Owen and I would stand under an arch and the wedding party would line down the sides to join us as we exchange our vows. Eide planned to cover the arch in white and yellow sunflowers. I could not wait for all this.

Joe interrupted my musings with his announcement that he was going to go fire up the barbeque, my dad told him he would go along and help. Eide said she should go check on Toby.

It seemed as if everyone else cleared out just as fast, leaving Owen and me alone in the barn.

"Hey hon?" Owen asked, sliding his arms around my waist, kissing me heatedly with such passion. "Hmm, that felt great, I've wanted to do that all day."

"Oh, well, I'm glad I could reward you accordingly, you guys did do all the demanding work."

"Yea, she tells Lane to move one more strand of light, he just might string her up." Owen said chuckling, holding me in his embrace.

"I think Ty might agree with him. It's kinda funny, though."

"This is going to be a wonderful wedding, Owen."

"Are you kidding me?" Owen said, looking deep into my eyes before kissing me again. There was so much fire in his soul, I thought I would lose all sense of feeling. "The best part's right here." We stood there holding each other for a moment, not needing to say a word, just sharing the quiet moment we'd both waited for all day. Owen quietly whispered in my ear, "I love you."

"Hmm, I love you, too." I said as I backed out of Owen's embrace and Arnold came bumping into us.

"Hey buddy, what are you doing here?" Owen asked, scratching his head. Arnold looked thoughtfully at us with his big, beautiful eyes.

The next morning, everyone seemed to descend on Rosie's kitchen early. She thought she didn't have enough coffee when Owen came home; well, this weekend might become a national emergency with all the Grainers in tow. Rosie set out a continental breakfast and everyone went their separate ways.

Eide, Molly and I planned to meet Elaine and Rachel in the barn later this morning to decorate the tables. Rosie and Mom held their ground about being on grandkid duty. Owen was taking Lane and Levi to Ty's to meet Max and get the meat ready for the meal. Darren and Joe seem to be unaccounted for; but I guess if I were them, I'd disappear too.

After lingering over our coffee, and cleaning up Rosie's kitchen, Eide, Molly and I headed out to the barn. We started with putting tablecloths on. We already had a few tablecloths situated according to Eide's specifications when she slumped down at the table at which she was working. "Oh, seriously Karla, why did I introduce you to Owen in the first place?" Eide said, mumbling and pounding her fist into the table. I could see tears starting to glisten her eyes.

"What?" I asked.

"Oh, you and Owen, you're perfect for each other." Eide said, slapping a tablecloth across the table. "But now he's dragging you all the way down here. I never should have introduced you two," Eide said nearly sobbing. "What was I thinking?"

"Hey now, this is a happy occasion!" I said, hugging Eide. "Let's put the water works away."

"It's gonna be okay." Molly said, moving over to console Eide. As she put her arms around us.

"Of course, it will." I told Eide. "Besides, If I remember correctly the day you wanted me to meet Owen, you told me you were tired of taking care of me."

"Yes, I know I said that. I didn't mean 'not wanting to take care of you' in the sense you feel the need to move five-hours away. I don't even know where down here is."

"Owen and I talked about it. I told Owen he had to fly me back. I promise, we'll be back for lots of visits." I said standing next to Eide.

"Hey ladies, is this where the party's at?" Rachel asked, stepping into the barn.

"Hi Rachel, did Elaine come?"

"She did, she picked me up. She just took the kids up to the house; she'll be out shortly. She has some boxes in the back of her car we could go unload, though."

"Oh, nice, she mentioned she had some things we might want use." I said, following Rachel out to Elaine's car.

Eide followed me and started picking items out of the box Rachel had picked up. There were tall marquee lights that said "LOVE" in another box.

"These are awesome!" Eide said, looking in the boxes as Rachel and I carried them in. "I know just where we're going put them."

"Take it away, Eide." I said, handing her a box.

We all went back to getting the tables ready. I had little sunflowers and small electric candles to set in small rustic candle holders for centerpieces. The barn was really starting to look fantastic. I could not believe Owen and I were going to be married here tomorrow— it sometimes made me think I was just dreaming.

"Hey, all." Ty said as we all walked into his garage that afternoon. "You ready for all this?"

Ty asked me, giving my shoulder a nudge and a sly-look, *I wondered when he'd take the plunge.*

"I've been ready, more than ready. When are we gonna do all this for you? When you finally gonna cash in at the bank?"

"Hmm, hmm, you'll never know," Ty said, smirking. "We're doing great, but not running any races, just enjoying each other's company. I haven't run off to meet her in San Francisco, yet."

"No, you just keep showing up at the bank every afternoon around four o'clock, huh?"

"Maybe something like that." Ty said.

"Thanks for doing all this, by the way. Really made it easy getting all the food and catering logistics figured out."

"Are you kidding? This is all pie in the sky." Ty said pumping his arms in the air.

"Any idea what we should do about these careless kids at the Flight School? You think a deposit situation will work?" I asked, taking the plastic wrapping off the roasts we were about to season.

"We should definitely implement a new policy of some sort." Ty said.

"You got any ideas?"

"No, but if we sit down together, I'm sure we can hammer it all out."

"What kinda of seasonings you got here?" Max asked Ty.

"Oh, I've got all kinds."

"I've been using some I found at the little meat market in the village, I should have brought them. Nice little place, going to miss it after we move back here. They have some great cuts of meat, nice quality too."

"Last time I was down there, I heard it was closing." Lane said. "The owner's kids don't have an interest in the business and he's ready to retire so he's going to close the store."

"Oh, no way, man. That's really going to leave a void down in the village."

"He probably got wind you were leaving town and knew his business was going to go downhill and decided it was time to close up shop." Levi joked.

"Ha, yea, I've always liked that place."

The next morning, I stepped out on the porch after grabbing a cup of coffee. Karla was leaning against the railing holding her cup, watching the sunrise. I walked up behind her and placed my hand around her, leaning my chin on her shoulder. "Good morning, beautiful!" I said, kissing the side of her neck. "How are you this morning?"

"Great, how are you?" Karla said, turning around, smiling beautifully at me.

"Wonderful, know what I get to do today?" I asked, taking Karla's hand.

"Hmm, gee, I don't know, Owen, what do you get to do today?"

"I get to marry the love of my life."

"Oh wow, sounds pretty exciting, do I know her?"

"Hmm, maybe?" I said, kissing her again. "Want to take that coffee for a walk?"

"Only if you're going." Karla said, smirking back at me.

Karla and I walked down to the corrals and into the hay field. So much had happened since last Thanksgiving, but my heart grew full of so much more love in the year that followed.

"I'm surprised we could sneak away so easily; I would have thought somebody in a house with that many people would have been up." Karla said. "Even your parents get up earlier than this."

"I think they may have been up; they just hadn't made it out to the kitchen." I told Karla. "Everybody's probably preparing for tonight?"

"I guess, but it's not like were planning a barn burner!" Karla said.

"Oh ho, just you wait." I said, taking a drink of coffee. "You thought Levi and Eide whooped it up when they got married. You've never been to a wedding in Kaster country, we've been known to kick up our heels a time or two."

"Kaster country—my, my, what have I gotten myself into?"

"Yep, this is your country now, too; 'cause as far as I'm concerned, you're a Kaster now."

"This sounds pretty serious, Owen."

"Owen, your parents have done so much work getting ready for this wedding; your dad working on the barn, your mom, my goodness, she did a total landscaping makeover of the yard. I didn't think of all the work they would go to when I said I wanted to get married here. We need to do something for them; but I'm not sure what. I was thinking about that, standing on the porch before you came out: your mom took such great care with all the beautiful fall flowers out here."

"I know, it is nice, and we'll come up with something. Ma and Dad were happy to help us; we saved a ton of money having the wedding here and that means a lot to them. If nothing else, we could always give Ma a few airplane rides and she'd be delighted."

"Owen."

"What, I'm serious, she hasn't gotten many of those recently. We'll think on it and come up with something nice for them."

Eide, Molly and I were getting ready that afternoon in the bedroom I had been staying in at Joe and Rosie's. We had all the dresses laid out on the bed in garment bags; waiting to be revealed.

"All right." Eide said. "Let's see this dress. I can't believe I didn't get to help you pick it out, darn bed rest."

"Oh, you're just jealous because you didn't get a final say."

"Well, maybe a little; and to top it off, you've kept it under wraps since you bought it."

"I haven't seen it either." Molly said.

"What?" Eide asked looking at Molly perturbed. "How come you didn't take her?"

"She says she got called to work." I said, looking skeptical at Molly.

"So, nobody's seen this dress?" Eide asked, sounding floored.

"Nope, I think she purposely got called into to work somehow. So, it was only Mom and I that picked out the dress, I brought it home and put it away. We'll be lucky if the thing even fits."

"Oh, come on, you'll look fabulous." Eide said. "Just pull the thing out, already."

I picked a simple gown. I knew being in the barn I did not want a long flowing gown or a train to have to contend with. I pulled a tea-length dress out of the garment bag and held it up. It was a V-neck dress with lace down the arms, just in case the late September evening air became cool; but otherwise, the dress was a clean, simple cut. There was a small diamond opening in the back of the neck. I held the dress up to me and turned around for Eide and Molly to see.

"Oh, wow. You did great." Eide said, picking up the arm of the dress, holding it out for a better look. "I love this. These sleeves are going to look great with your sunflower bouquet."

"She's right." Molly said. "Let's get you in this thing and see the whole package."

After Eide, Molly and I finished changing and getting our makeup and hair done; they left me and went down to the barn. I was there in the room with my own thoughts. Owen and I were supposed to wait for the designated picture time. I didn't really like waiting here like this, so I decided to text Owen. He may have only been a few doors away, but it was fun.

"Hey, Husband-to-be…"
"Hey, Wife-to-be…How's it going down there?" Owen replied.
"Oh, great! I think. Just keep me away from flammables, I think Eide sprayed a tank of hairspray in my hair, it may take me days to get it out." I added an emoji of a woman with flames coming out of her head just for fun.
"LOL! That's okay, I love you and your hair, no matter what happens to it."
"Good to know, 'cause it's not moving anywhere, anytime soon, that's for sure. Should we escape? Not real excited about this part."
"Me either!" Owen texted back. *"I don't like sitting here all alone, waiting. It's weird."*
"I know, it's our wedding, let's just go, now." I replied to Owen's text. This is our day; we can decide when we escape.

I stepped out in the hallway; to find Owen already standing there with his back to me. He was wearing tight-fitting jeans that sculpted his backside, a sharp white dress shirt and a charcoal tuxedo vest. "Hey, good-looking!" I said, walking up behind him, sliding my thumbs into his belt loops.

Owen took my hand, twirling me around, looking me over. "*Hello*, gorgeous. And here I thought you looked smoking in every other dress I have seen you in, oh wow. You know you'll never be able to take this off."

"Well, maybe I'll take it off later tonight." I said, mysteriously.

"You just want to have your way with me." Owen said, flashing his million-dollar smile.

"Hmm, you never know." I looked up at Owen with a slight smirk emerging. "Let's get married first, shall we?" I asked, taking Owen's hand, leading him down the hallway.

Chapter 4

Karla and I walked out to the barn where everyone had gathered, and many others were still arriving. Karla looked so gorgeous walking next to me as we headed down to exchange our vows. I had taken many walks with Karla in the last year or so but this one just might be my favorite.

"You guys, why are you together?" Elaine asked when she noticed Karla and me walking towards everyone.

"We're getting married. Last I checked she was on board with it."

"I know that ya dork." Elaine scolded me. "I mean now, before the pictures. I wanted to take pictures of you seeing her in her dress for the first time."

"Yea, we know." Karla said. "We don't care, our wedding. We had our moment together, without everyone watching."

"Isn't she good?" I said, smirking and pointing over to Karla.

"That's fine, but we should have gotten it on camera." Elaine said.

"We're good!" Karla said, smiling at me. "We're not soon to forget this day."

"Here, you want your moment?" I asked laughing. "Get your camera ready," I slide my arm around Karla's back, tipping her over in a flurry of passion, amid cheers.

"Oh wow, Owen!" Karla exclaimed, holding onto my shoulder for balance.

Shortly after our "moment," Lane and Levi came over, picking Karla up. "All right, picture time." Lane said.

"Is this the pose you two clowns want?" Karla asked, almost giggling, her head tipped back.

"Yep!" Lane said. Elaine grabbed a shot of Lane and Levi holding her on their forearms.

Owen took his place under the sunflower arch, with the minister near the LOVE marquee signs like we had rehearsed last night. We did not have a regular rehearsal dinner last night. The minister stopped by, and we visited for a while. Owen and I decided to forgo the formalities.

I stood just outside the barn doors with my dad. I noticed Arnold come wandering in the barn and took a seat next to Owen, he stood there like a statue looking like he knew he belonged there.

I could not help but laugh. "Dad, look!" I said, point out what Arnold was doing.

I noticed Owen lean down and talk to Arnold; they even shook hands and I heard laughter coming from up front.

"I guess Arnold thinks he's going to marry you, too." Dad joked.

Owen's niece, Caity, started walking down the center of the barn, scattering white sunflowers, and his nephew, Luke, carried the ring bearer pillow under Eide's direction. These two were adorable and took their job very seriously.

Eide and Ty, along with Molly and Todd left to walk down the aisle to join Owen and the minister at the sunflower arch.

Eide had told Dad and me to wait a few moments as she left her directing post.

"You look nice, Dad." I said when he took my arm in his.

"Yea, kinda surprised I didn't end up in a cobalt blue suit today."

"Well, no worries here, but you better be careful come December; Lane might have something up his sleeve."

"That kid, I tell ya." Dad said shaking his head. "He's going to torture poor Molly."

"Ah, Molly can handle him; she just feeds it right back. Shall we go?" I asked Dad. We started our way down the carpeted path. "Thank you, by the way."

I stood there at Dad's left side, slowly walking towards Owen in his charcoal vest, matching Ty, and Todd, listening to a song telling us "This is it, The Moment we'd all waited for." *It really is the moment we had waited for.* I thought. And Owen looked downright handsome.

Dad and I finally walked up to Owen; Dad held my hand out to Owen, and he stepped off to the side to wait for the minister to start.

"Thank you, sir." Owen told my dad, taking my hand.

"I think you're even more beautiful than when I saw you earlier." Owen whispered as we turned and stood under the arch to face the minister and prepared to say our vows.

"Good afternoon." the minister greeted everyone. I was having a hard time paying attention as I stood beside Karla, holding her hand entwined in mine. We had finally made it to our wedding. It had been a long road getting here, but I was grateful for every moment we had had and would have together.

The minister said it was time for us to share our vows. *Well, here goes nothing.* I thought, turning to face Karla.

"So, when you asked if we could share our vows today, I would have rather gotten Arnold here to say the vows for me. He is acting today; he probably would have done it. He's up here acting like he's marrying you." I pointed to Arnold lying at my feet. I heard a chuckle from everyone witnessing our vows. "I wanted to make you smile, Karla. I love seeing you smile. Am I right?" I said, gesturing at her beautiful smile as everyone laughed again. "See here's the deal, I didn't know how to put into words how I felt, and the other morning, after I got called out to work. I was driving along, and this song came on the radio, something about being speechless. It reminded me of a few things and got me thinking. I picked you up for several dates or to go to church, and one morning you came rushing down the stairs. You grabbed the door and ran back upstairs, you hollered back, 'I haven't put my makeup on yet.' Well makeup or no makeup, you looked great. When you came strolling back down the stairs, I was the one who was speechless. I could not even get my brain in gear to form one coherent thought. Your hair, your smile, the dress you were wearing that morning, you, just everything. I will forever have that morning in my memory. I was blessed you were going to church with me—me of all people, and I thanked God many times for that. I still do. You are the light of my life, Karla, I hope I get to enjoy many more 'speechless' moments with you."

"Karla, I have prayed for you even before I met you and when I did meet you, you lit up my soul with your smile. You are the most beautiful person, inside and out. As my bride, you hold my attention now and forever. It is my greatest joy to become your husband today and guide us faithfully under God's hands and wisdom, every day. I promise you today, as God and our family as my witnesses, to love God, love you, and protect our family and make you smile always, it makes me speechless."

"Owen, wow. Thank you!" I whispered, wiping back the tears that were fighting to escape. "I'm not so sure I can top that. Maybe we should just get straight to the 'I dos.'" I said, which ensued a round of laughter.

"Nah-uh." Owen whispered, flashing his million-dollar smile at me. "You're up."

Looking into Owen's deep, dark, gorgeous eyes. I began. "I once read somewhere that God sends his best angels to those in need, disguised as friends. I did not even know I needed an angel, let alone a friend. I got the best of both worlds when you came along. I see so many good things in you. You share the joy in my heart, and I live for the moments we cannot put into words. I love you more every day, Owen. I cannot wait to see what God has in store for us on this journey we call life. In First John Four: 12-15 scripture reads: *'No one has seen God at any time. If we love one another, God abides in us, and His love has been perfected in us. By this we know that we abide in Him, and He in us, because He has given us His Spirit. And we have seen and testify that the Father has sent the Son as Savior of the world. Whoever confesses that Jesus is the Son of God, God abides in him, and he in God.'*

"Thank you for letting me see him in you every day. I have seen God shine through you on countless occasions. I know we live in an imperfect world; and I promise to learn from God's guidance as you do daily to grow in his wisdom. I promise to give you the life and love within me; I love you with all my heart and soul, you're my rock, Owen."

We stood there holding hands, looking into each other's eyes like nobody else was around. I could have stayed like this forever. Owen truly was the light and love of my life. The minister spoke up just then, interrupting my thoughts.

"Karla mentions God sending angels in need. In Hebrews 13: 2 scripture it reads: *'Do not forget to show hospitality to strangers, for by so doing some people have shown hospitality to angels without knowing it.'* Psalms 91.11 scripture reads, *'For He will give His angels charge concerning you, to guard you in all your ways.'* God will instruct his angels to watch over his charges and give each of His angels a purpose, to guard those in need. Those who are faithful will be under the constant care of His angels, just like Owen and Karla.

"The apostle Paul compared the relationship between husband and wife to that between Christ and the church. Marriage is the choice of two individuals to share the life of Christian love described by Paul in I Corinthians 13:4-8: *'Love is patient, love is kind. It does not envy, it does not boast, it is not proud. It is not rude, it is not selfish, it is not easily angered, and it keeps no record of wrongs. Love does not delight in evil but rejoices with the truth. It always protects, always trusts, always hopes, and is always ready to endure whatever comes. Love never fails.'* Two lives, shared with this kind of love, can hold more fulfillment and happiness than either life alone."

"Owen, are you ready to enter into the sacrament of marriage with Karla, believing the love you share and your faith in God and in each other will endure all things? If so, say, 'I am.'"

"I am, with all my heart." Owen said, looking deeply into my eyes. Owen was holding my hands, smiling at me; I felt as if no one else was around, just Owen and me sharing in this moment.

"Do we have the ring?" the minister asked looking between Ty and Owen. Ty stepped up, grabbed his vest pocket, flipping through it.

"Come on, man!" Owen said, laughing at Ty.

"I know I put it in this pocket. Oh, yea, here it is." Ty pulled out the ring box, opened it up, and held it out to Owen.

Owen looked at it and just laughed shaking his head. In the box was a candy ring pop.

Owen took the ring and put it on my other hand. "I guess this one's from Arnold." Owen said laughing. "Now how about the ring I bought her?"

"Oh, sure." Ty said. "Just gotta find it." Ty pulled a hankie out of another pocket and flipped it onto his shoulder, followed by a set of keys, a handful of change that he handed to Todd, all the while getting chuckles and snickers from our family and friends. Finally, he turned around and asked Todd if he had the ring. Todd just smirked and shook his head no. "Oh, right. I know where it's at." Ty stepped down kneeling in front of Luke. "Hey buddy, remember that box I put in your pocket earlier? Can I have it back?"

Luke pulled the small box out and handed it to Ty, all business-like.

"Way to go buddy, thanks for helping me." Ty said, patting Luke's shoulder and then handing him a candy ring pop and another one for him to hand to Caity.

"Isn't he good? He'll be here all night." Owen said, pointing at Luke. "We all know who the responsible party is here."

"Okay, now that we've located Karla's ring." The minister said, chuckling, "Owen, repeat after me: 'I give you this ring, as a reminder—'"
"Karla, I give you this ring, as a reminder—"
"'That I will love, honor, and cherish you—'"
"That I will love, honor, and cherish you—"
"'In all times, in all places—'"
"In all times, in all places—"
"'And in all ways.'"
"And in all ways."
"'With this ring, I marry you. It is a symbol of my eternal love and life with you, my everlasting friendship, and the promise of all my days.'"
"With this ring, I marry you. It is a symbol of my eternal love and life with you, my everlasting friendship, and the promise of all my days."

The minister shared Proverbs 3:3-4: "Let love and faithfulness never leave you; bind them around you, write them on the heart. Then you will win favor and a good name in the sight of God and man."

"Karla, are you ready to enter into the sacrament of marriage with Owen, believing the love you share and your faith in God and in each other will endure all things? If so, say, 'I am.'"
"I am." I said looking between the minister and Owen.
"Does Luke have the other ring or is Caity harboring it?" the minister asked with a smirk on this face.
"Ah, no I have that one." Ty said, holding out a small white box to me.

"What's going to come out of this, Ty? I asked taking the box from him. "Small bugs, confetti, another candy ring pop?" Ty just stood there with a devilish grin on his face; I knew something was forthcoming.

Sure enough, I opened the small box and there was another candy ring pop, garnering yet another round of chuckles. Ty was turning this into a comedy show. I couldn't help but laugh along with them.

"Nice one, Ty!" Owen said.

I placed the ring pop on Owen's other hand just as he had done to me a few moments ago. Then without missing a beat, I looked up at Ty, extending my hand. "The ring, please?"

Ty handed me the ring, which brought roar of laughter.

The minister turned his attention back to Owen and me after watching Ty's comedy unfold. "Karla, repeat after me."

"Owen, I give you this ring, as a reminder—"

"'That I will love, honor, and cherish you—'"

"That I will love, honor, and cherish you—"

"'In all times, in all places—'"

"In all times, in all places—"

"'And in all ways.'"

"And in all ways."

"'With this ring, I marry you. It is a symbol of my eternal love and life with you, my everlasting friendship, and the promise of all my days.'"

"With this ring, I marry you. It is a symbol of my eternal love and life with you, my everlasting friendship, And the promise of all my days."

"I now pronounce you husband and wife!" the minister announced. "Owen, you may kiss your bride."

Chapter 5

I moved my hands around Karla's back, embraced her, kissing her passionately, and tipping her ever so slightly backwards. We stood there embraced for a moment, without a care in the world. The minister motioned for us to turn and face our family and friends as he told us, "Go forth, love one another and praise God."

Karla and I moved down the center of the aisle, greeting our family and friends. Arnold followed right alongside. We first met up with our parents, hugging them all. Of course, there were some tears involved.

Dad hugged me once Ma released me. "It's about time, Owen. I was getting tired of waiting on you, but it's okay, I think God set this all up for you two, anyways."

"I have no doubt about it. Dad." I said, smiling. "Thanks for everything, love you."

Dad stepped aside, and Karla and I continued through the crowd of well-wishers on our way out the back door of the barn.

When we reached the barn door after greeting everyone. Dad, Darren and Ole Man Erving were standing next a sweet-looking mustang with the top down. "What's all this about?" I asked them, standing there, holding Karla's hand, and looking the car over. "Hey, Erving, is this your car? The one you'd never let Ty and me drive?"

"The one and only, we thought you and the missus might like to go for a spin."

"Are you kidding? I'd love to—how about you, Karla?" I said, looking at her. "Besides, I have something to show you." I said in a lowered tone.

"Absolutely, let's go!" Karla said beaming.

I showed Karla to the passenger seat, and I ran back to get in the driver's seat. Arnold stood there waiting with a longing look in his eyes. "All right, buddy, hop in—I guess this is your day, too."

I sped off down the driveway. "Oh wow, Owen, this is incredible. I never imagined we would do anything like this on our wedding day. I do feel kinda bad about just ditching everyone back there."

"Ah, it's fine. We need a moment to ourselves." I said, cruising down the old country road as the breeze blew through our hair.

"I feel like I married you too, today, ya silly dog. Isn't that right, buddy." Karla told Arnold, scratching his neck. "Did you and your master cook all this up?"

"Don't look at me." I said, looking over at Karla and Arnold during their conversation. "He's behind this all the way—if I'd have planned this, I'd have at least gotten him a doggie bowtie. He knows what he's doing, don't ya, boy." I said laughing.

I pulled up to the Flight School, parked the car and we went into the hangar.

"Owen, what are you up to?" Karla asked, looking at me skeptically.

"I'm just showing you something. Don't get your hopes up, we're not taking a flight today. I kinda bought you a wedding present."

"Really, and it's here at the Flight School?"

"Yeah, well, we'll have to keep it here. You know we had to stop at the bank and sign those papers the other day? Well, I kinda deceived you. We did change some insurance things around; whatever Ty and Rachel were talking about. But we had to do it that day because I bought us a plane."

"Owen, you what?" Karla asked, looking astounded.

"I thought we could make trips back and forth to your family more often and not have to rely on just the few planes the Flight

School has. It's also an investment for the Flight School. Would you like to see the inside? I kinda want to see how well that dress comes off."

"Owen, here?" Karla said, half smirking.

"You bet, come on." I said, taking her hand to board the plane. After Karla and I stepped into the cabin, I closed the door.

About an hour later, Owen and I were back on the road headed to the barn as our reception was getting underway. "Owen, I can't believe you bought me a plane, which has to be like the all-time world's-greatest wedding gift."

"Yea, Ty and Max said I've set an incredibly high standard for anniversary gifts."

"Oh, don't worry about those two, they're just jealous they didn't think of something like this."

Owen parked Erving's incredible car, and we walked together back into the barn as I heard the DJ announce, "And now for the first time together as Husband and Wife, please welcome Owen and Karla Kaster." Everyone in Joe's barn was cheering and whistling for us.

Owen leaned over, "Doesn't that sound great? 'Owen and Karla Kaster'—now you're stuck with me."

"That's okay." I told Owen. "You're stuck with me, too."

Owen led me to the dance floor, and a song about praying for you started playing.

Owen and I danced together. Our first dance together as husband and wife. "Owen, this song is wonderful. You've done an excellent job with the music, thank you." I said, returning Owen's embrace. Together we swayed back and forth to the music.

"Well, you said you were struggling and after I started piecing things together, I could see why—this wedding music business is hard to navigate. I wanted songs that told our story."

"Me too. But maybe I didn't have as much patience as you did."

"It wasn't an easy feat. This song is for me. I've been praying for you even before I met you."

Owen and I danced to a few more songs together and then went to make the rounds to visit with family and friends.

We met up with Owen's aunt and uncle shortly after leaving the dance floor. Owen told me they've been doing missionary work in the Philippines, and I hadn't had a chance to meet them, yet. Owen's mom said they don't get back to the states very often. I could tell Owen was excited when he finally met up with them and found out they had made it into town just in time for our wedding.

"Hey guys, so glad you could make it!" Owen exclaimed, hugging his aunt.

"This is my beautiful wife, Karla."

"Karla, this is my Aunt Rene and my Uncle Riley. So glad you guys could make it." Owen said, hugging them again.

"Hey, honey. Congratulations!" Rene said, hugging me.

"How long do you guys get to stay?" Owen asked.

"Were not sure." Riley said. "We might stay awhile this time. We have some things around here we want to do; and we haven't seen you guys very much lately."

"We'd like to be around for the holidays this year, too." Rene said, looking excited.

"Oh, that's great." Owen said. "Looking forward to it. Did Ma tell you Karla and I are moving down here? I'm going back to work at the Flight School with Ty."

"Yes, she did." Rene said. "That's great. Your folks will be happy to have you closer, sweety. I think it was kinda hard on your mom when you moved to the big city."

"Good grief." Owen said, laughing and shaking his head. "I didn't move to the big city. They visited when I proposed to Karla. We live in a pretty small town, near Boulder, so they've decided I moved to the big city. Well, I'm glad you guys are sticking around for a while. Can we get together later—after we're moved, and catch up? I'd love to hear about your work in the Philippines."

"Of course, sweety. We'll be around, we'll even help you two get settled." Rene said, hugging Owen and kissing his cheek. "You guys enjoy your night, go visit with your guests. I'm going to find your mom." Rene said taking Riley's hand.

"Hi Karla." Craig said, coming up behind me and Owen as we were about to move on from talking to Owen's aunt and uncle. "This is a very nice wedding." Craig said. I had not spoken to Craig in several months. I briefly visited with him when I turned in my resignation, but that was the last time.

"Craig, so nice to see you. Craig, meet Owen."

"Owen, this is my boss from the firm I worked at in Denver."

"Craig, this is my Uber driver." I said laughing.

"Owen, nice to meet you." Craig said, extending his hand to shake Owen's. "So, you're the one that made Karla quit her job?"

"We'll there might be some truth in that statement." Owen said. "Nice to meet you, Craig."

"How's things at work?" I asked Craig.

"Marketable as always." Craig replied.

"How are you, Karla? You were having quite a rough time last we talked. I was delighted to get your invitation. I just had to drive down today and see you."

"I'm wonderful, Craig, I really am. Owen makes me complete." I said, placing my hand on Owens's chest as he stood by my side holding my other hand.

"I did have a lot going on when I resigned. But I cannot say that I regret making that decision; I am incredibly happy with my online work. It was a good move for me, and now Owen and I are moving down here. Owen's going back to work at his business with his partner at their Flight School."

"I'm glad to hear that." Craig said. "Although you were my best marketing associate." Craig said holding his hand around his mouth, attempting to say it discreetly.

"Oh sure, lay a major guilt trip on me. Thanks, Craig. You have some very good marketing associates on your team; Mindy does a wonderful job. If I remember correctly, she just stepped up and took over the Chattanooga account like she owned it when I could not finish it. I'm sure she did a much better job than I was doing with it."

"She did do an excellent job with that account; but a Ms. Lindstedt from San Francisco still calls and asks for you. I gave that account to Julia, and Julia says this Ms. Lindstedt seems perturbed that you are no longer with our firm. You must have gone above and beyond with that account."

"Oh, that's too bad, Ms. Lindstedt's team was great to work with. I hope it all works out for Julia."

"It's been great talking to you, Craig, but we need to make the rounds, we have lots of guests to thank. I will call you soon and check in, thank you for coming."

"Yes, I was heading out anyways, I just wanted to say hi, I didn't mean to talk shop talk so much."

"Thanks for coming." Owen said, holding his hand out to shake Craig's again. "It was nice meeting you. Safe travels."

"Can we get the bride and her father out on the dance floor for the father-daughter dance?" I heard the DJ announce. I turned to Owen. "I guess that's me—bye, Craig." I said, before heading off to find Dad. I had stepped away from Owen but decided to turn back after a couple steps. "Hey, what's Dad and I going to dance to?"

"A song!" Owen chuckled.

"Of course." I said leaving Owen's side.

"Hi Dad." I said as we met on the dance floor, and he took my hand.

"Hey, kiddo, may I have this dance?" Dad asked as the song started playing.

"It would be my honor."

"Pretty nice day you got going here." Dad said. "You look really beautiful in this dress, by the way."

"Oh wow, nice doesn't even begin to describe it—did you know Owen bought us a plane?"

"Yea, he told me about it. Said he was going to fly you home more often."

"Isn't he great?"

"Yea, he's pretty terrific. You did good, kiddo. He takes good care of you, that's what every father wants for their daughter."

"I know, Dad; you don't have to worry. I think Owen's been taking care of me since he laid eyes on me, and he will continue for a long time."

"You just make sure to take care of him, too. He needs looking after as well."

"Oh, don't worry, we've got each other's back." The song started winding down, I heard the DJ announce; "Can I get the groom and his mother out on the dance floor for the mother-son dance?"

"Can we dance again later?" I asked Dad.

"Of course, kiddo. I'll come find you." Dad said, pecking my cheek before we left the dance floor.

"Hey, Ma. You look pretty spectacular today."

"Thank you, son, you look pretty sharp, yourself."

"Thank you for everything you and Dad did for our wedding, we really appreciate it." I said as we started dancing to the song, I had picked for us.

"I can't tell you how excited I was when you and Karla told us your plans for your wedding. Kinda makes me wish I would have done something like this when your dad and I were getting married. I had a fun time getting ready for your wedding."

"You know, Ma, you and Dad have a pretty big anniversary, coming up. Some couples renew their vows—you and Dad could plan something like this and have a vow-renewal party here in the barn."

"Oh, I don't know, I told your dad maybe we should just take a trip together, that should be good enough."

"Ma, I know about you and Dad's trips. Ride around town, hit the Feed Store and if it's a really special night, you grab a burger at the Burger Barn.

You think on this, I think it's a great idea and if I ask Max, he'll agree. We could get all your friends and family together and celebrate you guys."

"Oh, Owen, you're always so full of it." Ma said, patting my chest.

"Hi Mom, how you doing over here? You're kinda rockin' the Granny Grainer thing, aren't ya?"

"It suits me just fine." Mom said shaking her head gently. "My heart could stand a few more of these little guys or gals."

"Ya, you think so, even though Lane thinks he a choir member already."

"You just never mind about Lane. Toby just has stories to tell, don't ya," Mom said, talking to Toby and nuzzling his chest, getting him to smile.

"Can you hold him while I go to the bathroom?" Mom asked before handing him to me.

"Of course, take your time, we'll be just fine, won't we, Toby?" I asked Toby as Owen came walking up.

"Hello, you two, how's my wife?" Owen asked. "You look pretty good holding that little guy," Owen said taking the seat Mom had just vacated.

"Yea, he looks pretty cute in his little tux, don't ya, Toby. Your mommy found a cute little outfit for our wedding."

"No, I mean I could do with us having one of these soon." Owen said.

"He is pretty cute, Owen. But we need more than cuteness overload to be ready for a baby. All in God's timing." I said, kissing Toby.

"Hey, you two." Eide said as she strolled up. "You look pretty good with that baby. You two planning on adding to the Grainer grandkid crop tonight?"

"Eide!!!"

"I was just trying to convince her of that." Owen chortled. "I think it's a great idea."

"Hey, back the stork truck up you two. All in God's time, all in God's time." I said as I played with Toby's chin.

"I'm just saying." Eide said, laughing. "Levi and I got it down pat."

"And we're all grateful for this little guy."

"Yes, we are." Mom said as she came walking back up. "I'll take my job back, now."

"Don't you want to go dance, Mom?" I asked.

"Yes, I'll dance with your dad and maybe with Owen if he'd like to at some point."

"I'd love to dance with you, Laurel." Owen said, holding out his hand. "Come on, may I have this dance?"

Mom and Owen left, leaving Edie and me with Toby.

"Eide you've done a wonderful job with our wedding; thank you so much."

"Hey, no thanks necessary." Eide said, taking the seat beside me. "You've had my back my entire life. Should the three of us go dance?" Edie asked. "It'll be fun."

Eide and I took Toby out on the dance floor and danced for a bit. When the song ended Owen came over and asked Edie if he could steal his wife.

"Oh sure!" Eide said. "I already hooked you guys up, and now you're moving down to no-man's-land. What's a dance or two?" Eide joked.

Owen took my hand, and we stepped into each other's embrace. I noticed Eide following Ty as they headed up to the DJ's booth and Ty took over the microphone.

"Good evening, everyone!" Ty announced when the song ended. "Can I have your attention—Eide and I have something we'd like to say."

"Oh, this ought to be good." Owen said.

"No doubt, with those two at the reins."

"Hi all, I'm Ty, best man, best friend of the groom and growing on the wife—isn't that right Karla?" Ty asked looking at me. I smiled back at Ty, wondering what was coming next.

"Most everyone here knows me and if you don't, well, I'm sorry about that and if you do, well, then, I'm sorry about that, too. I'll keep this short because I have to go to the bathroom.

"First off, I just want to say thank you, Karla, for putting up with Owe for more than five minutes. He really is a great guy. That just tells me what a great person you are. Ever since we met you, we knew you were a keeper, mostly because you laughed at my jokes when Owe just shook his head and called me an idiot. Owe told me when he wanted to move that he was being called to work with the Mountain Rescue Team; he couldn't really describe it, he said it was just something he needed to do. Well, they always say hindsight is twenty-twenty, but here's the deal, I think he was being called to find you. Nobody in this barn may believe it, but I believe it. To Owe and Karla, best wishes. Glad to have you all here tonight and now I'm going to go hug the bride and groom and go to the bathroom. Love you both."

"All right, my turn." Eide said, taking the mic from Ty. "Don't forget to wash your hands, Ty." "Anyhoo, Eide Grainer here, and I'm the reason we're all here today! Yeah, I introduced these two." Eide said, chuckling. I agree with Ty, I've prayed for a love story that makes people stand back and think, 'Yep God put these two together.' "I know, I'm good. Karla and I go way back. I jokingly told her one morning I was tired of taking care of her when I decided I was going to introduce her to Owen; I guess I got more than I bargained for with that guy. Owen stepped in and I have been as useless as these heels out there in Joe's corrals ever since. But I'm incredibly happy for you, Karla, you, and Owen deserve every ounce of happiness God sends your way. So, me and my heels will just be on our way, I guess. Love to you both."

"Ok, will you two go cut that cake. I could go for some cake right about now." Eide said, pointing to the cake table. "That one looks spectacular, so if you two would please go cut it and have your moment in front of the camera so the rest of us can indulge."

Following a round of laughing, whistling, and clapping; Karla and I moved over to the cake table after Eide's insistence. "Come on." I said, taking Karla's hand on the way. "Cake in the nose, ears, hair, or down the dress?" I asked Karla as we stood by the cake table. "This looks like a cool cake by the way; they made it look like birch bark."

"I know, that's what I asked for." Karla said. "And no, just a simple slice we cut together for the camera will do. I don't like this little ritual."

"Ah, come on, let's do it our way then, we are the Kasters, after all." I said chuckling.

"Hmm, nice." Karla said, kissing me. "We are the Kasters. Now let's cut this cake." Karla grabbed the knife and held it up.

"Wow, now wait a minute." I said holding up my hands, laughing. "Only married a few hours and we're grabbing weapons, are we?"

"Very nice, you two." the DJ announced after we had managed to cut the cake and only getting a little on each other's faces. "Now, we have a special request from the groom."
"Owen, what are you up to?" Karla asked.
"Just you wait and see."
"Grainer Party, front and center, it's dance-off time!" the DJ announced. "I understand the Grainers have some dance moves that are likely to scare off the locals."
"Get up there." I said, nudging Karla towards the dance floor. "This is your time with your family. Remember Mexico? I was watching and taking notes." I winked at Karla as she held her hand out to me.
"Come on, Owen, you gotta be a part of this, too." She hollered over the music. I took her hand following her. The DJ played a series of fast songs that got us all going much like Karla and her family did in Mexico; it was so much fun. It was awesome to see such a great smile on Karla's face; she looked to be having a wonderful time.

Eide was holding her arms out bopping to the beat of the music. "I think Owen's right. I think we scared the neighbors this time—maybe if we're lucky the homeowner's association won't let you move in," Eide hollered to me over the music.
"Good luck with that. There's not a homeowner's association for miles around." I hollered back to Eide. Karla smiled and shrugged her shoulders.
"Figures!" Eide said. "My last one true chance."

"Hey Kar, can I have this dance?" Lane asked when the music faded, and a slower song started.

"Of course." "Where have you been?" I asked, placing my hand on his shoulder.

"I've been around, you've been busy and looking to be having a fun time."

"How about you? Have you been having a good time?" I asked Lane.

"Oh yes, Molly and I've had a great time. Although, I wish she'd be having a terrible time."

"Lane!" I said, almost shocked. "That's not a nice thing to say. We're going to be doing this at your wedding soon."

"Don't remind me." Lane groaned shaking his head. "If Molly were having a terrible time; she might reconsider eloping." Lane said, laughing this time. "I've tried to get her to elope."

"We know, Lane, it's about every other phrase out of your mouth here lately. I think Molly's made it pretty clear what she wants for your wedding, and I think it's going to be great."

"I don't." Lane said. "I don't want to be the center of attention."

"Ha, what are you talking about, Lane Grainer? You're constantly the center of attention."

"Not with a wedding; it's like one big production at these things."

"Oh, stop it, Lane." I said, laughing. "Your whole life's been one big production, you'll be fine."

"Can I cut in here?" Levi asked. "I haven't gotten to dance with Karla all night."

"Sure, I'll catch you in a bit, Kar." Lane said, holding my hand out to Levi.

"Thanks for the dance, Lane."

"Geez, Karla. You've made tracks all over this barn tonight." Levi said, stepping in the dance with me.

"I know, that's what Lane was saying. He's also worried about his wedding."

"He is?" Levi asked. "Why?"

"He thinks it'll be too big of a production."

"Oh, ya, he's mentioned that a time or two. Molly's mom's really digging her heels in about things."

"Maybe we should stick Eide on her." I said, joking.

"Hey, can I borrow my wife for a moment?" Owen asked, interrupting our conversation.

"Uh, sure." Levi said. "That was kind of a short dance, though."

Owen laughed, taking my hand. "What's up, Owen?" I asked him.

"Ole Man Erving is leaving and would like to see us, so I said I'd come get you."

"Oh, sure, we can say goodbye. Sorry, Levi. We'll catch up in a bit."

"Hi Erving, did you have a nice time?" I asked walking up to him where he was standing next to the food table.

"I did, Karla, real nice time. But I was telling Owen I've got to go check some heifers yet tonight, but I wanted to be sure and give this to both of you."

"Well, thanks, Erving." Owen said, extending his hand to shake Erving's and take the envelope Erving was offering.

"Yes, thank you." I told Erving. "Thank you for coming."

"Oh sure, you kids get yourself something nice, I wouldn't know how to pick out a toaster if my life depended on it." Erving said, smirking. "Say you two, how long are you planning on hanging around after the wedding this weekend? Is there a chance you could stop by before you take off? Erving asked. "I'd like to visit you with you two."

"Of course." Owen said, looking at Erving and then at me for verification.

"Sure thing, we'd be glad to." I told Erving and Owen. "We need to clean up here tomorrow after church, so maybe later tomorrow afternoon we could drop by, would that work?"

"Yea, yea, whatever works for you two." Erving said slightly waving his hand. "We'll see you then." Erving took a sandwich and was out the door.

"Hmm, wonder what that's about?" I asked Owen.

"The guy's probably just lonely, he's said more than once that his daughters don't hardly ever come home anymore."

"Hmm, that's too bad. Once were moved, we need to make a point to stop and visit him or have him over to supper occasionally."

"I see why I fell in love with you." Owen said, holding my face in his hands and kissing me delicately—apparently for the whole barn to see, because there were some major whoops and hollers going on as he got with it.

"Hmm." Owen said, releasing me from our kiss. "I think they approve. Should I do it again?"

"Oh, sure. You just think because I married you can have your way with me?" Before I could finish the statement Owen had me bent over backwards, kissing me feverishly again.

Ty was standing nearby once Owen and I broke out of our embrace the second time. "I think that's about enough of that, at least for a while, public displays and all." Ty said laughing. "Can I have this dance?" Ty asked, holding his hand out.

"Why sure." Owen said reaching for Ty's hand. "I'd love to." Owen laughed at his joke with Ty.

"This young lady." Ty said, passing Owen up. "But if that's how this is going to go down, I'll be back for you later, big fella." Ty said winking at us with a smirk. "Come on, Karla." Ty said, taking my hand.

"How's it going?" I asked.

"This has all been great! How 'bout you? You've had a busy night."

"Oh, a wonderful day, for sure."

"Well, good, it's supposed to be a wonderful day. I hope it's turned out just the way you'd hoped." Ty said laughing.

"So, you're next?" I asked Ty.

Oh, sure." Ty scoffed. "You're gonna jump on Owe's bandwagon."

"Hey Ty, can I have my wife back?" Owen asked when the song winded down.

"Hmm, I don't know, Owe. She dances pretty well." Ty said laughing.

"I know, among other things." Owen told Ty. "So, I'll be cutting in now."

"Oh fine." Ty said, sounding dejected. "Thanks for the dance, Karla."

"You bet, Ty. We can do it again at your wedding, soon?" Ty just walked away smiling.

"This has been a wonderful day, Owen. Thank you for everything." I said laying my head on his shoulder as we swayed to the music playing.

"You're thanking me?" Owen said, repeating me. "You put all this together. This was your brainchild."

"Not hardly. You put just as much work into this as I did. And your parents, they did so much to get ready."

"I think they kinda of enjoyed it. Ma mentioned some things earlier while we were dancing. She wishes she would have had a wedding like this when she and Dad got married. I told her they should have an anniversary party out here in the barn. They have a big one coming up; I was thinking we'd talk to Max and Elaine about getting a party together for them."

"Owen, that's terrific idea."

"I kinda mentioned it to Ma, and she thought she and Dad would probably just take a trip, which knowing them it will probably consist of a drive to town and hit the Feed Store." Owen said laughing. "See how were going to be in forty years? The highlight of our Saturday night, making a run to the Feed Store."

"Hey, Owen, can I dance once more with the kiddo?" Darren asked, interrupting our moment together. "I promised her another dance earlier and haven't gotten back to it."

"Absolutely, Ty owes me a dance, anyways." Owen said laughing. "I'm going to collect."

I looked over as Dad and I started dancing; Ty and Owen came out onto the dance floor. They swayed back and forth like they were any ordinary couple, albeit garnering snickers from the crowd. Dad and I went back to our dance. When the song ended, the speaker screeched, and the lights flickered. Dad and I held up a bit to see what was going on.

Ty and Owen slipped on sunglasses and turned their backs to the crowd and put their hands on their hips as the song "Shout" started playing. Ty and Owen started shaking their hips, lip-syncing, and shuffling along to the music. It was great. Ty at one point did the splits and jumped backed up. Owen shook his booty. His booty shaking could send me shaking.

"Well, what do we have going on here?" Joe asked when he came up and standing next to me. "I don't think these two have danced together since their senior prom; even then, it wasn't very good." Joe was watching the performance intently, smirking and shaking his head.

"Seriously, Joe. Somebody's gonna have to tell me that story!" I said, laughing as the show went on. Soon, Owen was on his knees leaning back with his hands around his mouth like a megaphone singing *"come on now and shout,"* *"come on now and shout,"* *"you know you make me wanna shout,"* *"come on now, shout, come on now and shout,"* *"come on now and shout,"* *"you know you make me wanna shout,"* *"come on now, shout."* Then he jumped up as the song continued, *"wait a minute now."* He marched over and took my hand. *"I feel all right,"* he sang as he stuck his other hand in the air proclaiming, *"I got my woman now,"* so the song goes. Owen paraded me around with him and Ty on the dance floor. It was ridiculous, I was laughing so hard my sides were starting to hurt.

Owen put me at the front of the line he and Ty had assembled, and the crowd started shouting and clapping "*Hey, Hey, Hey"* for us as the song ended.

Owen turned me around and enveloped me in a soft embrace and kissed me. "Isn't this great?" The crowd had been singing along and was now cheering Owen on.

"That dance was awesome!" Owen proclaimed.

Chapter 6

Later in the night after all the guests had left, Karla was sitting on my lap and we were sitting at a table, our parents had gone to the house to put the grandkids to bed. Lane and Molly, Levi and Eide, Ty and Rachel, and Max and Elaine had joined us at the table.

"That dance was fabulous." Rachel said, looking from Owen to Ty.

"Yea, way better than the dance we had in Mexico." Eide chimed in. "Lane, Molly, you've got some big shoes to fill when it comes to your wedding dance."

"Elope!" cough. "Elope!" cough. "Hmm, I seem to have a tickle." Lane said laughing.

"You must be wearing her down, Lane, Molly didn't smack you this time!" I mentioned.

"She's too tired." Lane laughed.

"Too tired from the day, or the eloping jokes." Levi wanted to know.

"At this point, it's a toss-up." Molly said sounding more mysterious all the time.

"I think Owen and Ty need to give us an encore performance of that dance, it was epic." Edie said, laughing. "I got most of it on video; but I could do for a repeat session."

"Yes." Karla said. "I could see a repeat session, too. And what's this about a prom dance?"

"Wait, how'd you hear about that?" I asked, looking appalled.

"Your dad brought it up while you and Ty were dancing."

"Oh, well, we're gonna need some deets there." Rachel said laughing.

"No doubt." Karla said in agreement.

"Thanks, Dad. And here I thought that night was dead and buried."

"How'd your dad even know about that?" Ty asked.

"I think we need to change the subject." I spoke.

"Nope, the cat's out of the bag now, boys." Eide said laughing. "Let's hear it."

"Well, your boy Owe here was Prom King our senior year; so, we decided to mix things up a bit." Ty said.

"I didn't know you were Prom King, Owen." Karla said. "Not that it surprises me." She brushed her fingers across my forehead slightly adjusting my hair.

"I was his only real competition." Ty said.

"Competition, my butt." I said, mocking Ty.

"Well, I may have told a few people to vote for you." Ty said theatrically.

"Yea, sure ya did. You know I beat you by a landslide."

"Anyways, Owe and I are about the only real male specimens in the senior class, so we came out with black sunglasses, we had black tuxes and were boppin' around like a couple of—"

"Like a couple weirdos." I said, cutting him off. "We came out on stage to the song 'Can't Touch This,' our only rapping debut ever. It was pathetic."

"Oh my, does there happen to be a video of this somewhere? We need some footage of it." Rachel said laughing.

"Most definitely." Karla agreed.

"Well luckily for us, this was before the era of smart phones, videoing and the prominent YouTube." I said, sounding assured that there was not any evidence remaining.

"Oh, don't worry." Rachel said. "I'll ask around the bank—somebody, somewhere has a deep-seated crush on one you from high school and has something from that night."

"Owen, do you know what your mom has planned for breakfast?' Eide asked taking the conversation for a 360.

"Don't tell me you're hungry, Eide? You're in the middle of eating cake, anyways," Lane pointed out.

"Boo hoo, aren't you funny. You try breast-feeding a child. I was thinking we could get breakfast ready for everyone. She's fed us all weekend. She deserves a break, don't you think?"

"That so nice." Karla said. "Yes, Rosie does need a break and the three of us can get breakfast ready before we go to church."

"It won't happen, ladies. Mom doesn't plan to cook any of us breakfast tomorrow." I said laughing. "There's a breakfast at the church in the morning."

"Okay, well there goes that thought." Eide said, putting her cake plate and fork in the trash. "Come on, Mr. Grainer take me to bed." Eide extended her hand out to Levi. He got up along with the rest of us, who indicated leaving as well.

"We'll see you all in the morning." I said, taking Karla's hand to leave the barn.

"Thanks for everything, you guys." Karla said.

"Yes, thank you," I said. echoing Karla's sentiments.

We all started to head out of the barn; I took Karla's hand and started to lead her toward the loft stairs.

"Where you two headed?" Max asked.

"Well, Ma told me earlier that she put all the grandkids in my room, which leaves the room she's been sleeping in." I said, pointing to Karla. "You know, right between Ma and Dad's room and the room she gave Darren and Laurel. Funny, Ma, but joke's on you. I made up a place for Karla and me in the barn loft earlier today."

"Good going, Owen!" Eide laughed. "We'll see you cats tomorrow, sometime."

"Good night, all." I said leading her up the stairs.

I opened barn loft door; and Karla and I danced in, hugging one another.

"Welcome to the honeymoon suite, Mrs. Kaster."

"Well done, Mr. Kaster." Karla said, kissing me, unbuttoning the buttons of my dress shirt; the vest long since removed. "This is wonderful, Owen."

"You did pretty good yourself, we put on a pretty good party down there tonight."

"We did, didn't we, though, but I think that's enough talk for tonight." Karla said, kissing me.

Chapter 7

"Good morning, beautiful!" Owen said as we were both waking up, he kissed my forehead. How'd you sleep?"

"Wonderful, never slept in a barn before." I chuckled.

"I'm sorry, we never discussed this, and I really didn't want to drive to the motel in town."

"No, this was an awesome idea, Owen. I had no idea there was a loft up here. Way better than going to the motel." I said, returning Owen's kisses.

Later that morning, we quickly ran up to the house in time to change for church; ignoring all the snickers and comments from our parents about where we had been as we came through the kitchen. Everyone was sitting around Rosie's kitchen table visiting about last night while they enjoyed their coffee. "So much for coming in undetected." I whispered to Owen.

We got ready just in time to grab some coffee and follow the rest of our family into town.

I sat in the pew beside Owen, holding his hand, thinking back to the morning I met him. Eide had embarrassingly thrown us together; I wasn't even so sure I should meet anyone. Eide had mentioned the night before there was someone, she wanted me to meet, a pilot at the Mountain Rescue Center. I was so convinced that his ego would precede him; but oh, how wrong I had been.

I refocused my thoughts and tuned into the minister's sermon; this truly was a message for our little group this morning, he was discussing where friendship had developed into a little family which was perfect for us.

The minister continued: "A faithful friend should help strengthen you and your own biblical values." He noted that

Proverbs 27:17 explains it this way: "As iron sharpens iron, so one man sharpens another. In 1 Corinthians 15:33, we want to choose friends who will sharpen us, not corrupt us." I like the idea of Owen and I growing spiritually in this church together. The minister was a great speaker.

Karla and I met up with our families that afternoon to clean up the barn; I think it came down faster than it went up. It was kind of bittersweet. The time between when I asked Karla to marry me and now, cleaning up the barn the day after our wedding had gone so fast; I also could not wait to see what God has in store for us.

The ladies had picked up all the decorations while Lane, Levi, Ty, and I started tearing down tables and chairs while Dad and Darren loaded them in the trailer.

"Wow, Dad, you could have a plane in here again by nightfall." I said, joking, looking across the barn as everyone scurried to make a clean sweep.

"Well, it's a good thing there were no classes at the Flight School the last few days." Ty said. "We might have needed to bring something over for repair." I knew Ty was joking right now, but we really needed to come up with a plan for the next class.

"Don't worry about that; I'll have plane pieces in here in the morning." Dad said smiling, almost eager to get back to work.

"We're going to go start supper." Eide said, looking at Molly.

"I'll help." Elaine volunteered.

"Karla and I have an errand to run, otherwise we'd help, too."

"Now, just where do you two think you're headed?" Eide asked inquisitively.

"Ole Man Erving wanted us to come by." Karla said.

"Who's Ole Man Erving?" Molly asked.

"Erving, Ma and Dad's neighbor. Lives up the road a few miles. He's the one who had the car yesterday."

"Gotcha." Molly said, looking perplexed.

Karla and I jumped into the pickup, with Arnold following us close behind and we all left.

Erving was walking out towards the barn, coming through one of the corrals when we drove into his yard. He must have been checking some of his calves. "Maybe this isn't a good time." Karla commented.

"Hmm, I don't know. I'll ask. But I'm sure it's fine."

"Hey Erving. How ya doing?"

"Good, good, how you two doing?"

"Oh, we're great. Is this a good time?"

"Yea, yea, anytime." Erving said, waving his hand. "I wanted to visit with you two about something. Why don't we come up to the house; I'll get you something to drink. How was the wedding?"

"Oh, it was great!" Karla exclaimed. "We had a wonderful night. We danced and danced and danced some more."

"Yea, I think me, and the missus had quite the dance, too. That's been ages ago, though." Erving said as we approached the door to his house. "Come on inside." Erving said opened the door to his kitchen and motioned for us to have a seat.

"I made a pot of coffee just before I went out to check on those calves; can I get you a cup?"

"Oh, yes, a cup of coffee would be great." Karla said.

"Oh, I see why you married him." Erving joked. "You're just like this one, he was drinking coffee in elementary school, according to Kaster."

Erving set three cups of coffee on the table and then grabbed a chair and joined Karla and me.

"All right, you two." Erving said getting right to the point. "Word on the street is you're moving to the neighborhood?"

"Yes, why—do you need something?" I asked Erving, chuckling.

"Not exactly, you mentioned the other day when we talked that you didn't have a place to live."

"Not yet. Karla added. I could tell she was a bit confused. Having had this conversation with him before.

"Well, I've been thinking on that." Erving said fingering a wood grain mark in his table. "I'm getting up there in years. Heck, your old man even got smart and took his herd to market. I want to sell my place to you kids." Erving said, nearly causing us to choke on our coffees.

"Excuse me, you what?" I asked Erving once I was able to recover.

"Yea, I want you to buy this place." Erving repeated looking up at me.

"You need a place. I'm getting old, my girls hardly ever come home anymore. This place could definitely use a woman's touch again." Erving said, glancing at Karla then eyeing the walls around us.

"You're not that old, are you sure you want to give all this up, already?"

"Yes, Owen. I have given this a lot of thought. Especially the last few days. And I really am that old; you and Ty have been calling me Ole Man Erving since you two were in high school. This place needs new life, it needs a family. You two can give it that."

"But what will you do?" Karla asked.

"Oh, don't worry, Karla. There are some apartments at the far south end of town. Kaster and I went and looked at them the other day."

Dad knows about this. I thought. "What are you going to do with yourself in an apartment in town? That's not your style, Erving."

"I'm going to ease myself into this retirement business. I got this all planned out. I'm going to sell you this place; you're going to take on the herd and horses and I'll come out and see them off and on for a while, maybe help your dad some."

"That's some plan you got there, Erving. How many acres do you have here—what kind of price we talkin?" I asked.

"There's twenty acres with the house, barn and hayfield out back. And price, well, that I don't know." Erving said, shaking his head. "I was going to talk to you both. I want you two to move here, so we can work something out."

"I really don't know what to say. Have you talked to Ann and Katy about this?"

"Yes, Owen. I've thought about selling out off and on since your old man sold off his herd. Even before I heard you were moving back from the big city. This is no different than me putting a big For Sale sign out at the end of the drive. I figure this is just less hassle. You don't have to give me an answer today, Kaster. You two are leaving for your honeymoon tomorrow, right? Why don't you discuss it and come to see me when you get back? But really, I'd like you two to move here."

Karla and I walked in silence back down to the pickup we'd left parked by Erving's barn. I was stunned, I didn't know what to think about Ole Man Erving's offer. Or the fact he knew Ty and I called him that. Karla and I jumped in the pickup. I looked around and whistled for Arnold. "Come on, boy, let's go." I hollered. Arnold came moseying along. He had been snooping in a row of trees out behind the house. I opened the door for Arnold to jumped in with us; he launched himself into my lap and I moved him along into the backseat and drove off. We waved at Erving as we went by the house—he was probably going back to the barn to work on something else. Erving was always working in the barn or the shop; I couldn't see that he would be okay living in town. I drove to the end of the drive and stopped, putting the pickup in park, I turned myself in the seat to look at Karla.

"What just happened there?" Karla asked looking back at me.

"I think we just bought a house, or we're going to." I said, sitting there stunned. "What do you think about this?"

"I think it's wild. I mean, I didn't see much of the house, but what I did, it looks great. What do you think about Erving's plan about keeping the calves and horses?"

"Oh that, that's just until he can take them to market. But if this is God's plan for us; then I guess we shouldn't question it. If Erving feels the need to ease himself into retirement, who are we to stop him?" I said, laughing.

I pulled out of the driveway and drove back over to Ma and Dad's place, which only took about two minutes. I had been down this stretch of road countless times; just never thought I'd be living there. I pulled up in the yard and we got out. I noticed Dad was out by the grill just finishing when Karla and I walked up to him.

"You kids finished your errand?" Dad asked.

"Yea seems you knew all about this errand. Is everything ok with Erving?"

"I think so." Dad said. "Why do you ask?"

"This whole house business, it seems he's just up and decided to sell out. Seems a bit sudden."

"Oh, not really, Owen. You haven't seen much of Erving the last year or so. If he says he is ready to sell, then he's ready. He told me the other day he was going to offer it to you guys, and he found an apartment to rent. I even took Darren over to Erving's place and showed him around when we picked up his car."

"Oh, well, that settles it. If my dad knows then it's a done deal." Karla commented, snarly. We probably don't even have to tell the others; the rumor mill has probably been churning all weekend."

"Probably," I told Karla, laughing.

"So, you guys going to take him up on his offer?" Dad asked.

"I don't know, we don't have a price yet. We're going to think about it this week and then talk to him when we get back."

"Maybe a prayer or two wouldn't hurt, don't ya think?" Dad asked. "Anyways, better get these burgers inside before they get cold."

"Did you get your errand taken care of?" Eide quizzed when we sat down to eat.

"Hold that thought, Eide." Joe said. "Everyone, please bow your head for the blessing."

"Lord, it is truly your gift to be able to sit around this table and celebrate all that we are thankful for, good food, friends and family. We have much to celebrate for this evening as our families have been united and Owen and Karla begin their journey in this life under your guiding hand. We trust you will see everyone to have safe travels tomorrow. In your name we pray, amen."

At the end of Joe's prayer, Toby once again let out a numbered wail.

"Well, Joe, you must be doing good in the prayers department, according to Toby here." Eide said, getting up to pick Toby up.

"I think so, too." Ma said, tapping Dad's hand. I noticed she had placed her hand across his during the prayer. "He's kept me in prayers for nearly forty years."

"You must take after your dad." Karla whispered to me. "I've been the recipient of numerous prayers of yours."

"Hmm, vice versa." I whispered in Karla's ear.

"What are you two whispering about?" Eide asked as she returned to the table after getting Toby settled. "Are you talking about your errand?"

"No, but we can." Karla said, nearly smirking.

"So, where'd you go?" Eide quizzed again.

"Well," Karla said, looking at me. "We went and looked at a possible home to buy."

"Really? That's awesome!" Molly exclaimed.

"Where's it at?" Ma asked. "You weren't gone very long."

"Just a couple miles from here." I said, waiting for Ma to pick up on it all.

"A few miles." She said, still looking confused. "In what direction?"

"South." I said matter of factly.

"That could only be Erving's." Ma said. The confusion look was still there but diminishing.

"Is Erving the neighbor with car?" Laurel asked. "Is that not a good thing, Rosie?"

"No, not at all, just a bit surprising. Did you know about this, Joe? You haven't said a word."

"Yea, Darren and I talked to Erving about it the other day. Said he's been thinking about selling out for a while and with Owen and Karla moving back this just seemed right."

"You knew about this too, Darren?" Laurel asked, looking at Darren and tapping his shoulder.

"Well, the guy told us when we were moving his car around; it was all good timing."

"So, you going to buy this guy's house or what?" Eide asked.

"Well, it's more than the house." Karla said. "It's more of a farm."

"You guys are buying a farm?" Lane asked, shaking his head. "Didn't see this one coming. When do the chickens show up?"

"I think this is a great idea." Darren said. "It's a nice little out-of-the-way place. When you're ready to move let us know, we'll be ready to help."

"Seriously, again." Levi said, laughing. "You're moving again, Karla—I moved twice in fifteen years and one of them I did it all by myself."

"Yea, me too, Kar." Lane joined in the heckling. "This will be your what, fourth move in two-years. You think you'd be a pro by now."

"Ha-ha, very funny, guys." Karla said giving them a sly look.

"What about your uh, the uh." Eide said, stuttering and finally blurting out, "Well Garratt's rental?"

"What about it?" Karla asked.

"Don't you have to pack it up and basically move out of there too?"

"No, not really. Owen and I went over there awhile back and packed it all up; when we put our houses on the market. All we have to do is load everything and pack at Owen's house."

"I can come help you pack when you get back from your honeymoon." Eide offered. "You are taking a honeymoon? I haven't really heard either of you say much about it."

"Yes, we are." Karla said, looking at me. "Although, we don't really have a plan."

"Who doesn't have a plan for their honeymoon?" Lane chastised. "Do you two even understand the meaning of a honeymoon?"

"Ah, yes, we got that part, Lane."

"So, you're planning to take off in the morning to an unknown destination?" Darren asked.

"Pretty much." Karla said flippantly answering her dad.

"And how long do you plan to be gone?" Laurel asked.

"We'll be back here Wednesday or Thursday." I told everyone, thinking. *I should have planned better and taken Karla to a fancy beach vacation.*

"And you're flying?" Dad asked.

"Of course, Dad, we did just buy a plane." I said, looking at Karla and smiling.

"Well, you better get a plan together right quick," Darren said. "We'd like to hear about it before we leave in the morning."

Chapter 8

The next morning, everyone rose early to get going. My family was all headed home this morning. The guys were out packing the vehicles and Owen helped with bags from the kitchen to the vehicles. Rosie and I along with Mom, Eide and Molly were visiting over a cup coffee as the guys made laps around us.

"We could help them." Molly mentioned to Eide.

"Eh, probably not." Eide said.

"We're all stuck together for the next five hours as we make our way out of Juarez." Eide joked.

"Oh, stop. You're not in Juarez." I said laughing.

"She's really not that far off." Rosie commented. "You'll be even closer if you and Owen buy Erving's place."

"Seriously, Rosie!" I said, chuckling. "Don't add fuel to the fire. She already has it in her head that we live in Mexico. Once we're settled, we'll take a girl's trip; maybe like Taos or something."

"That is a great idea, I've heard they have great art and jewelry collections. You ladies should come too." Molly said, looking at Laurel and Rosie.

"Oh no, I'll stay home with this little guy." Mom said, leaning down and giving Toby a sweet kiss as she held him, gently rocking him.

"I could handle the grandkid detail, too." Rosie said. "Then you could ask Elaine and Rachel to join you."

"Sounds like a plan. But with all that's going on in Karla's world, we might as well pencil it in for ten o'clock next summer." Eide said laughing.

The guys stepped into the kitchen and announced they were all packed and wanted to know if everyone was ready to go. Levi said their vehicle was all packed, too.

"Yea, three-fourths of it belongs to the smallest person in the tribe; how is that even possible?" Lane wanted to know.

"Diapers, Lane Grainer, and you're changing the next one." Eide joked.

"Hmm, I feel a nap coming on." Lane said, stretching. "I just don't feel fully prepared for it."

"We're going to get you prepared for it." Molly said, laughing as she patted Lane's chest.

"Don't rush me, we can wait ten or fifteen years." Lane said with a big ole grin.

"I think not, Lane." Molly said.

"Okay, you two." Dad said, looking at Owen and me.

"Don't look at us." Owen said. 'We're not harboring a little Toby anywhere."

"Where ya goin' on your honeymoon? Not this grandkid business."

"Oh, they can add to the Grainer/Kaster grandkid crop this week." Eide said snidely. "Give my kid some competition."

"We're goin flying, it's what we do best." Owen said, putting his arm around my shoulder.

"That's helpful," Joe said.

"We're heading up in the Glacier region and possibly do some camping, if we can grab some camping gear from Ty. All my stuff's at home."

"All right, you kids, be careful. Joe, Rosie, thank you for a nice weekend." Dad said, extending his hand to shake hands with Joe.

"Yes." Mom said. "Thank you for putting up with all of us."

"It was nice having you all here. A great reason to get together." Rosie said. "Sounds like we'll get the chance again soon in a few weeks."

All my family left a few moments later. Owen and I grabbed our bags and a cup of coffee.

"I texted Ty, he's going to meet us at the Flight School with some camping gear."

"You guys sure you don't want some breakfast first?" Rosie asked.

"Nah, we're good, Ma, give you and Dad some peace and quiet this morning."

"Oh, we're not worried about that, there's always time for that." Rosie said.

"Speak for yourself, Rosie dear, I'm planning on a nap." Joe said. "Maybe even again later this morning."

"Okay, well, the king has spoken." Owen joked. "We're going to head out for a few days. Thank you both for everything." Owen leaned over and hugged his mom before walking towards the door.

"I don't know how we'll ever be able to properly thank you for everything you've done." I said to Rosie after Owen released her from their embrace.

"Oh, honey, just seeing you two happy is thanks enough. Now go have some fun before you start this big move."

"Oh, this is gonna be fun. He plans the greatest adventures for us." I said, pointing at Owen.

Karla and I got out of the pickup after I parked next to Ty's Jeep at the Flight School and saw that he was putting his tent into the cargo area of the plane we had just bought.

"Morning, Owe. Karla." Ty said, stepping out of the cargo area. "How's things going?"

"Great! And you?" I asked Ty.

"Actually, I'm draggin' butt a little this morning. I don't have that just married glow to keep me going." Ty said, smiling at us.

"You could. I see how Rachel looks at you."

"Hmm, maybe." Ty said, a small smile sneaking out.

"Did you buy a ring yet?" I asked Ty.

"I'm not telling you."

"Ah, ha. What got to you, Ty? Was it when we exchanged vows, the I do's, the whole nine yards?"

"We should just go buy a ring right now." *I remember all this razing last winter when I had come down for a visit while Karla was out of town for work. Ty and Max had themselves convinced we should go to town that night and get a ring.*

"Oh, just get out of here, you two." Ty said. "I brought you the tent and a couple sleeping bags but wasn't sure what else you wanted or needed. How long you going to be gone for?"

"Just a couple nights. We're coming back to visit with Ole Man Erving Wednesday or Thursday."

"Why does Ole Man Erving care when you come back?" Ty asked, looking confused at what I had just said.

"Well, for one he knows we call him Ole Man Erving, and two he wants to sell us his place."

"What, that came out of left field." Ty said. "You, living at Ole Man Erving's? That's just kind of unfathomable."

"Yea, but he seems pretty set on the notion. I want to check this baby out." I said, looking the plane over. "You've been up with this girl, yet? What can you tell me?"

"Actually, no." Ty said. It was delivered right before your wedding, and I haven't had the chance. This will be her maiden voyage, so to speak, I'm kinda bummed, though, I mean it's the Cessna 172. We've never had a plane this awesome."

"You'll get your chance. Let's do pre-flight checks so we can head out."

Following the pre-flight checks, I loaded our bags into the cargo area along with the camping gear Ty brought. We settled into the cockpit and told Ty goodbye. I radioed the control tower and taxied out onto the runway.

We were having a smooth flight. I always loved watching Karla when I took us on a flight. Last spring, we flew over the Grand Canyon. The views were spectacular. This morning was not much different flying, Karla was looking out and appeared to be enjoying the view once again when things took a sharp turn. I noticed that I was losing thrust and air pressure. I quickly started descending to account for this change.

"Why are we descending?" Karla asked me. "We're not landing, are we?" Karla and I usually didn't visit much during our flights. She was taking it all in. This morning, I was having trouble, and did not want to tell her that just yet, no need for her to worry. "No." I said, briskly. "We're not landing yet; I need to descend to a lower altitude."

I was quickly making adjustments and radioed air traffic control. I needed to find a place for us to land, and soon. Is something wrong?" Karla asked.

"Hmm, possibly. We're close to Kalispell, and we'll need to land and get things checked out." I told Karla, when the plane took another sudden descent, shaking the plane, us included.

"What's going on, Owen?" Karla asked shrieking again, loudly. I could hear how scared she was in her voice, but now there was nothing I could do about it.

"We're going to land, soon. Hang on tight. Put your seatbelt on." I yelled back when the plane shook terrible again. I was trying to counter act the situation and wasn't doing very good job. The plane continued shaking and descending rapidly.

Once we'd stabilized, I radioed into Kalispell air traffic control again requesting inbound traffic and I reported possible engine failure, they cleared us for landing. Air traffic control instructed me to contact ground control for further instructions.

"Owen, is everything all right?" Karla asked loudly. "I've never heard you contact the control tower like that before."

"Just hang tight, we might be in for a bumpy landing, as soon as we land quickly take the seat belt off and be prepared to jump out. I'll come around and get you." The plane jolted and descended even further. At this point I was beginning to wonder if we would make it to Kalispell.

"Owen!" Karla screamed again, I noticed she laid her head in between her knees, and I could hear her heavy breathing. Karla had been terribly upset, of course she didn't know what was going on and could only feel the plane every time it dropped even further. This might be the hardest part of all this; not being there for Karla. It was so tough seeing her like this.

The tires hit the runway and bounced up again as I cleared the runway, I radioed ground control for instructions upon entering the runway. Two men came walking towards us. One of the men was directing me into position as the rotor suddenly stopped.

I would have given anything to take Karla's hand as we landed; I didn't figure this would be too easy of a landing and she was already very scared.

"Karla, you can look up now; we're on the ground, you can take your seatbelt off and be ready to get out." We hit the runway with minimal problems and taxied into the airfield. Ground Control directed to a nearby hangar. Two gentlemen came walking towards the plane as I finished shutting down.

"Hi." The gentlemen greeted me as I got out of my side of the plane. I quickly walked around to Karla's side and was finally able to take her hand.

"We were notified by air traffic control this plane was having engine troubles, is that correct?" one of the gentlemen asked.

"Yes. I lost an engine prior to landing."

"Really, I was questioning if we even had the right plane as we watched you land. I know you were having a rough landing but to be in engine failure and land a plane that well, well that takes skill. So, do you know what seems to be going on?"

"Possibly a piston and ring failure, I lost thrust and air pressure early on, then later lost oil pressure. I thought I'd missed moisture in the fuel line during pre-flight checks. But now after getting landed and thinking back through protocol I'm certain it's the piston and ring."

"Okay, well, I'm Jimmy, one of the mechanics here at the hangar. I can help you take care of it if you like."

"Hi, Jimmy. Nice to meet you. I'm Owen." I said extending my hand to shake his.

"This is my wife, Karla. We were headed for a flight over Glacier today as a start to our honeymoon and then check out a place to do some camping tonight."

"Nice!" Jimmy said. "Congratulations. Well, not sure what you're thinking about with this, but I could get your plane fixed up if you guys want to get a rental car—not exactly as exciting as a plane."

"You'd do that for us?" Karla asked.

"You bet, I got everything over in the mechanics hangar; we'll just push the plane over there. I can get to work on it yet today. It's been slow here lately."

"Thanks, Jimmy. I appreciate it. I can help you push it over to your shop; and then if you want to point us in the direction of the rental car counter."

Jimmy and I moved the plane over to the mechanics shop and unloaded the cargo area of the plane. "I can drive you guys up to the rental car booth; you can throw your things in the back of my pickup." Jimmy offered.

Jimmy drove up to the front of the building and Karla and I got out. Jimmy said he would just wait here until we had a vehicle.

"We can take our things now if you'd like, it's not that far of a walk." I told Jimmy.

"No worries." Jimmy said. "You won't be that long."

Jimmy was right, we were back outside the terminal in about five minutes with a rented Jeep.

"See, that didn't take long." Jimmy said. "Which row?"

"We got a Jeep, ah, section E5." I told Jimmy after looking at the paperwork. Jimmy pulled up behind the Jeep. I opened the hatchback to the Jeep and started putting our luggage in the back.

When Karla and I had our things transferred over; I wrote my cell number on a post-it note I had gotten from the car rental clerk and gave it to Jimmy, along with a twenty-dollar bill. "Hey Jimmy, thanks for your help today, I appreciate it. Call if you have any questions."

"I'll take your phone number, and here's my business card, but the tip isn't necessary, just part of the job."

"Nah." I said. "You take it. You went above and beyond today."

"Thanks, Owen. See you in a couple days."

After Jimmy drove off, I took Karla's hands and then wrapped my arms around her holding her tightly. "Are you okay?"

"Yes, a little shaky, but this helps. What happened back there? I've never seen you land like that before."

"Well, yes, I've landed like that before; just not very often. Sorry you had to see that, but it's a part of the aviation world."

"Those guys thought you did an excellent job." Karla said, finally smiling.

"Yea, I guess. I was trying to make the landing as smooth as possible. Let's talk about this later and get some lunch. I'm starving. Should we find a burger joint and then make some plans for the rest of the day?" I asked as I drove out of the airport parking lot.

Chapter 9

Owen found a pub in town, and we went in and grabbed a table. "This looks fun." I said, looking around. "There's a lot of car parts on the walls."

"Yea, and they'll bring your meal in an oil pan." Owen said smirking. The waitress came and brought us menus and a glass of water, leaving just as quickly as she arrived. Moments later she returned and took our orders.

Owen pulled out his phone after the waitress left with our orders. "Should we check out some campgrounds?" Owen asked.

"Yes!" I said, still looking at the car parts hanging on the wall.

"Do you want to use the tent Ty sent, or do you want to see about getting a cabin; looks like they have some available. It might get a little cold at night." Owen suggested.

"I'm good with tent camping." I said smirking.

"I see how it is." Owen said looking up at me with a smirk and a glimmer in his eyes. "Tent camping it is, now we just need to find a location."

"How about this one." I said, turning my phone around for Owen to see the listing.

"That looks like a good choice. Says here they have kayaking, probably don't offer it this time of year, though. Would you be game for that, if they did?" Owen asked as the waiter brought our burgers.

"Yes. I would totally be up for some kayaking. We should definitely take a drive across the Going-to-the-Sun Road, too."

"That sounds great." Owen said, agreeing with me. We ate our lunch and left the pub. Owen slipped his arm around my waist, kissing my forehead as we walked back to the Jeep.

"Do we want to stop anywhere in town before we head out to the campground?" Owen asked.

"Yea, actually I was thinking we should probably stop at a place like Target. Grab some bedding, some stuff for a camp cookout and ooh, some s'mores." I told him.

"Hmm, ha. Yes, I think we can handle some s'mores." Owen said laughing at me. "Let's hit up an REI, get some bedding first."

"Much better idea, I didn't think about this place." I told Owen as he pulled into the parking lot.

We made our way into the store and back to the sleeping bags and bedding department to look things over.

"Hey Owen, look at this one. Did you know they have double sleeping bags?"

"Yea, but I hadn't seen them yet. You want to get this one?"

"Yes, actually I think it would be perfect for us."

"Do you want a pillow?" Owen asked, looking a little further down the aisle.

"Hmm, yea, might be nice."

Owen grabbed a couple and put them in the cart. "What else, do you think?"

"Hmm, I don't know, we're only here a couple nights. What more could we need?"

"Let's go see about some chairs." Owen said, taking off with the cart.

On the way to the chairs, Owen stopped. "Hey, look at these, aren't they cool?"

"Oh, please, you and Eide. Child hiking carriers. Seriously, Owen. I think that's a ways off."

"Hmm, maybe not so far off." Owen said, putting his arm around my shoulder as we stood looking at the carriers.

"All in God's timing; we don't rush these things, remember, and we definitely don't need one this trip. So, moving on." I said, taking the cart from Owen and continuing down the aisle.

Owen and I left the store. He drove a couple blocks and came to a grocery store. "Should we stop here?" Owen asked pulling into the parking lot.

It was a cute little market, I noticed, as we walked up to the building.

"So, what are you thinking here?" Owen asked.

"S'mores, remember. Childish, I know. But I haven't had one in years."

"Hey, no complaining here." Owen exclaimed. "It's a camping tradition. But what would you like besides that? Not sure we can survive on s'mores alone."

"Um, your choice."

Owen and I picked up a few items and a cup of coffee and left the store. Owen drove down the highway out of town to the campground.

"So, Owen. I said interrupting our silence as he drove along. "What happened back there, with the plane?"

"Oh, I think just a piston and ring went out." Owen said distantly. "Should be no big deal, nothing to worry about."

"Owen, you keep telling me not to worry about things; first off, I'm going to worry about things even if you tell me not to, and quite likely I'm going to worry about you more when you tell me not to. Number two, we are married now. We need to share our concerns with each other, you know—that includes you, too, bucko!" I said sternly.

"Okay, there's the fiery little gal we all know and love." Owen said, laughing and pulling the Jeep over to the side of the road.

"Karla." Owen said, turning in his seat looking at me. "You're my entire world, you know that. I just don't want you to worry."

Owen said reaching over to adjust the hair from my forehead and then took my hand.

"I know you don't want me worrying. It's okay. I want to know these things; I am not some delicate flower about to break. You always went off on rescues and came back and usually just told me you had a successful outcome but not much beyond that."

"Okay, okay. I get where you are coming from. But we can't sit here on the side of the road and have this conversation. I promise after we set up camp, I will tell you everything."

"Owen."

"Yes, Karla. I promise." Owen said as he merged back onto the highway.

"This is nice." I said as he drove into the campground. Owen followed the signs and pulled up in front of the cabin with a sign out front that read "OFFICE." Owen and I both went in to see about a campsite. The gentleman behind the counter welcomed us as we came in and asked us how long we would be staying.

"Two, possibly three nights." Owen told the gentleman.

"Sure." the gentleman said. "I'll just keep your card on file and when you leave, stop in and settle up, that'll be fine. You pretty much have the pick of the grounds—being early October we're a little slow, so just drive around and find yourselves a nice little spot."

"Thanks." Owen said. "Is there a place nearby to get coffee later or in the morning?"

"Yeah, there's the Lake Lodge, just up the way, across the road. They have coffees and other drinks, breakfast items, grilling items, all sorts of things. Almost to the point a guy'd never have to leave the campgrounds up here at all."

"Perfect, we'll check it out." I told Owen.

"Yea." Owen said. "Might be time for a cup of coffee."

"Thanks for your help, sir." Owen said as we left.

"So, any preference on where we set up camp?" Owen asked once we had gotten back in the Jeep.

"Hmm, somewhere back out of the way."

"That's kinda what I was thinking." Owen said, driving down the camp roads looking for a spot.

We were both scanning the sides of the road like we thought Bigfoot himself was going to come out and lie on the hood of the Jeep.

"Look at this spot." Owen said as he pulled to the side of the road and parked the Jeep.

We both got out. Owen came around to my door and took my hand and we looked around in front of the Jeep.

"What do you think?" Owen asked.

"It looks great." I said, looking over at Owen.

"Oh, you think so." Owen said, taking me around the waist and twirling me around. As he sat me down, Owen kissed me passionately, melting away the concerns that had filled me earlier.

"Should we make camp here?" Owen asked.

"Yes, we should."

Owen and I went to the Jeep and grabbed Ty's tent from the back and started unpacking it. I helped Owen put the tent most of the way up and then when all that was left was staking it down, I started getting our other things out of the Jeep, our new sleeping bag, pillows, and luggage. Owen set our chairs up in front of the tent, it looked cute. "Sit in one of the chairs." I told Owen. "I'm gonna take your picture."

After I snapped the picture. Owen said, standing up, "Okay, now it's your turn."

When we had finished with the pictures; Owen got the fire pit that was sitting off to the side of our camping spot to set it up.

"Want to go for a walk, find some kindling and firewood with me?" Owen asked, offering his hand to me.

"Absolutely!" I said, taking hold of his offered hand.

We walked in silence for a brief time as Owen was picking up a few kindling items here and there for the fire. It was nice walking along the backside of the campground, so peaceful. We could see the mountains; the colors of fall were all around us.

Chapter 10

"Okay, Karla." I said, stopping and turning to look at her, interrupting the silence. *I decided it was time to talk to her about the plane.* "You asked about the plane earlier."

"Yes, what happened?"

"I lost an engine, I think it's a piston and ring failure, but nonetheless it's a mechanical failure."

"What's all that mean?"

"Well, in our case, I should have arranged to take another plane for this trip. I let my excitement get the better of me. We had just gotten this plane and I wanted to take it out. I'm not even sure we have received the inspection report on it. Ty and I should have checked it out ourselves first.

"The really bad part," I said, putting my arm around Karla after I set the kindling on the ground, "when you lose an engine, you only have a certain amount of time to land. We were just lucky to be that close to the airport."

"Are you telling me we may not have had such a controlled landing—those guys at the airport referenced that, didn't they?" Karla asked.

"That's exactly what I'm saying. Even though there's no mechanics left to a plane and no engine left to work with, you still have to continue flying the plane."

"How do you do that, though, when you're in a car and the thing's dead, it's dead."

I chuckled at Karla's reference. "In this situation, you work to find the best glide and speed, it's all about precision; and in my case, I just pray to God."

"But we're okay, Owen. Everything is going to be okay. You did an impressive job today. Even those guys at the airport were impressed with how well you handled things. And see, I didn't break when you told me."

"You sure about that?" I asked Karla, lightly embracing her swaying back and forth.

"You know it, honey." Karla said, laughing and giggling with me. We were slowly dancing amongst the trees laughing and carrying on. We eventually tripped over each other, falling to the ground, and crunching the leaves beneath us.

Owen and I laid there in the weeds looking deep into each other's eyes. Owen rolled over, on top of me, kissing me heatedly. There was so much fire and passion in him.

He was kissing down my neck and starting to unbutton my shirt when we heard twigs breaking in the distance. Owen looked at me, and I stared into his dark gorgeous eyes.

"Let's continue this in the tent." Owen said breathlessly, forgetting about the kindling he had gathered earlier.

"I think that was better than our wedding night." Owen said as we laid together in the tent, later.

"I don't. You made that night pretty special, too. That entire day was special."

"I was just talking about the few hours we spent in the barn loft alone." Owen said, running his thumb along the bottom of my chin, exploring it. His other arm slide under my neck.

"I know what you were talking about, cowboy."

"Oh woah, easy there with the 'cowboy' talk. I don't wear spurs, or boots for that matter."

"I'm going to get you some if we buy Erving's place; you're going to need them to muck out the barn stalls."

"And here I thought this was such a good idea to buy Ole Man Erving's place and then you go and remind me about the barn stalls." Owen groaned, attempting to move away from our embrace. "We should get dressed and go get the fire going; it's gonna start getting cold."

"I'm warm and cozy in here." I said before Owen could get up.

"Yea, me too." Owen said playfully. "Supper's not going to cook itself, though."

Owen snuggled back in next to me, playfully kissing the side of my neck. "Only for a little longer; then we'll go work on supper."

We never left our spot last night, Owen and I cozied in together and stayed there the rest of the night. "Should we grab some coffee and take a road trip; maybe pick up some breakfast, since we, uh, skipped supper last night?" Owen mentioned as we dressed.

"That sounds like a great idea." I spoke.

We grabbed coffees and breakfast burritos at the Lake Lodge and headed toward the Going-to-the-Sun Road. We drove along for a while and saw beautiful snow-capped mountains, mountain goats perched on the side of a cliff, deer and elk munching in the morning dewy grass. Owen pulled up to a lake and we got out. He took my hand and we started walking down to the shore.

"Almost as pretty as our spot back home." I spoke.

"They're both spectacular in their own way." Owen said.

"Any good spots in our new home?" I asked Owen, looking out across the water.

"Oh, plenty, just you wait and see. I'll show ya." Owen said smiling.

"Let's head back to the campground and see if we can do some kayaking." I suggested to Owen.

"Yes, I knew there was a reason I brought you on this trip." Owen said, smiling back at me.

We arrived at the campground and stopped at the office to inquire about the kayaking.

Owen parked and ran inside to ask the clerk, but soon stepped back out on the sidewalk and motioned for me to roll the window down.

"Do you want your own or do want to share one?" Owen asked.

"Let's share." I said giddily.

Owen went back in the office for a short time and came back out and hopped in the Jeep and asked if I was ready.

"Absolutely, where we headed?"

"Kayaking, silly."

"Oh, right. I thought we were going ice skating."

Owen drove down the road a few miles from our campsite and a gentleman met us at a storage shed along the riverbank.

"Hello." Owen said approaching the gentleman, who was sent to get us started on our kayaking trip.

"Hi, I'm James. I'll help you get rigged-up."

"Thanks." Owen said.

"The office said you just wanted the one kayak, is that correct?"

"Yea, we're going to share." Owen said. "Is that okay?

"Sure, no problem. If you want to change your mind after you're rigged-up, just let me know." James said. "We can change the ticket."

"Oh, okay. Thanks." Owen said.

James went to work getting the kayak, paddles, life jackets and helmets out and carried them down to the edge of the river. He handed us the life jackets and helmets and instructed us to put them on. James slide the kayak down to the water and told us we could get in when we were ready.

"Ready?" Owen asked me, taking my hand.

"Let's go." I said, shaking my head. *Yes, let's go before creepy James here dumps us in the river.* I thought.

James gave us a shove and we were off.

"I'll pick you up down the road about three miles and bring you back here when you're finished." James told us. "You'll see a sign that says where to get out, but I'll be waiting to help.

Karla and I started out after James gave us a boost.

"It's so peaceful out here, look at the water, it's so crystal-clear blue." Karla said looking around admiring the scenery.

"Don't look now, there's mountain goats coming down over there." I pointed out to Karla.

"This is nice, Owen. I'm glad you wanted to do this. It's just the two of us out here."

"Hey, look over there; there's some deer over there on the bank." I told Karla. "Did you see? It was a momma and her fawn?"

"Yes, Owen, I saw the momma and her fawn, and don't you think for a moment that I didn't see the pun in that comment."

"Hey, that was purely incidental." I laughed. "And I am on board with you about it being in God's timing, but we have to do our part too."

"Owen, look up ahead. What is that lying in the river? Is that a moose? It almost has to be, as big as it. It looks like it's bathing." Karla said laughing. "I've never seen a moose or any other animal for that matter taking a bath."

"Yea, I think it is a moose. Get a picture of it, Karla, that's cool."

As we got closer, I could tell it was a moose looking like he was taking a swim in the river. Karla snapped a picture before he got to his feet and sauntered out of the water, up the bank and into the tree coverings.

"That was awesome. Don't see that every day."

"No kidding, glad I could get a picture."

It wasn't much longer that we came up to the sign and saw James waiting for us in his UTV with a rack on top to hold the kayak. Karla and I paddled up to the designated spot in the riverbank.

James stepped out of the UTV and leaned down the riverbank and I helped him pull the kayak up.

"How was your trip?" James asked.

"Oh, great!" I exclaimed.

"It was." Karla confirmed. "We even saw a moose taking a swim. Of course, we interrupted him, and he took off."

"Yea, they're a little skittish." James said, setting the kayak and paddles on top of the UTV and tying them down. "I've heard of them doing that few times. Hop in and I'll take you back to your Jeep." James took off down the road toward the shed we had started from. I think he was practicing for the Indy 500—wow, we made record time. Maybe he was late for something; this guy was a fast and reckless driver in this thing, but it was kinda fun.

We handed the lifejackets to James and went to the Jeep. After we settled in, I pulled out. "I guess the UTV ride back must be part of the adventure they don't tell you about when you pay." I said chuckling.

"Must be why you had to pay up-front, so if James kills you on the way back, you're all paid-up." Karla said laughing. "It was kinda fun."

"What now?" I asked Karla.

"Hmm, I'm game for about anything. I would just like to cleanup back at the campground first. What do you have in mind?"

"Well, the clean-up thing sounds great. Then maybe taking a walk, getting some coffee, have a little camp cookout, a little moonlight dance. Just hanging out at camp with you, if you know what I mean. But if you had something else in mind, then I'm happy to oblige."

"Oh, I know what you mean, Owen." Karla said laughing. "But I'm good, this sounds like a wonderful plan. Have I told you today that I love you?"

"No, I don't remember you saying that today." I said chuckling, I parked the Jeep at our campsite; I went around to Karla's side, meeting her as she was getting out. I slid my hands around her middle. "Well, Mrs. Kaster, I love you, too." I picked Karla up off the ground, twirling her around. "And don't you ever forget." I said before placing a few delicately placed, sweet little kisses along her cheek.

"Oh, don't worry. I haven't forgotten and it won't ever fade." I carried her into the tent kissing her neck off and on.

"So much for cleaning up." Karla said

Owen and I lay snuggled tightly in the sleeping bag sharing the moment. "How about some coffee?" Owen asked later.

"Yes, I'm all for coffee, even a couple cups. But I'm going to take a shower first or you're not going to want to share a tent with me anymore."

"Hmm, I'm not worried about that." Owen said nuzzling my neck.

"I am." I said, moving out of Owen's embrace.

"Okay." Owen said, sounding dejected.

We started grabbing our clothes and I noticed Owen looking at his phone.

"Something wrong?" I asked.

"No, I just have a message. Must be from Jimmy at the airport." Owen said, listening.

Owen listened to his message and then put his phone back in his bag.

"That was Jimmy from the airport; he has the plane fixed and we can give him a call when we're ready to head out and he'll pick us up at the rental car place where he dropped us off."

"Oh, good."

"Yea, it is." Owen said, looking in his bag; not seeming to be engaged in what I had said.

"I'm going to the showers, are you coming?"

"Yep, right behind you, just need to grab my stuff." I stepped outside the tent and decided to wait and walk with Owen over to the showers.

"Oh, geez. You scared me." Owen said opening the tent flap. "What are you doing here? I thought you went to the showers."

"I was going, but then decided to wait and walk with you."

"Oh, you know what that means, don't you?" Owen asked seductively.

"Yea, I know. I can see the gears cranking in your head, cowboy. I want to know what you think about the plane, first."

"Oh, that. Well, I think he might have fixed it pretty quickly, but maybe there isn't much wrong with it." Owen said with a shrug as we walked into the shower.

"Maybe we should take it for a test flight tomorrow and find out for ourselves." I suggested to Owen.

"I like how you think." Owen said, surrounding my face with this gentle hands. The steamy shower flowing over us.

"I knew there was a reason you kept me around."

"I could think of a few others." Owen said, kissing me, standing there, held in each other's embrace.

"That was a steamy shower." Owen said smirking, as we were dressing.

"Umhmm. That's okay." I said, smiling sweetly back at Owen. "We should go get that cup of coffee you mentioned earlier."

"Coffee coming up!" Owen said, taking my hand as we walked outside to put our things away in the tent. "Let's take the Jeep, it's gonna be dark soon—do you want to go somewhere else?"

"No sir, I like the campfire-cookout idea."

"I'll get the fire started." Owen offered, after we had returned from getting coffee.

"I think I'll stay here while you get the kindling this time or we may never actually get a fire going." I said, snickering.

"All right, if you insist." Owen said, laughing. "I'll make it quick."

I grabbed my book and sat in the chair and started reading while Owen went to gather the kindling. Yesterday, we went to gather kindling and came back with nothing. I mused, trying to delve into my book. My mind wandered to the house and farm that Erving had offered to sell us. I was excited at the prospect of living in the country. We spent most of the summer wondering where we were going to live and then all the sudden a house and farm is practically dumped in our laps. Owen said all summer we needed to leave it in God's hands.

I was deep in thought when Owen returned, I was not sure how long he had been back working on the fire when I looked up, he was looking over at me.

"Hi." I said, watching Owen work his magic with the campfire. "Nice to have you back."

"Nice to be back." Owen said. "I got a pretty good fire going while you were off in another world over there. You should have said something sooner, we could have gotten back here earlier so you could spend some time reading."

"Of course not, I wanted to go kayaking with you."

"Yea, it was nice out there, peaceful. All right, well, I'll make us some supper and you finish your story, sound good?"

"No, I'm good." I said, closing the book. "I wasn't reading as much as thinking. I'll help with supper, and we can talk."

"Oh, no. Here we go. We're not even married a week and I'm already in trouble; what'd I do this time?" Owen asked, laughing.

"You? In trouble? Just you wait, buddy." I teased Owen as we got the burgers ready.

"Anytime the wife says we need to talk, usually means the husband's in trouble. Am I right?" Owen asked, holding up his hands in jest.

"Good point, I'll keep that in mind. So, I guess you're in trouble." I said, laughing.

"That's right." Owen said, putting his arms around my neck and kissing me. "We're good together."

"I'd hope we're good together, Owen. We did just say 'I do' a couple days ago."

"So, what did you want to talk about?"

"Erving's house." I told Owen.

"Oh, yea. You don't want to buy it?"

"No, that's not it at all. I want to know what you think about it. We never really talked about buying a farm."

"Well, it's more of an acreage. How do you feel about living out in the country?"

"I actually kinda like the idea. I was thinking about things while you were gathering kindling. You know I spent all summer worried about where we were going to live and then suddenly, a house and farm is practically dropped in our laps."

"I knew you were worried, that's why I kept telling you to leave it up to God. And he would come through. We still need to leave it in God's hands; we can go look things over, talk to Erving, and see what comes about. We don't even have a price yet, that might be a showstopper. Here's your burger. Let's just enjoy the night and we can cross these bridges later. What would you like to do tomorrow?" Owen asked putting his burger together.

"Tomorrow? I thought we were going flying."

"I thought I'd go for a quick trip and check things out." Owen said as he took a bite of his burger.

"Umm, let me think about that for a second. Nope. We're going together."

"I don't know, Karla. I feel like I should go by myself."

"No, you lose. We're a team; remember we face these things together."

"All right, all right." Owen said, holding his hands up his hands in jest. "We'll go together. What else do you want to do?"

"Just that, fly around Glacier. Go see Erving and his house."

"Seriously, you're ready to go home already?"

"Well yea, I'm excited about this house."

"Wow, Lane was right. We didn't do very well in the honeymoon department, if we're ready to go home after two days." Owen said laughing, nuzzling, and kissing my neck as we sat side by side on the picnic table.

"I've had a wonderful time, Owen—we didn't plan anything, if you remember right. I like your off-the-cuff trips."

"Hmm, maybe." Owen said, not sounding convinced. "We should look into something more resort-style after the first of the year. Do the honeymoon thing right. You deserve a proper honeymoon."

"Oh, please. What exactly do you think constitutes a proper honeymoon?"

"I don't know, glitz and glamour, fancy hotels, a resort."

"Ha-ha, I disagree. Owen. I so disagree. I have been to fancy hotels, remember and that does not constitute a proper honeymoon. We're spending time together and it doesn't matter where that's at. That's what constitutes a proper honeymoon to me. I'm just happy being with you."

"We'll see what you have to say about that after being with me a year." Owen said, laughing.

"I've been with you a year, remember. And I still married you, so there. You flew out to San Francisco and surprised me about a year ago, remember? That was awesome. So, I think, my feelings will only grow stronger for you."

"Oh, well, San Francisco." Owen said. "That was just kinda thrown together on a whim."

"See? My point exactly. You flew in on a whim and we had a wonderful weekend, I love your whims."

"Oh yea, a whim is what you want. I got a whim for you." Owen said, taking my hand.

I figured Owen was going to lure me into the tent, but he turned some music on his phone, and we started dancing by the fire under the stars. It was sweet dancing next to him, much different than at our wedding. "See, this is nice, Owen."

"Yea." Owen said smiling.

"You're a great dancer. That duet you and Ty performed at the wedding, fabulous."

"Oh no, you had to bring that up. Let's just hope it doesn't end up on YouTube somewhere."

"Well, you never know. Eide said she got most of it recorded."

"We might just have to get filming rights from her." Owen joked, dipping me to the music.

Owen and I danced under the stars and moonlight for quite a while, hand in hand, shoulder to shoulder. Most of the time I laid my head on his chest and we just enjoyed the quiet night until the campfire burned itself out and the night air grew cool.

"Are you getting cold?" Owen asked when I leaned into him a little more.

"Yea, actually I am."

"We can move this inside." Owen said, taking my hand.

"Do you have a sweatshirt you want me to get you?" Owen asked as I kicked my shoes off and went and laid in the sleeping bag.

"No, thank you. Just come lay beside me."

"Oh, I get it, now." Owen said snickering. "Of course, I'll come lay beside you."

"Oh, just get in here, I'm freezing." I said, giggling as Owen rooted his way around the sleeping bag and put his arm around me.

Chapter 11

The next morning, I got up and was packing my things. Karla was still in the tent, but I could hear her moving about and figured she would be stepping out soon. A moment later, I looked up and wow, she made an ordinary sweatshirt and jeans talk. She took my breath away and now she was my wife. "How'd you sleep last night, you finally get warmed up?" I asked her once I found my voice.

"Good and yes, I got warmed up thanks to you. Could use some coffee, though."

"Do you even have to ask that question?" I asked, laughing. "Let's run down to the Lake Lodge and grab some and then we can finish packing up. I saw some t-shirts to get Luke and Caity. They have some bears on the front and said something about pooping in the park. I think they'll get a kick out of 'em."

"Nice, bucking for some uncle points again." Karla said, getting into the Jeep. "He sure kept my ring safe at the wedding when Ty was goofing around."

"Yea, I saw Ty give him that, told him we were going to give it to Uncle Owe in a little while. He was all excited when Ty put the box in his pocket and told him not to mess with it. But then I noticed he kept looking at his pocket like it was going to fall out."

"Poor kid, you guys probably gave him so much anxiety."

"Ah, he's fine. He got a sucker out of the deal."

"Yea, Ty's a turd. Just wait until his wedding—we're pulling out all the stops." Karla said while we were filling our coffee cups.

"Nice, sounds like your planning paybacks and he isn't even engaged."

"You better believe it." Karla said, giggling. "And don't worry, he'll be engaged soon."

"Any special places you'd like to go on your flight?" I asked Karla later after we had left the campground and I was driving down the road towards the airport.

"I was looking up a few places, if you don't mind."

"Of course, whatcha got?"

"I was looking at Hyalite Canyon and Kootenai Falls. And then maybe a pass into Banff National Park?"

"Sounds great. And you say I'm the one with all the good ideas."

"Do you think everything's good with the plane?"

"I hope so." I said, pulling into the rental car parking lot at the airport. "We'll talk to Jimmy and take things one step at a time—most importantly, we'll say a prayer." I pulled my phone out and dialed Jimmy to see if he was still available to give us a ride around back. He arrived a short time later, and I transferred our things to the back of his pickup.

Mid-afternoon, I taxied into the Flight School runway. *We could not have asked for a better day; the views were fantastic.* I thought. *The weather was great, and the plane seem to be doing well. I did not have any mechanical failures after Jimmy took care of things; the landing was spot-on. The guy seemed like he knew his stuff pretty well, but just to be on the safe side, I think it would be a good idea for Ty and me to look.*

"You're doing it again." Karla said.

"Doing what?" I asked, collecting things out of the plane.

"You look like a thought or two is consuming you."

"Oh, yea a little bit. I was thinking about this plane and what the mechanic at Kalispell told me about the repairs he had made. But I think just to be on the safe side, Ty and I should check it out."

"Well, I don't know anything about plane mechanics, but today's flight was awesome. The flight, the scenery, the landing—heck, even the mountain goats playing out there. The pilot was pretty darn good, too, and handsome to boot."

"No, I'm not disagreeing with you. It was a textbook flight."

"So, then what's to worry about?"

"Yea, you're probably right. Let's get some coffee." We had all our things loaded in the pickup when Ty pulled up alongside of us.

"That was a pretty short honeymoon." Ty said, parking his Jeep next to my pickup.

"That's what I told her last night. But we didn't really have any solid plans."

"Hey, I don't know about him, but I had a wonderful time!" Karla said sounding excited.

"Here, let me grab your tent." I said jumping out of the pickup. "Thanks for letting us borrow it."

"No problem." Ty said.

"We're going after a cup of coffee, so we'll catch you later." I said, getting back in the pickup.

"Coffee still!" Ty said, shaking his head. "I think your ole man is right, you're addicted to that stuff. Get you some Dr. Pepper, it's better for ya."

"First thing I'm bringing back to work is a coffee pot. You probably threw my old one out just as soon as I left. See ya later, Ty."

"Bye, Ty." Karla waved to Ty as I backed away from the hangar.

Driving down the road towards town, I decided to call Erving. See if he was still available. I told Erving we would be out after getting coffee. "That work good for you?" I asked Karla, after I had hung up with Erving.

"Yes, that's fine, but let's go back to your parents' house and freshen up first."

"Oh, honey, I don't know. That seems so far out of the way. I mean so many miles down the road. I-I... I'm just not sure if I can handle the drive." I said, laughing.

"Hmm, well if the driving is too much for you." Karla sarcastically countered back, "then maybe I should drive. In fact, I think I will."

Arnold came barreling out of the barn like he hadn't seen us in ages when I pulled in the driveway. I stepped out of the pickup, and he jumped up on me like we were going to dance or something, all the while trying to sniff me out and detect if I had cheated on him.

"Arnold, buddy, we were only gone two days. Just wait until we're gone to move, or we take a weeklong honeymoon, you'll probably forget about us." When Karla got out of the pickup and came around to my side, Arnold noticed her and decided he had a newfound love. He was done with me; he only had affection for Karla.

"What—am I expired now? We marry her together and somehow, she's your new buddy now? Traitor."

"Nope." Karla said. "We're all married now. Isn't that right, Arnold?"

Arnold barked at us as if he intended to answer Karla.

"That dog howls a lot." Dad said as he came walking up from the barn. "Especially in the evenings. He's stood at the back door the last two evenings and howled; I think he was waiting for you two to come in. Your mother thought he missed you both. I told her was just being a pest." Dad said, watching Arnold continue his dance around Karla.

"Were you being a pest?" I asked Arnold. Arnold just ignored me; he was more concerned with Karla and could care less that I was around.

"What are you doing home already?" Dad asked.

"We didn't really have any definite plans."

"Anybody ever tell you kids how to honeymoon?" Dad asked, shaking his head.

"Don't you worry about our honeymoon." I told Dad, laughing at his comment.

"Yes, Joe. We had a great honeymoon. I told Owen to come back today and we'd go talk to Erving."

"Is Ma in the house? We were looking for a cup of coffee."

"Sure, should have known the only reason you stopped by was for coffee." Dad said, smirking as we headed to the house. And, no, your mother isn't here, she went to town early today. She has her Bible study on Wednesday evenings and wanted to run a few errands. You remember she leaves me to fend for myself on Wednesdays."

"Ah, come on Dad, you'll be fine. Let's get that coffee. I at least know how to make that."

"Yea, you're addicted to it." Dad said sitting down at the table.

"Well, that's kinda funny. Every time we sit down to have a cup, I don't see you passing one up. You seem to have plenty yourself. So better stop judging." I said, laughing.

"So, you kids are going to see Erving this afternoon?" Dad asked.

"Yea, I called him after we left the Flight School and said we'd be over after we get a cup of coffee."

"Well, I think he's actually been waiting on you two. He's been over a couple times. He rented that apartment in town and asked for some help moving things."

"What's he moving?" Karla asked.

"Furniture, mostly." Dad said. "I think he's been working on this move since Sunday."

"What, why?" I asked. "We haven't even agreed to buy his property. I just hope once the dust settles, he's still good with living in town. There were times I remember him not leaving that place for months on end."

"I'm going to go freshen up." Karla said, leaving the table.

"Yea, well, times change, Owen, you'll see that as priorities change." Dad said. "Why don't you two drive over there and see what he's been up to today. I'm going back to the barn; I'll see you later."

"What are you working on, Dad?"

"Just a couple plane wheels, nothing exciting. The bearings went out. Ty dropped them off earlier this afternoon. I should have them changed out this evening. You've seen one of them, you've seen a dozen. I'll see you kids later."

"Well, we'll talk to Erving and then be back to pick you up for supper; would hate to leave you to your own devices, again." I joked with Dad.

"Yea, okay. Are you kids sure you want to have supper with your ole man?" Karla had returned and we were all walking outside together.

"Oh, please, Joe." Karla said. "Yes, we'll be by to pick you up."

"I think we'll bring Erving, too." I spoke.

"Even better." Dad said. "Supper with two old farts. See what's happened to you two, and you haven't even been married a week. See you later." Dad said, waving his arm over his shoulder as he headed out to the barn.

I turned toward the pickup to find Karla in the driver's seat and Arnold in the passenger seat.

"Have I been exiled from my own pickup? Ha-ha. Very funny. Get in the back, Arnold. Ya practical joker."

I could see Erving moving about in the barn as Karla pulled into the driveway.

"Just pull up over here by the barn." I pointed as Karla came to a stop, and Erving came out.

"Hey, kids. Thought I might see you today. How was your trip?"

"It was great, Owen sure can fly a plane!" Karla exclaimed.

"Yea, I guess being a pilot could come in handy." Erving commented. "You kids give any thought about this place?"

"Yea, actually we've given it a lot of thought. Dad said you've been moving things."

"Yep, been working on it. I have some things left to get rid of; the place needs a good cleaning and a few repairs. I'm slowly getting it done. Why don't we go on up to the house and sit down and talk some business?" Erving suggested.

"You don't have to be in this big of a hurry." Karla said. "Especially not on our account."

"We have things we need to work out on our end, first." I added to Karla's comment.

"I know that Owen, these things take time. I also know that you guys need a place to live even in the interim, so you might as well live here. Have a seat at the table and I'll get us a cup of coffee—you still drink coffee, don't you, Kaster?" Erving asked, chuckling.

"Uh, yeah, the sun came up this morning, there Erving. So how much are you asking for this place? That's our biggest question."

"Well, I didn't really know. I went down to the bank to talk to ole Walter about it. You remember Walter Canning. Well, seems he's up and retired. They got some young girl in there took his place, name slips me now, starts with an R." Erving said, scratching his chin, thinking intently.

"Is it Rachel?" Karla asked.

"Yea, believe it is." Erving said, pointing his finger in the air. "How do you know her?"

"She's dating Ty." Karla said. "She was at the wedding with him."

"You don't say. Well, I sat down and talked to her about our plans, and she was going to come up with a market study for me. Whatever that's supposed to mean. Said she would have it ready for me in a couple of days. Then if both parties were agreeable, she could draw up a purchase agreement."

"Erving, do you care if I look around?" Karla asked.

"Oh, heavens, yes. I got ahead of myself. I forgot you've never been here. Owen's been here quite a few times. Listen, I have a load of things I am taking to town. You kids look things over as much as you like; be much easier if I'm not breathing down your neck."

"We're taking Dad to the Burger Barn in a while for supper, why don't you join us?"

"Uh, yea, sure. What's your ole man up to anyways? I'll swing in, maybe he can ride to town with me and help me unload."

"He was replacing some wheel bearings, child's play."

"Well, I'll see you kids in town, take your time." Erving said, replacing his cap, standing by the door.

"Thanks, Erving." Karla said, looking around the kitchen and heading into the dining room. Erving went outside and I joined Karla as she started a tour of the house.

"Owen, this is quite the house. You come to visit a particular neighbor girl, quite a bit?" Karla asked with a chuckle.

"No, nothing like that. Ann and I were in the same grade and Katy's just a year behind. But in this town, it's not exactly your school grade that matters. If anybody had a birthday party in the same age range, we were all invited. Luke's and Caity's parties will be the same way. It the same way for our kids, small-town living. The house could use some updating, don't you think?"

"Yea, I suppose. Some of its country charm though." Karla said.

"Come on." I said, taking Karla's hand. "Let's go upstairs."

"You don't even feel a bit weirded out checking out your friends' bedrooms when they're not here?" Karla asked.

"No, Ann and Katy haven't lived here in years, and Marsha before that. Erving probably hasn't touched these rooms in years, until maybe recently."

"Owen, there's four rooms up here, what are we going to with all this space?"

"I got a few ideas." I said, nuzzling the side of Karla's neck and kissing her cheek while leaned up against the wall.

"Now we just have to work on the family part." I told Karla between the kisses shooting back and forth between us.

"I agree." Karla said through a muffled kiss. "All in his time."

"Let's go finish looking downstairs. I think this staircase leads to the living room. I said, taking Karla's hand again and descending the staircase.

"That fireplace is great, and floor-to-ceiling bookshelves." Karla exclaimed as the room came into view as we descended the stairs. "Your mom's gotten me to be quite the reader these last few months;' at least with us moving down here she won't feel she has to mail me books, she can drop them off. She's probably spent a small fortune on postage."

"Don't worry about Ma, it's those kinds of things that bring her joy in life, sharing something with you. She'll be jealous of all the bookshelves you've got now. I think Marsha was an avid reader and Erving probably built her those shelves."

"Ah, that's so sweet." Karla said, walking past the fireplace. "Hey Owen, come back here. This room would be great for my office."

"I didn't even know this room was here. Only you'd find an office space this quick."

"This is great, perfect-sized space and has a small window. I can put my file cabinet here behind the door. I think my desk will fit here and I have that big painting of the mountains that will look great right above it."

"Look at you go." I said, coming up behind Karla and slowly reaching around her waist. "You better knock it down a notch before you hurt yourself. Maybe focus on where to put the Christmas tree."

"Oh honey, the Christmas tree is easy—you saw the big bay window, it goes there. Besides, who said we were having just one, we're buying a farm. We're having a country Christmas."

"Whoa, whoa, rein that excitement in there, darlin.' This is an acreage, which we haven't bought yet, and I have a two-tree minimum."

"Do I hear a little scrooge piping up? Just have a little faith, Owen. I will decide the decorating scheme. That is, unless I decide to let Eide help."

"Oh, my, look at the time, we better get going and catch up to Dad and Ole Man Erving before they cook up another plan for our lives."

Chapter 12

A few days after looking at Erving's house, he called, asking us to meet with him and Rachel at the bank. We had been in limbo since coming back from our honeymoon. Owen said not to worry, Erving's been on a mission and would be in touch soon. Owen and I walked up to Rachel's office, Erving hadn't arrived yet and Rachel was on the phone, so we held back a moment. Rachel waved us in and motioned for us to have a seat. She wound down her phone call and told the caller thanks for calling, telling them they would talk again soon, and shortly thereafter she replaced the receiver.

"Hey guys, how's it going?" Rachel asked when she finished on the phone.
"We're good. How are you?"
"Good, glad to hear it." Rachel said. "So, you guys are buying Mr. Erving's acreage?"
"Wait, I thought Erving was his first name." I said, looking to Owen for confirmation.
"No." Owen said, laughing. "I think his name's Jack. But everyone around here calls him Erving."
"Good grief, I thought all this time his name was Erving."
"That's right, I go by Erving." He said, stepping into Rachel's office. "I've been Erving for as long as I can remember. Should we get down to business?"
"I got to remind you." Owen said, "We still haven't sold our houses back home yet."
"Don't worry about such minor details, Kaster." Erving said. "I'm moving to town; you kids move out to my place and buy

when you can. I don't 'spect it'll take that long to get your houses sold."

"Well, that's quite a plan you've got worked out there." Owen said. "Can we at least rent the place from you; keep the business side kosher, at least for insurance purposes?"

"That's what I suggested." Rachel said. "It's a fairly common real estate practice when purchasing property."

"What are you going to do, Kaster, burn the place down? I don't figure you will, and I like to keep things simple, especially when it comes to the banking world. So, she said we needed to sign a purchase agreement or some such thing and then we'll close when you two are ready."

"Are you sure about this Erving?" Owen asked again.

"Simple, Kaster, simple." Erving said with a goofy-looking smile. "Besides, you're getting some barnyard animals and a neighbor a few miles north that said you might not be too keen on the idea."

"Hmm, well, not exactly." Owen said, smirking.

"He's warming up to the idea." I said, patting Owen's shoulder.

"Geez, thanks, Karla!"

"Don't worry." Erving said. "I'll help you for a while, get you re-acquainted to the ole gals, anyways. I got a few things to finish and then I'll bring the keys over to you in a few days—sound good?"

"By all means. Take your time. Do you need help with anything?" Owen asked. "Dad and I can come by and help you."

"No, no nothing like that. I have a few repairs in the house and I have someone lined up to give the place a good cleaning."

"Oh, no, Erving, ah Jack. That's not necessary." I told him. "I will take care of that. Especially what you're doing for us."

"Karla's right, we'll take care of the cleaning."

"You kids have enough to take care of. I have it all lined up."

We all signed the papers Rachel had drawn up. As soon as Erving finished with his part, he spoke up, "Are we good here?" He looked over to Owen and I and then at Rachel for confirmation.

"Yes, everything looks in order." Rachel said. "We'll all be in touch soon. Thanks, Mr. Erving."

"Thank you, miss." Erving said. I suspected he still couldn't remember Rachel's name. "Thank you, you two." Erving said, turning to Owen and me.

"Thanks Erving." Owen said, shaking his hand.

"Okay, I'll see you all later." Erving said leaving Rachel's office.

"Does he even know our names?" I asked Owen.

"It's very possible he doesn't. He should mine, he's known it for thirty-some-odd years; but Rachel, well, he wasn't too excited to find out that you'd replaced Walter." Owen said laughing.

"He's always called me 'miss' after he got over the fact that he wouldn't be getting a meeting with Walter."

"Well, we need to get going. Max, Elaine and the kids are coming for supper tonight." Owen reminded me.

"Ah, that's nice." Rachel said. "Once you guys are all settled, let's get together, I know Ty will be up for it. We'll tell him it's his treat." We all chuckled.

"Thanks for everything. Rachel."

"Yes, thank you." I said following Owen's statement.

Owen and I walked out to the pickup and got in. Did we just buy a farm?" I asked Owen.

"No." Owen flipped back. "It's not a farm. Even Rachel called it an acreage."

"Okay, okay. Technicalities." I said excitedly. "I think we should get some chickens or maybe turkeys and ducks; oh, we need to get some llamas."

"Whoa, back the funny farm up." Owen said as my phone started ringing. "Don't think this conversation is going by the wayside 'cause you're answering the phone."

"Hey Eide." I answered as Owen was still giving me his ultimatum.

"Karla, what are you doing? You sound like a windbag."

"Owen and I were just discussing some things. I was giving him some ideas and got excited, Owen not so much."

"Awe, are you two having a fight?" Eide asked. "Didn't you two just get back from your honeymoon?"

"We're not having a fight." I said, grinning at Owen. "Yes, we did just get back from our honeymoon and we bought the farm."

"Acreage." Owen interjected and chuckled as he drove down the highway heading to his parents' farm.

"What are you two doing?" Eide asked.

"Owen and I kinda sorta bought a house, a herd of cows and a few horses down the road from his parents' house, clearly out in the country. I call it a farm; Owen calls it an acreage. I was suggesting we get chickens, turkeys, ducks, llamas."

"You should get some sheep, goats—ohh, you could do goat yoga. How about those fainting goats, those would be cool?" Eide suggested.

"I heard that, Edie." Owen said. "No fainting goats. We're not getting into the barnyard animal business."

"I might get into the barnyard animal business." I said, smirking.

"Just remember." Owen said. "They make terrible smells, do obscene things and they're hard work."

"So, when are you moving?" Eide asked. "When do I get to see this place, is this the place you went and checked out the other day?"

"Yes, and soon, actually."

"I knew it," Eide said dejectedly. "I knew you wouldn't be coming back."

"Well, not to live, but we'll be back to visit, don't worry. Lane and Molly's wedding is coming up, we'll obviously be there for that."

"That's still two months' away and still time for things to change, the way those wedding plans are going."

"I know. Molly and her mom will work things out, we just need to pray for them. I'll call you later when we finalize moving details."

"Oh, fine. Goodbye. Go plan your fancy new life. Just leave us lowlifes back in the hood!"

"Bye, Eide." I said laughing at her famous statement.

"Is she alright?" Owen asked as he pulled down his parents' driveway. "She seemed a bit more fired up than usual. And what's going on with Lane and Molly?"

"She's not happy about our move. I think once we're settled, and we all get into a routine and go back for visits she'll be all right. We've been best friends forever, so it's kinda like losing an appendage."

"Now you know how Ty felt when I left town."

"Yeah, he told me."

"Oh God, what else did he tell you? What's up with Lane and Molly?"

"I think things are good with them; at least for now. Molly and her mom are having some trouble and if that keeps up Lane might not hold up. They could use some extra prayers though. I'm guessing Lane saw the writing on the wall long ago and wasn't just joking about eloping."

"Well, the prayers we can do." Owen said, getting out of the pickup coming around to my side.

"Come here, you." Owen said, embracing me in a hug and twirling me around. "Come on, Max, Elaine and the kids will be getting here soon. Where's those shirts we got for them?"

"Oh, yes. I will get them ready. And then I'll help your mom with supper."

"I'm going to go see what Dad's doing in the barn first; tell Ma if she's got something to grill, I'll be back to fire it up in a bit."

"Hey, Dad. What are you up to?"

"Owen, hi. I'm just cleaning up a bit. Your mom said you kids would be coming around for supper soon. What did you and Erving get figure out?"

"Erving says he's moving to town. In fact, I think he's almost done. Gave Karla and me a purchase agreement and told us to move in. I asked him about renting until our houses sold to keep everything business-kosher, Rachel even suggested it. Erving wouldn't hear of it; said he wanted to keep it simple."

"Sounds about like Erving; he's always wanted a simplistic life. Do you guys want to live out here and can you afford it?"

"Yea, we're good on both fronts. I mean, after we sell our houses back in Silver City."

"Don't forget to work in a few prayers for yourselves. It helps, you know."

"Already on it, Dad. I'm going back to the house. I told Karla I'd come fire up the grill."

"Hey Owen." Dad said, catching my attention before I had slipped out of the barn.

"Yea, Dad."

"It'll be good having you live down the road instead of in the big city."

"I know." I said, chuckling. "Thanks, Dad." I left the barn and was walking back to the house.

I noticed Ty driving in hauling a trailer with what looked like a very interesting piece of equipment.

"Ty, what in the name of Christmas Eve?" I asked him as he came to a stop beside me. I could tell he was clearly upset about something.

"Today was nearly a disaster." Ty said, running his hand through his hair.

"What happened?"

"I'm getting too old for this, Owe, these kids have no respect." Ty said, pulling away. Ty backed the trailer up to the front of the barn. I stood there watching him unhook it. When he finished, he drove back over to where I was watching him.

"Hey, Ty. You should stay for supper. Karla and I have something to tell you, anyways."

"Please tell me its good news, after the day I've had I don't want—"

"Ty, calm down." I said, cutting him off. I pointed my finger towards the house. "I'm going to fire up the grill, you park and meet me on the deck."

"Ty, you alright?" I asked when he stepped up on the deck. "Can I get you something to drink? Ma usually has some iced tea in the fridge; or she always has coffee for Karla and me."

"I'll take a glass of iced tea." Ty said sitting in one of the chairs at the patio table.

"I'll be right back."

I stepped in the house. Ma and Karla were at the counter preparing food. "Hey Ma, Karla, we're going to have an extra one for supper. Ty's here. I'm getting him a glass of iced tea and then I'll take whatever you're planning for the grill."

"Yea, we want to get the burgers going. The kids'll be here soon, and they'll be hungry." Ma said.

"How's Ty doing?" Karla asked.

"He's had a terrible day; he brought a trailer load of something for Dad to repair and he's all bent out of shape about how it got that way."

"Hey, Owen."

"Yea. What's up?"

"Tell him about our llama farm; that'll cheer him." She said, smirking.

"Acreage, and no llamas." I said, smirking and shaking my head as I went back out the door.

"Here Ty." I said, handing him the iced tea and setting the burgers by the grill.

"Who's getting llamas?" Ty asked.

"No one." I said, laughing. "This has been an ongoing joke between Karla and me today. We're moving to Ole Man Erving's soon and she's been giving me a hard time about it, including buying llamas and moving to a farm."

"How soon is soon?" Ty asked.

"Possibly in the next few weeks. Wait—didn't Rachel tell you any of this?"

"Why would Rach tell me any of this?"

"She set it all up for Ole Man Erving and then Karla and I went in to sign the purchase agreement at the bank today."

"Rach and I don't talk bank talk." Ty said shaking his head.

"Erving has a few things to finish at the house and then he said he'd bring the keys by in a few days. Rachel didn't tell you any of this?"

"No, man. Her job's confidential, we don't discuss her clients or their situations."

"Oh, well, it's us, man."

"No exceptions with Rach. But I'm glad you told me. This is best thing I've heard all day." Ty said, finally smiling. "Seriously, you're going to live in Ole Man Erving's house."

"Yep, that's the plan—well, his plan, he cooked this whole thing up. He's moving to town."

"Erving, living in town." Ty said, shaking his head. "Yeah, that's just out there."

"Oh, and get this, he's leaving his herd of cattle and horses out there. Says he's going to introduce me to his gals, and he'll take care of them until I get up to speed. I figure he'll take them to market, soon."

"Introduce you to his gals!" Ty said, laughing again. "Well, it's not like you need much training, you've done it your whole life. Sounds like Ole Man Erving's not ready to give up the herd or his horses. And here comes two kids you could take for a horsey ride." Ty said, motioning to Max and Elaine pulling in the driveway.

"Well, let's just hope they stay on a horse better than you did as a kid." I said, laughing.

"Gampa, Gampa." We could hear the kids clamoring for attention before Max and Elaine got their doors opened.

Caity and Luke came running up to the deck as soon as they were free from their booster seats. "Where's Gampa? Well hello Max, Caity." I said, teasing them.

"I'm Luke. Max is my dad."

"You're Luke! I exclaimed. "Ty, this guy looks just like my brother, don't you think?" I told Luke comically.

"Yes, he does, Owe."

"Dad. Owen called me Max." Luke said when Max and Elaine walked up on the deck.

"Well, that's not very nice, what did he say that for?" Max asked Luke.

"Said I look like you."

"Oh, well in that case, I'd take it as a compliment." Max said, chuckling.

"What's a compement, Dad?" Luke asked, not getting the word pronounced correctly.

"Compliment. Just say, 'Thanks, Owe.'"

"Here." Karla said stepping out the door, handing me the gift bags. "Since you've totally confused the two maybe they'd like a present."

"Yeah. Yeah." Luke said, Caity repeating shortly after him.

"Thank you, Karla, it's not my birthday yet; you shouldn't have."

"Those aren't for you, Uncle Owen. Come on, kids; tell Uncle Owen you want your presents." Karla said, teasing me.

"Uncle Owen?"

"Yes, Caity."

"She said those were for us." Caity said, pointing at Karla and the bags.

"She's Karla and she's your aunt now. Don't you remember? You were at our wedding. Remember the ring pops Ty got you." I said, smirking at Ty. Ty was just sitting back taking it all in.

"I remember." Luke said.

"I just told Owe to take you kids on a horsey ride. You want to do that?" Ty piped in.

"Can we please?" Caity cajoled.

"Not tonight." I said, trying to get the kids to stop begging. "I might have something else for you." I said, passing the pink and blue bags to the respective kid.

"Can we go tomorrow?" Luke wanted to know.

"No, Luke, you can't go tomorrow, you're in trouble, mister, remember?" Max asked Luke.

"Wait, I thought Dad said you moved away." Caity asked, pondering.

"I did but Aunt Karla and I are going to move down the road real soon."

"You can move in with us." Luke offered.

"No, way. I can't move in with you."

"Why?"

"Why, 'cause you snore buddy. Why did your dad say you're in trouble?"

"Yea, Luke. Tell your Uncle Owen why you're in trouble." Max said, trying to hold back a laugh.

"I ordered Cheerios from Mamazon." Luke said, quietly and dejected.

"Sorry—you did what?" Ty said laughing. "You ordered Cheerios? Max, are you not feeding these kids or what?"

"Don't you two laugh. I have to punish this kid." Max said.

"Seriously, Luke, you ordered Cheerios from Amazon—what'd you do, just call them up and order a bowl for breakfast?"

"Hey, how come you two haven't opened your presents?" Karla asked, changing the subject.

"Mom said we can't open presents until we're told we can." Caity said.

"Open them, my clothes are going' out of style waitin' on you two." I told the kids boisterously, getting them to giggle again. The kids tore into the bags Karla had nicely prepared for them, found the t-shirts, and started looking at them. Luke started laughing as soon as he realized what was on his shirt.

"Hey guys, whatcha got there?" Elaine asked.

"A shirt with a bear on it that looks like it's pooping." Luke said, giggling.

"Do you know what it says?" I asked Luke.

"No, I don't read, Uncle Owen, you know that."

"Hold it up and I'll read it for you. 'Who Pooped in the Park? Glacier National Park.' Do you know what animals are on it?"

"Deer, elk, moose, buffalo." Luke said.

"What's this one?" I asked, pointing at the animal on the shirt he was holding up.

"Hmm, I don't know. Dad, what's that one?"

"That's a mountain lion, you know what that animal is."

"Oh right, I forgot."

"What'd you get, Caity?" Elaine asked.

"Mine has pretty flowers on it." Caity said. "Not a poopy shirt like his."

"What do you kids say?" Elaine asked.

"Thank you, Owen." Luke and Caity said in unison.

"What about Karla?"

"What about her?" Luke asked.

"Thank her for your shirt." Max said. "They were from her, too. Owen and Karla went to Glacier National Park and brought you those shirts back—wasn't that nice?"

"You went camping in a park?" Luke asked Karla.

"We sure did."

"Can we go camping, Dad?" Luke asked.

"No, Luke." Max said, sounding irritated. "Now thank you aunt and uncle for the shirts like your mom told you."

"Thank you." Caity said, and Luke repeated her.

"Ok you two little monsters, let's go wash up and see if your grandma needs help setting the table before you get into any more trouble," Elaine said as she herded the two into the door. I could hear Ma fussing over the kids. I looked over towards the barn as dusk was just settling over the hay field behind it. Dad and Arnold were coming out of the barn and looking the trailer over that Ty had parked there earlier. I could see the confused look on Dad's face as he started walking this way. Dad turned and said something to Arnold.

"Ty did you blow up a plane as one of your lessons at the Flight School today?" Dad asked him as he stepped onto to the deck joining us.

"No sir, but I think that would have made my day a whole lot easier."

"But I think a kid ordering Cheerios on Amazon made up for whatever did happen over there today." I told Dad.

"What'd Luke do now?" Dad asked.

"He watched Elaine place an Amazon order on the Alexa the other day; so yesterday he wanted Cheerios for breakfast and Elaine said they weren't here yet and he had to finish up the other cereal we had." Max said still sounding irritated. "Well, I guess Luke didn't like that idea—Elaine came back from the laundry room in time to hear Luke say, 'Yes, place order.'"

"Nice!" Ty said, laughing again. "I'm impressed he can even run or talk to the thing."

"Yea, me too. Let's go in and join the ladies and eat some burgers, shall we, gents?"

"I got burgers ready." I said as we came into the kitchen making a blanket statement.

"Ah, thanks for cooking them, honey." Ma said as she came up alongside of me, half-hugging me.

"Sure thing, Ma. As long as you made the dessert."

"I did, a pie and some cookies. Either of those interest you?"

"I won't complain about either."

"You made cookies, Gramma?" Luke asked.

"That's what she said." I told Luke. "But she made 'em for me."

"Owen, be nice." Karla scolded. "Luke, you just wait, we'll make sure you get his share for teasing you."

"Yes!" Luke said, raising his arms in the air.

"All right, let's take a seat and bow our heads." Dad said, intent on offering a blessing.

"Dear Lord, we come to you this evening with blessed hearts and possibly some troubled minds. We thank you for any blessings you send our way to ease our sufferings and focus on the good you bring to us. We are blessed to spend our time with family, friends, and with the good food so wonderfully prepared. Bless us one and all. Amen."

"So, Owen, you were saying before we came in to eat that you're moving down the road soon." Max said, looking inquisitive. "I take it you and Erving got things squared away."

"I guess you could say that. He's been moving to town this week."

"Oh wow, really." Max said, looking shocked as he took a bite of his burger.

"Yea, he told us today that he'll bring the keys to us in a few days."

"So, when are you moving in?" Elaine asked.

"I don't know, we haven't really decided." I said, looking at Karla. "I think our heads are still spinning from all this."

"I'll tell you when you're moving, right now." Ty said, driving his finger into the table." If I have to hire an army to do it, you're moving this weekend."

"What do you mean this weekend, Ty?"

"You're moving this weekend. I'll fly us all up in the morning; we still have one decent plane left. Karla, does your family have a couple trailers to drive back with?"

"Uh, yea." Karla started to say.

"Toe, Toe." Luke said, standing in his chair, interrupting Karla.

"Luke, what are you doing?" Max asked him. "You need to sit down."

"I have a question." Luke said.

"Not like that you don't." Max said. "Now sit down and eat."

"Toe." Luke said again.

"What's wrong with your toe?" Elaine asked.

"Uncle Toe." Luke said, pointing at Owen, while everyone laughed.

"Where did you get that idea?" Max asked.

"You called him Toe outside, Dad."

"No, I called him Owe. But maybe we should start calling you Uncle Toe." Max said looking at me.

"I think we'll stick with Owe. What do you need, buddy?"

"Can I go in the plane with you tomorrow?" Luke asked.

"Yep." Ty said. Your whole family's going in the plane."

"Okay, thanks for volunteering us there, Ty." Max said.

"Sure thing, the kid wants to go in the plane—see, it'll be fun." Ty told Max.

"And I'll end up with a neck ache lugging his furniture around." Max said, nudging me in the arm.

"Hey, you didn't even know when I moved up there and I helped you move twice before—you owe me."

"Yea, who's fault is that?" Ty asked. "You just kinda left town in the dead of night."

"Not really, just early in the morning and I told you I was leaving. Besides, that's all water under bridge, I'm back." I said, holding my hands in the air.

"Yes, yes. Thank you, ladies and gentlemen." Ty said, standing and bowing, causing an eruption of laughter. "I take full credit and not a minute too soon, I might add."

"I for one am glad." Ma said, smiling. "Five hours away was getting to be a bit much for this mother's heart."

"Hey now, come on—what am I, the ugly stepson?" Max asked, laughing.

"No, of course not." Ma told Max. "But you only come around when I ask you guys to come for supper."

"Well therein lies your problem, Rosie dear." Dad said.

"What's that?" Ma said.

"You should offer to feed them more." Dad said, laughing.

"Well, if that's what it takes, you're all invited to supper every night." Ma said.

"Does that include me, too, Mrs. Kaster?" Ty asked.

"Yes, that's always included you, Ty."

"So, Ty, tell us about that hunk of junk on your trailer out there." Dad said.

"Oh, and the evening was going so well." Ty said, sighing, running his hand through his hair. "This has been a very trying class. In fact, it was so trying, I just up and canceled classes all next week."

"You've never canceled an entire week of classes before, Ty. Things must be really bad."

"Yea, I thought everyone could use a reset. Most of all me. Since Owe left, I have been giving students independent instructions to take care of while I went up with students on flights. For the most part, it's worked out; but this class has just gotten worse, especially the last few months. There's one guy in particular—he doesn't listen very well and his attitude leaves something to be desired. He in turn convinces this other guy to mess around with stuff. They were messing around with that older Bonanza parked in the back. They were trying to rewire something, the battery compartment overheated, damaging the battery and caused an explosion. So now we need a battery box rebuilt and some panels straightened or possibly re-machined."

"Wow, Ty, I had no idea things had gotten so bad. Of course, I'll be back on Monday, and we can get a plan together to get things straightened around."

"Well, I don't know about Monday. I'm serious about helping you guys move this weekend."

"What about Rachel?"

"Rach's leaving to see her sister in the morning."

"Ah, so you're just a lost pup looking for—"

"Don't even go there." Ty said, cutting me off.

But then Luke interrupted me. "Dad, are we going in the plane?"

"Yea, Dad, are we?" Caity wanted to know.

"How about some dessert?" Ma asked, deflecting the kids' question.

"Yes, yes, Gamma, cookie cookie," Luke said, fidgeting in his seat.

"I thought I was getting the cookies." I said, joking as Ma set a plate of cookies in the center of the table with one hand and a pie next to it, and then stepped back to the counter to get dessert plates and whipped topping.

"Everyone, feel free to help yourself." Ma said.

"Just one, Luke." Max said as Luke was jumping toward the cookie plate.

"Would someone mind handing me that pie?" Dad asked. "Seems your mother only makes pie when you kids come around; I think she thinks one of you likes em better'n me, another reason to tell your mother you'd stop by more often."

"I think she does that on purpose. Dad."

"At my age, I don't really care about that purpose." Dad said. "So, what time's this moving party start tomorrow?"

"Owe and I take care of pre-flight checks at six-thirty, take off at seven? That be ok with everyone?" Ty asked.

"Well then, we better get some little honyocks to bed." Elaine said.

"Is all this on the up-and-up with you guys, Elaine? It was just kind of dumped on you. If this doesn't work for you guys to go along, it's all good, just say. We know you're busy."

"Oh no, we know when we're being railroading into something." Elaine said, laughing. "Ty just railroaded all of us, including you. I think it's a pretty slow day tomorrow. Besides, now the kids are all excited for a plane ride, I don't think we can get out of it."

"Thanks for supper, Mom." Max said as he and Elaine were herding the kids out the door. "See how that worked out? You'll get to see us two days in a row. How you like them apples?"

"Yes, maybe I'll get Ty to get you involved in more projects around here. So, you can at least make a landing occasionally. See you in the morning. Bye, Luke. Bye, Caity. Gramma loves you."

"Bye, Gramma." Caity said.

"It looks like Luke and Elaine are already out to the van." Max said. "Night, Mom."

"Here you two, let me take care of the dishes." Ma said to Karla and me as she stepped back into the kitchen from saying goodbye to Max, Elaine, and the kids.
"We're almost done, Ma."
"I'm helping, too." Ty said.
"Oh Ty, I didn't realize you were still here." Ma said, startled as she turned around to see Ty close the fridge door.
"Your ketchup and mustard might not be in the right spot, but at least I got them in the fridge." Ty said, laughing.
"Oh, any ole spot's good in there. Thank you, all. I'm going to check for some things in the freezer then, if you all have the dishes covered." Ma said, leaving the kitchen.

"So, if we land in Denver, can someone from your family come get us, Karla?" Ty asked when we all sat down at the table after we had the dishes finished.
"Well, her dad would come get us, I'm sure." I said, pointing to Karla. "I texted Aaron from Mountain Rescue to see if we could land out there and he said yeah, no problem. So, we might as well fly in there."
"That will be so much closer and easier." Ty said. "Good thinking."
"Ty, you sure about doing all this tomorrow?" I asked. "Karla and I can run up in a couple weekends and take care of things. As a matter of fact, we haven't even sold our houses."
"Yes, I like this idea, get everyone together and be done quickly. It would take the two of you like six weeks to pack up your houses."
"I need to text Dad and maybe call Eide." Karla said. "I'll leave you guys to your flight plans. Thanks for your help, Ty."

"Hey Karla, didn't we just talk a few hours ago? Or am I getting my days mixed around?" Eide asked, answering the phone.

"Hi. Yes, we did talk this afternoon. Can't I talk to you twice in one day? We've done that before."

"Yes, we've done that before." Eide said. "But something tells me I'm not going to like this conversation. Did you buy a llama or a fainting goat?" Eide asked, laughing.

"Why would Karla be buying a fainting goat?" I could hear Levi ask in the background.

"Hold on, Karla, I didn't tell Levi I talked to you this afternoon; let me put you on speaker phone and you can tell him about the fainting goats."

"Hey, Levi."

"Hey, what's going on? Have a good honeymoon?"

"Yes, good honeymoon. Different subject, though. When Eide called me today, Owen and I had just more or less bought a farm—acreage —whatever Owen and I are calling it, and we were discussing buying a llama and Eide suggested buying a fainting goat. Well, anyways, the exotic animal purchases have kinda been put on hold."

"Oh, no, here it comes." Eide said. "I can just tell it's going to be bad. Everything's been bad since you said yes to Owen's marriage proposal."

"Eide, just hear me out. What are you guys doing tomorrow?"

"Lane and I have some grass to plant but shouldn't take more than a couple hours." Levi said.

"Toby and I are going to see if we could break his diaper-changing record tomorrow; we hit eight today. Gonna try for nine tomorrow and possibly suck a thumb or two. Why, what's going on?" Eide asked.

"Ty's decided we're moving this weekend. He's flying us all up there in the morning to pack up and move."

"All in one day?" Eide asked. "Good grief, they elect you mayor of this little hotshot town or what? How can you even move yet, you said you just bought the house?"

"Well, I doubt we'll be done tomorrow, but at the rate Ty's going who knows. I said, laughing. "And technically we haven't bought it yet; Erving cooked this whole thing up. We buy the house when we sell ours up there and move in now."

"What's he, the outgoing mayor?" Eide asked sarcastically.

"No, he's not the mayor. You guys want to meet at Owen's house and help pack? I asked Eide and Levi.

Chapter 13

"Good morning, Ma, what are you doing in here?" Owen asked, walking into the kitchen, and pouring himself a cup of coffee.

"I thought I'd make us some breakfast burritos."

"Good grief, Ma, you didn't have to go to all this work."

"It's not that much work; I have the filling about done and the tortillas were in the freezer. I'll roll 'em up here right quick and be done."

"Listen to yourself: filling, tortillas in the freezer, roll 'em up. Sounds like a manufacturing plant. We could have picked things up when we got to Silver City."

"I know" Rosie said. "This will be faster, and the grandkids will be hungry by then."

"Oh, wow, sure smells fabulous in here." I said, following Owen into the kitchen.

"Yeah, look at what Ma here is concocting."

"Man, Rosie, you're going to a lot of work."

"I'm gonna head out and meet Ty." Owen said. "You want to come with me or with my folks?"

"I'll stay and help your mom."

"Ah, thanks, honey. We'll be right behind you." Rosie said as Owen went out the door.

"Sounds good, ladies, don't want to make the drill sergeant wait."

Rosie and I finished the burritos and headed over to the Flight School to meet everyone. Joe went with Owen earlier, so it was just Rosie and me. I wondered if there would be more opportunities for Rosie and me to have outings in the future now that we were moving down here; she was such a kind mother-in-law.

We met everyone at the Flight School just as Owen and Ty were finishing the pre-flight checks. Rosie passed out her breakfast burritos as everyone boarded the plane. I think Rosie was just as excited as the kids to go on the plane. Did they not realize how much work was involved at the other end? This was going to be a terribly busy weekend.

We landed at the Mountain Rescue hangar a little over an hour later. It had been a while since Ty, and I had been pilot and co-pilot. "That was a pretty sweet flight." Ty said.

"You're telling me! I'm glad you suggested this, Ty. We should do this more often."

"Well maybe not the moving part." Ty said.

Ty gave the typical arrival instructions to the passengers but was pretty casual. We started to disembark the plane. I waited for Karla to come up from her seat.

"Good morning, again." I said as we met up to walk down the stairs together. "How was your flight?"

"Delightful." Karla said, laughing as I put my hand around her neck, and we walked toward her dad waiting at his SUV.

"Hi, Dad." Karla said, smiling at him. "Thanks for picking us up."

"Hey kiddo, hi Owen—you two sure took your time getting off the plane," Darren said skeptically.

"Don't worry about it, Dad." Karla said.

"Are your brothers coming?" Darren asked Karla as we got in and Darren started to drive off. "I haven't gotten ahold of them this morning. I thought they could go to the recycle center to get boxes."

"We already have a bunch of boxes at Owen's house we were saving. Lane and Levi are planting grass today, but they'll be by later. Eide's coming by sometime later, so for now you're looking at the moving crew." Karla mentioned.

"Well let's get to it." Darren said as we pulled up to my house. I noticed Laurel parked out front. Everyone exchanged greetings with Laurel as we headed inside to get organized.

Laurel and Ma headed for the kitchen and started pulling things out of the cupboards. I had never seen anything like it before. It was like they were all programmed, like robots. Karla and I stood back in amazement; it took us nearly six hours pack up her kitchen and here our mothers had the kitchen ransacked in about ten minutes.

"Owen, don't just stand there." Ma said. "Get the packing supplies."

"Sorry, Ma, just a little surprised."

Ty was in the living room disassembling the tv and entertainment center. Max was taking pictures off the walls and Elaine and the kids were helping him. It looked like a home robbery was in progress.

"I think you might be right; we might be moved out by noon." Karla said, laughing.

"Yeah, no kidding, you might want to get started on your office before some four-foot-tall kid packs it up and you're out of business."

I heard Eide and Toby come in a while later. "Hello," Eide said. "I brought donuts, coffee and breast milk. Anyone interested?"

Karla and I met her in a now-empty kitchen. "I'd love a cup of coffee; I'll pass on the breast milk, though." The rest of the clan came looking for the coffee and donuts as well.

"Wow, you guys have really gone to town packing this place up. Are you sure you're not going back to be mayor?" Eide asked, looking at Karla.

"Of course, she is. Mayor of Owen." I said laughing, putting my arm around her, and taking a donut.

I went back to my room and continued packing after the short coffee break. I looked out my bedroom window at the excited voices coming from the backyard. It looked nice out. Luke and Caity had given up on the moving endeavors going on in the house and rediscovered the massive fort system I had put together before they all came to visit last summer, when I proposed to Karla. *I think I will just leave that here in hopes another family can enjoy it. I can always get another set and assemble it at Erving's place.*

"Hey how's it going in here?" Karla asked. She was leaning up against the door frame; it was the best-looking thing I'd seen since we landed.

"Hey, guess I got distracted." I said, referencing the activity going on in the backyard.

"Yeah, you could say that. Everything has been going full steam ahead since last night; we walked in here this morning, and everyone is just going at it. Even Luke and Caity are little troopers."

"I know, did you see our mothers? It's like they just ransacked the kitchen like heathens, it was kinda funny."

"I'm grateful for all their help though." Karla said. "You remember how long it took us to pack up my house."

"Hey there, where are you two?" Ty asked from down the hall. "We need one of you to go to Karla's and get her vehicle, so we can hook up a trailer." Ty said as he knocked on the door.

"Uh, this is all you." I said, looking at Karla. "If you're planning to get llamas, you gotta drive your vehicle and trailer home."

"What? That's not fair." Karla said, looking shocked. "What does me pulling a trailer load of our belongings on a five-hour road trip have to do with getting a llama?"

"When you get a llama, how you gonna get it home? Tuck it in the backseat? Get it a car seat? I'm still rooting for the two-legged species that requires the car seat, you know."

"You better watch yourself, there, Mr. Kaster." Karla said, laughing at me.

"Oh my, come on Karla." Ty said.

We all finished packing; Owen and I were ready to leave Silver City by late afternoon. I did not figure it could be done. Lane and Levi were pulling in just as we were about to head out.

"Wow, you two have the absolute perfect timing." Dad said, shaking his head. "A second later, everyone and everything would have been gone."

"We've been sitting down at the corner watching y'all, waiting for the right moment," Lane said. "Haven't we helped you move like twelve times, Kar? You ought to have a system by now."

"Actually, this move was way different than any other move. And now Elaine and I are taking a road trip this evening."

"Wait, you're pulling the trailer?" Lane asked. "This is a joke, right?"

"Owen sure seems to think so."

"How's everything with you and Molly? The wedding?"

"Molly and I are great, always have been." Lane said. "The wedding and her mom are a different story. How did you and Mom do it?"

"I don't know, we just did it. Mom knew when step back and let me do my thing and she knew when to step up and help. Our mom and Molly's mom are two different people, though."

"I keep telling Molly we just need to elope and forgo any more heartache."

"You've been telling Molly that since before you were even engaged, Lane." I said, laughing.

"We can discuss this later—you guys need to get on the road. I will call you next week. Be careful."

"Love ya, brother, sorry you missed out on all the fun."

"Yeah, me too. Glad you got to see me." Lane said smiling as I pulled my Durango and Dad's cargo trailer down the street with Owen and Max following me with Dad's pickup and trailer.

"I'm glad you let the kids go with Joe and Rosie for the night and are riding back with me." I told Elaine as we hit the highway after fueling up at the gas station.

"Of course, I'm glad you asked." Elaine said. "Although Joe and Rosie might be in for an interesting night with those two. They have been quite active lately. The things they come up with." Elaine shook her head, laughing. "If one doesn't come up with it the other will for sure. You heard about Luke's Amazon order, right?"

"Yes, the guys were laughing at him, poor kid."

"Did Rosie tell you about the garage door?" Elaine asked.

"No, what happened with the garage door?"

"A week or so ago the kids and I came back from the grocery store. I didn't pull into the garage because we were going to leave again when Max got home. I was just going to run the groceries in the house. I grabbed the groceries and walked by punching the button to open the overhead garage door. I thought the kids were still buckled in their seats; well, I thought wrong. Next thing I know, Caity's out of the van riding the garage door as it rolls up and Luke's mad that he doesn't get to ride it."

"Oh, wow." I said, laughing. "What made her decide to do that?"

"Who knows. That's why Max calls them our little monsters. A couple months ago I get a call from one of the neighbors; Luke and Caity had just left the neighbor's house being little salespeople."

"Ohh, how cute. What were they trying to sell?"

"Not so cute, they were trying to sell the cat."

"No way." I said, laughing. "Whatever for?"

"They claim they needed money to buy cupcakes."

"Well, come on, Elaine, are you not contributing to their daily sugar intake or what? I wonder If Max and Owen were holy terrors when they were that age?" I asked Elaine. "Owen's talked some about being that age, but it was mostly about him and Ty."

"Yeah, Max never has really said much about them when he and Owen were that age. Just when they worked out in the corrals taking care of the cattle. He grew old of it pretty quick; it wasn't his thing. He said Owen and Ty were way better at it than him."

"Owen told me they helped their dad, too. Ty wasn't particularly good at it and kept falling off the horses." Elaine and I both laughed at Ty.

"Did you meet Max in college?" I asked Elaine.

"No, I didn't meet Max until after we were both out of college. Max had moved back to West Creek and was already working at the high school. I was working at a bank in Colorado Springs and making weekly trips to the branch in Durango. One week on the way home, my car broke down, and who should find me? Max Kaster." Elaine said smiling, shaking her head. "He tried to help me with my car, but that didn't work out and we went over to the mechanic, who was nowhere to be found. So, he told me he would help me get a motel room for the night and he knew a guy outside of town that could help with my car in the morning. Well, when we got to the motel, they didn't have any rooms. So, beings that Durango's a forty-mile drive and Colorado Springs is over an hour away, Max asked me how I felt about staying at his house."

"Seriously. Max took you to his house?" I asked Elaine. "Weren't you freaked out?"

"Not exactly freaked out, I think Max might have been. He stayed in his pickup in the garage. I think he was trying to figure out how to help me that night and this was the best way he could come up with. All he'd have had to do was go stay in the basement. It had a separate entrance. I told him he was a weirdo."

"No way, that's funny." I said, laughing.

"Anyways, I think he got cold. He came in the kitchen around four that morning. I was making coffee in the kitchen; I nearly scared the wits out of him. We sat at the table talking for hours, it was great. Later that morning, we went out to Joe and Rosie's and talked to them and of course Joe fixed my car. After that, Max and I met up almost every weekend when I was done in Durango."

"Oh my, that's quite a story. I need to stop and go to the bathroom—would you call the guys and tell them I'm making a pit stop."

"Hey ladies, how's the trip going?" Owen asked when we got out and was heading to the store.

"Clearly, a lot longer trip than running down the interstate. But we're having a nice visit." I said, sharing a glance with Elaine.

"It's not much longer." Owen said. "Couple more hours. Let's get something to eat while we're here, 'cause it's a while before the next stop. How are you doing on gas?"

"I fueled up before we left town, when we got coffee. Hence, the pitstop. I'll finish this conversation after I visit the little girls' room."

"Ha, right, don't wet your pants. Might be a rough ride home from here, hon." Owen said, trailing after me.

"You're so funny." I hollered back at him.

We got home later that evening and parked the trailers out by Joe's barn and took Max and Elaine out to the Flight School to pick up their van.

"Thanks for riding back with us." Owen said. "It was good catching up with you, Max. I'll talk to Karla about the Harvest Festival. I had forgotten all about it. But we'll probably go with you guys. Maybe Ty and Rachel will go, too."

"Oh, yea, the Harvest Festival is coming up." Elaine said. "You missed it last year."

"He's missed the last two years." Max said.

"What's the Harvest Festival?" I asked. "And how come you missed it, Owen?"

"I was in San Francisco with a good-looking woman."

"This sounds fun, we'll be there." I said, ignoring Owen's comment. "We'll call later and make plans."

"See you both at church in the morning." Owen said. "Good night, thanks again."

"Owen, what's the Harvest Festival—and how come you ditched your family at your birthday?"

"Yep, I did. I went to San Francisco and stalked a beautiful woman. One of the best birthdays I've ever had."

"Well, play your cards right and you might actually get a birthday gift this year." I said, laughing.

"I've gotten one of the best gifts, ever." Owen said, taking my hand as he drove down the driveway of the Flight School to head back to his parents' house.

Chapter 14

Karla and I settled into Erving's house over the next few weeks, and I joined Ty back at the Flight School. We agreed on splitting up the sessions like we'd always done; I took the classroom and instructional materials. Ty took the flight sessions.

"Morning, Owe." Ty said as he walked into the shop. "What are you doing here so early?"

"Hey Ty, I haven't really been cleaning up after classes, lately. Thought I should come in and do some organizing, try to find some things back, so to speak."

"You guys getting all settled in over at Ole Man Erving's?" Ty asked, laughing. "I still can't believe you're living there."

"Yea, well, I wasn't so sure we should move there, either, but then after you railroaded us back to town Erving brought the keys by a few days later. That night after Erving left, the realtor called and had an offer on my house. So, I took it as a sign."

"Karla wanted me to mention Thanksgiving to you. We're hosting this year."

"Oh, yeah." Ty said, chuckling. "Does she want me to smoke a turkey or something?"

"No, you crazy fool. You know I'm better at it than you are. She volunteered you to fly up, pick them all up, including Eide." I laughed widening my eyes.

"She what? Where'd this idea come from?"

"Yep, you're flying up Wednesday afternoon. Welcome to the family, you started all this flight stuff." I said, laughing.

"All right, all right." Ty said. "Sure thing. You tell Karla, I'll do it, on one condition."

"What's that?"

"She makes me my own pumpkin pie."

"I'll relay your terms. But for now, I better get things organized or I'll be in the same boat as when I came in here."

"I'll help ya." Ty offered. "I want to talk to you about those kids that were messing around with the battery compartment a few weeks ago. They came to see me yesterday."

"Oh yea?"

"Yea, they want their spots back in the class." Ty said, rubbing his face and looking distressed.

"What did you tell them?"

"I said I had talk to you. I wanted your thoughts on the whole thing."

"What do you think, can we get them through? They're about three weeks behind."

"That's the other thing, getting them caught up; it'll be tight to finish up by the end of the session, with the holidays." Ty said.

"Tell you what, send 'em in and I will talk to them. Maybe we can work something out; have some after-hours sessions."

"Just be careful, Owe. They could have done some considerable damage this last round. Not to mention hurt themselves or somebody else."

"Hey, hon, I'm home. How was your day?" I called out. Karla immediately looked up from her office in the little room off the living room, which is usually where she's at when I leave for work and where I find her when I get back. "Seriously, Karla, have you even gotten up at all, today? You were here when I left, and I went to work early."

"Hi, honey. Yes, I have gotten up. Arnold and I had to go to the bathroom."

"Are you about done for the day? It's about seven."

"Seven, seven p.m." Karla said, stammering. "Really, that late? Goodness, why are you getting home so late?"

"Long story, let me grab a shower and then I'll tell you about it over supper. What are we having for supper, anyways?"

"Um, I don't know—let me close this file out and I'll go figure it out. I lost track of time, otherwise I would have it ready. Oops," Karla said, laughing as she covered her mouth. I headed upstairs, chuckling at Karla.

I came back downstairs about a half hour later to find Karla still at the computer in her office. "Whatever you're working on, honey, sure has drawn your attention to it. I'm going to make a sandwich and go check on the calves. You take whatever time you need; we can talk later. But make sure you stop and eat something tonight."

I went out to the barn and looked in on the horses. Erving had left five horses and about twenty head of cow-calf pairs out here. When we first moved in, Erving was making about three trips a day out here to check on things. But now that it has gotten colder and we've had a couple light snows, his trips have dwindled. A few days, like today, he's trusted me enough to check the herd in the evening and make sure there's enough hay and muck out the stalls. All the animals seem content, so I moved to the barn office. I'd only been in there a few times. Erving said Dad still had some things stored in there from when Karla and I got married in his barn. I stepped in there, planning to look at all the old rodeo pictures on the wall and noticed there were a few boxes left. *I will have to remember to tell Dad he still has things over here.* I flipped through a few things on the top box. I noticed a newspaper that seemed older than me sticking out. I picked it up, looking it over. I skimmed through other papers in the box and put it back, not finding much to catch my attention. I noticed some other papers and an older picture. The older picture fell from between the newspapers. *I suppose Dad's forgotten about these boxes being in here.* I picked up the picture that had fallen to the floor; it was of a little girl. *Hmm, cute kid—maybe these were Erving's boxes with the picture of the little girl.* I heard the barn door open, interrupting my thoughts.

"Owen?" Karla called out. "Are you in here?"

I set the papers and picture in the box and turned to meet her out by the stalls.

"Hey, workaholic lady. What's up? You finally tear yourself away from that computer?" I asked, smiling.

"Owen, I'm sorry about supper not being done when you got home." Karla said as she put her hands around me.

"Hey, it's okay. Whatever you're working on must be really interesting. What are you working on, anyways?" I asked as we sat down on the square hay bales stacked next to the horse stalls.

"I got this new account in Durango. I'm really excited about it."

"I can tell. Who's the account for?"

"A saddle shop—this opens up a whole new avenue for me."

"That's great, hon, just remember to come up for air occasionally. Did you eat today?"

"No, they emailed their signed contract this morning and I got started on things and just kept rolling with it. I didn't realize what time it was until you came home. Why were you so late today?"

"I went in early to clean and organize the shop. Let's go in and at least make you a sandwich." I said, taking Karla's hand, leaving the barn. "Shortly after I got started Ty came in and wanted to talk. I mentioned to him that you volunteered him to fly everyone in for Thanksgiving."

"Oh good, is he game for that?" Karla asked.

"He is, if you supply his own pumpkin pie."

"The drill sergeant's negotiating now?" Karla asked, laughing.

"Yeah, he's kinda earned the right." I said, laughing. It's a wonder he doesn't have permanent back damage. He loaded and unloaded two trailer loads of our belonging in less than two weeks' time. So, I say if all he wants is a pumpkin pie, he gets a pumpkin pie."

"I suppose you're right." Karla said, getting a sandwich ready. "But this doesn't explain why you were so late."

"The two students that caused the severe plane damage a few weeks ago, came to the Flight School yesterday and talked to Ty about getting back into class. Ty told them he had to talk to me."

"So, what are you guys going to do?" Karla asked while she finished putting her sandwich together.

"Do we have any cookies?" I asked, rummaging through the cupboard.

"Yea," Karla said. "Try the top shelf."

I had just glanced up there to see the package of chocolate chip cookies, so I grabbed them, and we sat down at the table together.

"So, Ty and I talked it over this morning, and I told him to have them come in and we'd discuss this and see if we could put a plan together. This afternoon, they came back, and Ty and I talked to them together and they are committed to completing the class. They wanted to jump back in today. I told them I would work with them after class for the next couple weeks and get them caught up."

"Do you think they can get through this time?"

"Yea, Ty and I agreed they're not to be left alone at any time. They're either in the classroom setting or up flying with one of us and then they need to leave the property. I know that sounds harsh, but that's the reality of the situation."

"No, that sound like a good plan."

"You want any of these cookies before I put them away?" I asked Karla.

"No, I'm good." Karla said. "I'm going to bed."

"You're going to bed? Are you all right?"

"Yep, perfectly fine. It's just time for bed." Karla said, standing at the staircase, smiling back at me.

"Oh, oh, bedtime, you say." I said smirking.

Chapter 15

"Good grief, Karla, what are you doing up so early jammin' out down here in the kitchen for?" Owen asked as he came up behind me and twirled me around to the music, kissing my neck.

"We dance in the kitchen pretty well, ya know, Owen."

"I know, you're always jammin' out in here—the floorings just right, hon. So, what are you doing up so early?" Owen asked as we swayed back and forth to the tune of the music. "I thought Ma was coming to help you with things later. Do you have work to take care of? If you do, I can help more, too."

"I pretty well have things tied up for my clients for the year; nobody really has marketing aspirations at the end of the year. I learned that a long time ago. I was just awake and thinking about Thanksgiving plans for tomorrow and decided to come down and get organized. I didn't wake you, did I?"

"No, you didn't wake me. I'm headed to work here in a bit. So, do you mean you're not working for over a month? Nice. Let's do something for a few days, maybe before Lane and Molly's wedding."

"Well, I didn't say I wasn't working; but what did you have in mind, Owen?"

"Anything that involves being warm and cozy with you, hon. You decide. I'm going to go check the calves and then I'm going to meet with Matt and Ryan up at the Flight School to get an extra lesson in."

"Hey, what time is Ty leaving for Silver City?"

"I think he said about noon. Apparently, Eide called him and told him she wanted to get here about two this afternoon."

"She didn't tell me they were coming that early. I really better kick it in gear."

"Don't kick it in gear that much, I'll be back to help you in a few hours. And I am sure Eide plans to help, too."

"Hello, anybody home?" Eide called out as she came in the kitchen door that afternoon.

"Yep—Rosie and I are here. Where's everyone else?" I asked Eide as she stepped into the kitchen carrying Toby, who was pretty content sitting back in the crook of Eide's arm, sucking on his pacifier.

"Oh, they're outside with Ty, unloading his Jeep. We kinda overloaded him," Eide said, snickering. "Six adults, a baby and luggage. A bit much for his Jeep. I wanted to see your house, so I just ditched everyone."

"How was your flight?"

"It was great. Toby slept the whole time. He's had worse trips to the grocery store. We may have to get Ty to come and take him for a flight when he won't go to sleep at night."

"Hey, Kar, how's it going?" Lane said as he and Levi came in, loaded down with luggage. "I'd hug ya, but it'll have to wait; I think Levi and Eide brought the entire nursery."

"I did convince her to leave the crib." Levi said, joking. *At least I think Levi was joking.* "Hi Karla. How's it going?" Levi asked, piping into my thoughts.

"It's great, you guys bring whatever you like."

"Hey, kiddo." Dad said.

"Hi honey. How are you?" Mom asked.

"I'm great!"

"Speak for yourself there, Karla." Ty said, laughing. He walked in behind my parents also carrying an armload of things I presumed belonged to Toby. "It's not your Jeep. Where's Owe, by the way?"

"Hmm, I don't know—he hasn't gotten back yet. He met with Ryan and Matt; said he would be back early to help. He'll be rolling in anytime."

"I figured he was out getting turkeys ready."

"Karla. Show us around, make sure this place is up to snuff." Eide said.

"Yes. Okay. I will at least show you to your room. You're acting like a little kid." I said, laughing. "Bring your bags, I think the bellhops are off-duty today. Mom, you're coming, right?" I asked looking back to see Mom picking up her luggage and tailing behind Eide and me. We went up the kitchen stairs to the upstairs bedrooms. I started by showing Mom and Eide the rooms in which they would be staying.

"These are great. Cute little country charm." Eide said.

"Yes," Mom said. "Very cute. What are there—four bedrooms up here?"

"Yea, and then one downstairs. Owen and I have a bedroom up here for now. We debated about taking the one downstairs but in the end, Owen liked the idea of being upstairs. He said when we get older, we're going to have to be downstairs; we'll be too old and crippled."

"Yea, and when you have kids, you don't want to be running upstairs all the time in the night. Eide said, very matter-of-factly.

"You and Owen think a baby's just going drop out of thin air." I said, laughing. "Speak of the devil. I just heard Owen come in the kitchen and I think Ty's giving him the riot act. Let's go this way and we can go down through the living room."

I intended to be home several hours earlier today to help Karla and Ma prepare for tomorrow's dinner but got distracted going over the lessons with Matt and Ryan.

"Hello, everyone." I said, coming in the back door. "How was your flight?"

I looked around the kitchen table where everyone was sitting; well, at least the guys.

"Where's Karla?" I asked. "I was supposed to be back earlier, I lost track of time."

"I didn't even realize you hadn't made it back when we landed earlier." Ty said.

"She went with Eide and Laurel to take a tour upstairs."

"I need to go talk to Karla; I'll be back." I said, slipping out of the kitchen.

"Karla," I called out, trying to get her attention.

"Owen, we're in the living room." Karla hollered back. "Everything go ok today?" she asked when we met in the living room by the fireplace.

"Hey, hon." I said, turning and putting my arm around her. "I'm sorry I didn't get back here earlier. I lost track of time. You and Ma got things ready, or you want some help, now? I talked to her briefly when I pulled in, but she was leaving, so I didn't want to hold her up."

"Yea, she said she was going to go home for a little while and would be back with your aunts and uncles. Poor Rosie, I probably wore her out."

"Do you need help with anything?"

"We can help, too." Eide said.

"No, I think we're all good. Rosie and I whipped everything out pretty well today. Rosie's got a good system."

"Well then, I'm anxious for the rest of your tour, if you're done feeling guilty, Owen?" Eide said, chastising me.

"Be my guest, enjoy yourselves. I'm going to go clean up and then I'll get the turkeys ready for the smoker."

"Okay, thanks, honey." Karla said, kissing my cheek.

"What's up with you guys?" I asked, sitting down at the table joining everyone else when I had finished showering.

"How'd things go with Matt?" Ty wanted to know.

"I had classroom and shop time with Ryan and Matt this morning; then Ryan had to leave early so I took Matt up for a flight lesson; he was doing very well. It was a good session today."

"Yea," Ty said. "Just be careful with those two."

"I need to get some turkeys ready for the smoker—anybody coming along?"

"Yeah." Darren said, looking up from the newspaper he had been reading. "How's this little farm of yours coming anyways?"

"Huh!" I said, chuckling. "You talk to Karla too much; she calls it a farm. I call it an acreage. And it's going great."

"Hey, Owe." Ty said, interrupting. "Are you opening all five of these packages in the fridge?"

"Yea, I think there's going to be quite few people here this weekend, so might as well."

"The cousin platoon." Ty and I said in unison.

"Have you ever been to a family event where all your cousins showed up? Do you even know all of them?" Ty asked.

"No, I don't think so."

"Wait, wait." Lane said. "You don't know all your cousins, or you haven't been to a family event where they all showed up? Just how many cousins do you have?"

"A platoon!" Ty and I said in unison again. "It's kind of a family joke. One of my aunts and uncles randomly take kids in. They've fostered kids for years; so, it's always changing. One summer they visited for a week. They had just taken in this young boy. Do you remember that boy, Ty? We took him horseback riding; he thought it was the greatest thing ever. I don't think he wanted to go to bed the entire time he was here." I pondered spending that week with that kid for a moment as I seasoned a turkey. *Hmm, I wonder what happened to him.*

"How's the cattle business out here?" Darren asked, pulling me from my thoughts. I looked up and he was looking out at the corrals.

"Oh, it's not so bad. Erving comes out occasionally. He still owns them; Karla and I are just helping him out until he can take them to market."

"I think Owe and Karla are going to own that herd and the horses before too long."

"What, who are you kidding, Ty!" I said, shaking my head, laughing. "Erving's going to take them to market, probably after the first of the year."

"Nuh-uh, mark my words. That herd will be you and Karla's in short order; it's all part of Ole Man Erving's master plan."

"Good morning, Karla," I said, rolling over in bed when I heard her rousing. I wrapped my arm around her, and we laid there visiting for a moment.

"Good morning. Happy Thanksgiving, Owen. How was your night?"

"Good, I was just laying here thinking. Are you ready for today? There could be forty-some people here, you know."

"Please, your mom got me so organized yesterday. She is a pro at these things. What are you thinking about?"

"Yesterday, Ty and I were talking about the cousin platoon. The foster kids my aunt and uncle have brought around through the years. This one summer they brought this boy, he rode the horses over at Ma and Dad's, he loved it. I was wondering what happened to that kid."

"How old was he?" Karla asked.

"Well, I'd guess him to be around seven or nine that summer. I will have to ask Aunt Regina later. I haven't thought about that boy in years."

"You've been thinking about kids a lot lately. Haven't you?"

"Hmm-hmm. Something about you does that to me." I said, nuzzling Karla's neck.

"Sorry, not today, cowboy. I love you, but as you just pointed out we could have forty-some people coming to hang out with us today. I'm going to go fire up the coffee pot." Karla said, flashing me a big smile.

"You mean to tell me I'm getting stood up by the coffee pot?"

"Yep, you just put that mood on simmer for a few days and well pick it up. I hear there's a storm moving in first of the week. We might need an activity and some cuddling."

"Oh, I like how you think. I'll meet you at the coffee pot, shortly."

"Hey, do you think Erving will come for dinner today?" Karla asked as I poured us some coffee.

"I don't know." I said, shaking my head. "I haven't seen or heard from him since I asked him when we fed calves the other night. I think he was waiting to see what Ann and Katy were doing. You notice how he's been coming out less and less?"

"Yea, I have. Are you good with all that, Owen? I know you weren't too excited to be taking all that on."

"Oh, it's no problem, it's not near the size of herds Dad used to have." I said, looking out the kitchen window out to the barn. "I'm going to head out to do morning rounds. I will be back to help you in here. I won't get lost this time; I promise." I said, smiling, turning back to kiss Karla's cheek a couple times, and then headed out the door.

"Morning honey, Happy Thanksgiving." Mom said, just barely missing Owen's goodbye. "Whatcha got goin on in here? Can I help you with anything?"

"Happy Thanksgiving, Mom. I didn't realize you were up. I'm just getting a good start."

"I think your dad's headed this way, too, and I heard Toby rustling earlier so I'm guessing Levi and Eide will be down soon. Is Owen up?" Mom asked, reaching in the cupboard to get a coffee cup.

"Yea, he went out to the barn to do chores."

"Your dad said he helped him feed last night."

"What did I do last night?" Dad asked. "Morning, kiddo."

"Mom said you helped Owen feed the calves last night."

"Yea, is that where Owen's at now?"

"Yes." I said, laughing at Dad's enthusiasm.

"Oh, well give me some coffee and I'll go out and help him. Maybe this time he'll let me muck out a stall out two—said last night I'd get too dirty."

"Good morning, ladies. Happy Thanksgiving!" Eide said, coming down the stairs into the kitchen holding Toby.

"Good morning, Happy Thanksgiving." Mom said.

"Good morning, Eide, how was your night? How's the Tobster?" I asked, poking at Toby's chin, getting a slight smile out of him.

"Oh, he's quite active, and an early riser. Sometimes before four a.m. Don't ya, little turd. Sure as heck can't let Mom or Dad sleep in." Eide said, tapping and nudging Toby's pacifier at his chin.

"Would you like some coffee?" I asked. "And then I wouldn't mind holding him; if he's up for it."

"He's up for it, aren't ya dude." Eide said, leaning over to hand Toby to me.

"Hi there, little guy." I said, setting down with Toby. "What do you have on your shirt? Did Mom put a turkey shirt on you this morning?" I was getting almost a full-on giggle out of him. "I take it Levi and Lane are still sleeping?"

Levi was awake and I haven't heard a word from Lane; well, I take that back." Eide said thoughtfully. "I think he was talking to Molly later last night."

"I'm sorry she's working. I feel bad, we always plan our holidays around her work schedule. She needs to start putting in time off on holidays."

"Yes, she does." Mom said.

"Morning, morning. Happy Turkey Day everyone." Levi said as he came into the kitchen, rubbing his eyes. "There's my little chatterbox son. I wondered where he made off to, it got quiet in the room. Come see Dad."

"Hey, I just got him. Get yourself some coffee and then I might think about returning the merchandise."

"I was going to take him out to see the horses."

"Oh fine." I told Levi. "You better make sure I get to see him later, you hear?"

"Yes, Auntie Karla." Levi said, taking Toby and putting him in his snowsuit and hat.

"Good morning y'all. What's a guy gotta do to buy a cup of coffee down here in these parts?" Lane asked, yawning, sitting down at the table between Mom and me.

"Good morning, Lane." Mom said. "Happy Thanksgiving; are you okay this morning?"

"Yea, I'm fine. Just tired."

"I'll get you some coffee. Did we wake you?"

"No, there's a three-month-old chatterbox next door that woke me. He did not seem upset at anything, he wasn't crying, yelling, or screaming. He was just talking away to someone." Lane said, theatrically. "Someday he'll make a heck of a politician or minister. It would have been cute and funny if it weren't three-thirty in the morning. What are you feeding that kid, Eide?" Lane asked as I set a cup of coffee in front of him.

"Breast milk, Lane. Do you want some? Toby seems to be ruling the world with it; maybe we all could be, too." Eide said, laughing.

"Might be time to try a little rice cereal in his nighttime bottle." Mom suggested.

"Yeah, Levi and I have been discussing that. I just need to add it to my next order." Eide said.

"Hey Lane, what's Molly's schedule this weekend?"

"She's working today through Sunday. She's pulling a double on Saturday."

"Why a double?" I asked.

"She planned her schedule this way because of the wedding; she requested two and half weeks off at Christmas."

"She really needs to start requesting some holidays off. She's worked more than her fair share."

"Well good luck telling her that," Lane said. "I think she's more married to her job than she'll ever be married to me."

"Good morning, everyone." Rosie said as she came in the kitchen carrying a handful of things. "Happy Thanksgiving, Rosie. Wow, Rosie, let me help you with that. What are you doing bringing all this? I thought we got everything ready yesterday."

"We did, I just worked on a couple things this morning."

"Would you listen to her? We sit around drinking coffee and chit-chatting, and she makes more food."

"Oh, it was nothing." Rosie said, waving her hand. "My sisters are right behind me."

"Have a seat and I'll get some coffee. I also have hot tea, ladies." I said after Rosie's sisters made it into the house.

"I think I'm outnumbered here, ladies." Lane said, laughing. "I think I'll go find the party out in the barn. Even the three-month-old politician is out there."

"So, how's things been over here this morning?" Rosie asked, taking a cup of coffee.

"Very nice. We have just been chatting it up. It's been a while since we have been able to just sit and do this. Last time we were together, Ty had us on a marathon moving day and before that was the wedding."

"Hello, hello. We're back. Do you have anything warm to drink?" Owen asked, carrying two kids, upside down by their pants.
"Oh my, what do we have here?" I asked chuckling.
"I caught two little turkeys strutting around the yard. I thought we could use them for dinner."
"Nuh-uh, Uncle Owen." Luke said squirming and laughing.
"Weren't you just strutting in the yard?" Owen asked them.
"We're not turkeys!" Caity exclaimed.
"You could have fooled me; I think you're both a couple turkeys." Owen said, setting them down.
"Oh great, now my underwear's all messed up." Luke said. "It's sticking out of my jeans." Luke squirmed around, trying to look at his backside.
"Ah, you'll be fine, buddy." Owen said, laughing. "Next time you go to the bathroom everything will be back to normal."
"Owen, be nice to him. Luke, come here, honey. You want some help with your pants?" I asked him before he ran off. Where's Max and Elaine? I asked Owen after Luke didn't want help with his pants.
"They're getting things out of the van with Dad." Owen said.

Joe, along with Max and Elaine came in with a few trays of food and two big boxes. "Well, what do we have here?" I asked as they were setting their boxes down.
"These are for dinner." Elaine said. "Hopefully, you can put them in the fridge. Otherwise, we can set them back outside until we're ready to eat; it's a regular icebox out there today."
"Of course, I have room. These look wonderful. Thank you. What's up with the boxes, if you don't mind my asking."

"Oh, you're going to love these, if I don't say so myself. These are wedding pictures."

"Oh wow, really? Already? How exciting. Ladies, clear the table, I gotta see these."

"Aunt Karly—" Caity came running up, interrupting.

"Yes, honey. What is it?"

"Can we play with those games we were playing last time we were here?"

"Yes, of course, honey. Do you need help getting them out?"

"No, Daddy's getting them. He said we had to ask you first." Caity said, running back toward the hall closet where I kept the kids' games.

"She's been calling you Karly at home, too." Elaine said after Caity left. "I've tried to correct her, but she keeps at." Elaine said, shaking her head as she set some packages out of the box and started unwrapping them.

"It's fine, she's five. So, I have a nickname." I said, dramatically bopping my head back. "I think it's cute, she's said it a few times around here when they've came to play. So, did you and Max already look at these?" I asked as we all waited patiently for the pictures to be unwrapped.

"No." Elaine said. "I unwrapped a couple and was pretty excited about them for you guys but then I realized how close we were to Thanksgiving Day and thought we could enjoy them all together. I hope that's okay."

"No, this is great. Isn't it, Owen? This way everyone gets a chance to see."

"Let's just start an assembly line." Owen suggested. "You start there Elaine, since you're unwrapping and then you can hand them down to Aunt Karly and I." Owen said, mocking Caity's nickname for me.

"Hello? Hello, am I interrupting anything?" Erving asked, knocking on the back porch door, coming into the kitchen.

"Hey, Erving." Owen said. "Glad you could make. You're not interrupting anything. Elaine brought wedding pictures and we were just starting to unwrap them. You want to come take a look with us?"

"Happy Thanksgiving, Erving." I said before returning my attention to the pictures.

"Hi Karla, you kids look at your pictures. Maybe I'll have a look later. Where's Kaster at?"

"Dads in the living room." Owen told Erving. "Go on in and make yourself comfortable."

"Come on, Erving." Rosie said, joining him in stride to the living room.

I heard Erving tell her something about Karla making the place look nice. *Owen and I talked about making updates to the house right away, but I told him to put those thoughts on the back burner for a while and just settle in first.*

"Elaine, my goodness. These pictures are wonderful. I love this one with Owen and me standing in the barn shadow. Ah. Look at us holding Luke and Caity's hands, that's so sweet."

"Yes, I want to know how my children turned out to be so sweet and innocent that day." Elaine asked.

"Ty fed 'em the Kool-Aid." Owen said, laughing.

"Oh my, this one's hilarious. Ty and Owen's dance. I'm glad you got shots of that, for sure."

"Let me see that." Edie said.

"I told Karla we're going to have to get filming rights, so you don't put anything out on YouTube." Owen said, laying down the law for Eide.

"Oh, hold on." I said, backing away from the table. "I better go do some stirring and check the oven, so something doesn't burn."

"You keep looking." Rene said. "I got it covered."

"Thank you, Rene." I said, joining the picture unveiling again.

"Oh, ho, looky here, cowboy. Ooh, wee!" Eide said, exclaiming over the picture she held.

"What?" Owen asked. "What did you do, Elaine?"

"Ah, yea." Elaine said, leaning over to see about the picture that had Eide so excited. "I added a little photoshopping after you guys bought this place." Elaine explained.

"You added, wait—is that Erving's herd out there in the corral?"

"Guilty."

"Elaine, you took a picture of Erving's calves and photoshopped them in behind Karla and me standing in front of the corrals. I think *'The Kasters Est. 2019'* is great. But the herd? That's not even our herd." Owen exclaimed.

"Oh well." Elaine said, shrugging her shoulders. "Ty thinks they will be someday soon anyways.

"Oh please, Ty and his big ideas." I said, laughing along with everyone else.

"What about Ty and his big ideas?" Ty asked, coming into the kitchen. "Why are you all talking about me behind my back?"

"Yes, we are talking behind your back." Owen said, looking up at Ty. "You're spreading vicious rumors about me and Erving's herd."

"That's not a rumor. It'll turn out to be true, soon enough."

"Whatever, Ty." Owen said, shaking his head. "Where's Rachel?"

"She went to see her aunt and sisters today."

"Ah look at this picture." Eide said. "Can I get a copy? I just love it."

"Yes, of course." Elaine said. "I can get copies."

"What picture are you looking at?" I asked Eide.

"Levi and me dancing. Levi's holding Toby—ah, just melts my heart. I almost forgot that Granny Grainer didn't have him kidnapped the whole night."

"As much as I love looking at these pictures, we better look later and get the meal on the table. I'm sure there's some hungry people around."

"I'll get the turkeys out." Owen said. "Can I get a volunteer there, Ty?"

Eide and I, along with Owen's mom and aunt, helped me set everything else up on the counters. We soon had lids off and spoons in.

"Okay, everyone. Gather around." I announced. "We have everything set up buffet-style so as soon as Joe leads us in a blessing, we'll let him, and Rosie start us off through the line."

"Sounds good to me." Joe remarked. "Everyone bow yer heads." Joe took ahold of Rosie's hand and as if on cue they both bowed their heads.

"Dear Heavenly Father. We join you today on this most special of days, Thanksgiving.

We thank you for walking with us through the seasons of our lives and helping us see the blessing you provide every day. We thank you for the opportunities to spend time with family and friends and we thank you for the blessing those have bestowed upon us.

And most importantly we thank you for the unconditional love you share, the food and fellowship we are about to share. In your name we pray, Amen."

"We all shared an amen, including Toby, who started chattering as if on cue.

"Joe I'm convinced there's something to your prayers." Eide said, chuckling.

"Hey, Owen. How are things? Aunt Regina asked me I sat down across the table from her.

"Hey, Aunt Regina. I was hoping I'd get chance to visit with you today."

I'm glad you came to sit next to me, too. It's been quite a while since you sat and chatted with your ole aunt. It's nice of you and Karla to host Thanksgiving."

"Oh yes, of course. Although Ma and Karla did all the work yesterday."

"Are you glad to be back home? Your mom sure seems glad to have you back from the big city."

"I am glad to be back, but that's where I met Karla, so it was all good."

"Hey, Aunt Regina, I wanted to ask you something."

"Sure honey, anything."

"You ever keep in contact with any of the foster kids you and Nate ever took in?"

"Some of them. But some of them only stayed with us a brief time; at this point in my life, I'd be hard-pressed to even remember some of their names. Why do you ask?"

"Well for quite a while, Ty and I have called it the 'cousin platoon.'"

"Oh goodness." Regina laughed. "I guess that's one way of describing it."

"We were discussing it with Karla's brothers yesterday afternoon and it got me thinking about one boy you brought out that week you guys stayed with us. We rode horses with him. I think he might have been about seven or nine. Man, that kid loved riding horses with us; he would have stayed in the saddle all night if we would have let him. Do you remember that kid? Kinda seems like his name was Oliver."

"Hmm. Kinda seems familiar. We had quite a few kids over the years, Owen. This memory isn't what it used to be. Why do you ask about this one?"

"Oh, no reason. Like I said, we were just talking about the kids you used to take in and this one just came to light and got me thinking. I wondered how he was doing."

"I often wonder about that with any number of kids we had. But many times, the foster kids we had moved on quickly. Some went back to their biological parents or were adopted into their forever homes."

"Wasn't that hard? I mean you'd just get to know them and then they'd have to go."

"We knew that all along that we were providing temporary care. God entrusted us to provide a safe haven for youngsters in all sorts of circumstances. That might have been an overnight stay or in some cases up to a year and we happily complied."

"That's cause you both have such good hearts."

"Well honey, we just did what we thought God was calling us to do."

"Hey, Owen." Karla said, sitting down next to me.

"Hi honey. This is my Aunt Regina, remember meeting her at the wedding?"

"Hi, Regina. Nice to see you again. How is everything?" Karla asked, gesturing to the meals.

"Oh, it's absolutely wonderful. I'm just enjoying it and the company."

"I wondered what happened to you." Karla said. "Eide got out some more wedding pictures, she found one of you and Ty dancing to a slow song—right before you started dancing to the 'Shout' song. This shot might be the most hilarious."

"We have to hide those shots." I told Karla, laughing.

"Ty said he's getting some framed for the Flight School."

"Oh no you don't, Ty." I hollered out. "I asked Regina about that boy I told you about this morning. But she doesn't remember him."

"I'll ask Nate later, see if he remembers him or what become of him."

"I'm going to go get some more turkey." I said, getting up and leaving Karla and Aunt Regina to continue visiting.

"How'd you make the turkey?" Aunt Regina asked looking at Karla.

"I smoked it out by the barn." I said surprising Aunt Regina.

"Well, it's wonderful. I've never had turkey like this before."

"Hey Karla." Eide said, sitting down taking Owen's seat when he left the table.

"What's up?" I asked Eide.

"We need to frame some of these pictures for you tomorrow and get them hung, they're fabulous." Eide said, kissing her fingertips.

"That's a great idea, but I don't have any frames, just yet."

"Yes, you do." Eide said. "What about those you got for wedding gifts?"

"Oh yes. Of course. Do you know what? Those are still over at Joe and Rosie's. I need to go over and get that stuff."

"I can help you do that." Eide offered. "Then we can decide on the frames for the pictures. I have some ideas."

"Thanks, I always love your ideas. But I like your cleanup ideas, too. We need to go clean up the counters and put out the desserts—you want to help with that, too?"

"Yes, of course. That one pumpkin fluffy cake-looking thing looked absolutely scrumptious; did you make it?"

"I don't know what you're talking about. Rosie and I made about a hundred pies, though. That woman is a pie-making machine; I learned that last year."

"Hey Mom." I said, sitting down next to her on the couch as the ladies gathered in the living room that evening with a cup of coffee when the guys went out to the barn to check on the animals.

"What, dear?"

"I missed talking to Aunt Jane, today. I missed her somewhere along the line."

"I forgot to tell you earlier. Jane called me. She and Martin weren't coming. Martin wasn't feeling well, and Jane wasn't up to making the drive alone."

"Darn it, I'm sorry to hear that. I hope he gets to feeling better soon. I'll try and give her a call soon."

"Rosie." I said, changing the subject. "Do you remember that Owen and I have wedding gifts stored in that back bedroom?"

"Oh, yes, dear. They're still there." Rosie said.

"Eide asked me about some picture frames this afternoon and reminded me of those. Do you care if we come over and get those tomorrow?"

"Yes, of course, except your mother and I going to go to a few stores in town tomorrow morning. Would you two like to join us, first?" Rosie asked.

"No, I don't think I'll take Toby to town." Eide said, looking down at him sleeping on her lap.

"Yea, I think Eide, and I'll work on pictures. Do you want to come help with pictures?" I asked Elaine.

"Yea, that'd be great." Elaine said as we heard a lot of commotion in the kitchen. The guys must be finished with the evening feeding. I got up in time to hear Owen asking if we had fresh coffee.

"Owen, in a house with this many people, the coffee's always fresh." I joked when I met him by the kitchen counter.

"Well, that's perfect for us, but the little knuckleheads can't have my coffee." Owen said, laughing.

"Hey, we're not knuckleheads." Luke said.

"You are." Caity said, teasing Luke.

"How about some hot chocolate?" I asked the kids.

"Can we?" Caity asked.

"Coming right up."

"Here, I can make that." Owen said getting cups out of the cupboard.

"That's all right, I can do it." I said, letting the water heat up.

"Uncle Owen." Luke said. "Can we play a game?"

"Sure, buddy, go pick one out and Karla and I will bring you your hot chocolate."

Luke went scampering into the living room as we followed shortly behind with their drinks.

"What are two doing getting a game out?" Max asked.

"Owen said we could play."

"We need to leave soon." Elaine said.

"So," Luke said, matter-of-factly. "You and Dad can leave. Let Caity and me play the game."

"Well, if Dad and I leave, how do you think you're going to get home?"

"Owen, he always takes us." Luke said, picking pieces out of the game box.

"Owen's not going to take you home after you finish your game tonight." Max said, sarcastically.

"Fine." Luke said. "We'll just spend the night." *Boy this kid is a tough negotiator, tonight.*

"I don't think so, you crazy kid. Karla and Owen don't need two little monsters staying the night." Max said, growing more impatient with Luke all the time.

"Sure, they do." Luke said.

"It's ok if they want to stay. I can run them home in the morning." Owen said.

"You kids don't even have any clothes here." Elaine said.

"Actually, they do." I interjected, hoping I was not causing problems for Max and Elaine. "Owen's left them here a few other times. Said we'd get them back to you later; the kids didn't need to carry them around school all day."

"Oh, fine." Elaine said, tossing her hands in the air. "You two better behave. I will see you in the morning. I'm coming back to work on pictures, so I'll get you then."

Luke and Caity said a unified Yes! and proceeded to jump up and down.

"That's enough—sit down and play your game." Max said. "We'll see you tomorrow."

"You might as well tag along, too, Max." Owen suggested.

"Hmm, yeah maybe." Max said. "Thank you, guys. It was a nice day."

Chapter 16

"Ugh, I'm so tired. I don't think I'm ever getting up off this couch." Karla said, sitting down on the couch and laying her head back.

"Hon, you should have said something. You didn't have to help me out in the barn this afternoon." I sat down on the couch next to Karla and I could see it written all over face, she was exhausted. Everyone all left this morning, after a very fun, busy Thanksgiving weekend.

"Did you and Eide get all the pictures framed yesterday like she wanted?"

"You have to ask? She even got Levi and Lane to move a few pieces of furniture. I told her she couldn't ever come back again. She looked at me and just flipped her hand at me and muttered 'phish phish.'"

"Ha-ha. I heard her coercing Lane and Levi into something. Do I need to move anything back?"

"No, she really is good at this sort of thing—she just has a knack for it, and she knows it, so she flaunts it. But we love her all the same. And besides, at this point, I'm too tired to care." Karla said sounding as exhausted as she said.

"How did you even make it through church this morning?"

"That was a struggle, honey. You didn't see me."

"Why are you so tired? It's not like we stayed up real late, and you weren't up any earlier than normal."

"I don't know, but I'm definitely going to bed early tonight. I don't know how your mom hosted Thanksgiving dinners for everyone; she made it look so easy last year."

"She's always made it look easy; it must be your family that tipped the scales."

"Hey, now." Karla said, slapping my leg.

"I'll get us some supper and bring you a plate and you can keep your vigilance up here on the couch."

"Hmm, thank you." Karla said as I left for the kitchen.

When I returned from the kitchen, Karla had dozed off on the couch and slumped her head down toward her shoulder. *Ohh, that's gonna cause a neck ache.* I set our plates with turkey sandwiches on the coffee table and sat down beside her.

"Hey, Karla." I said, leaning over and kissing her cheek. "I got us a turkey sandwich. You should sit up, your gonna give yourself a neck, or headache or both laying like that." I handed Karla the plate with her turkey sandwich.

"Hmm, thanks." Karla said, sitting up. "This looks good."

"Are you all right? I know you said you were tired but you just out-and-out crashed."

"Yea, I'm fine." Karla said, diving into her turkey sandwich. "Wow you even make a killer turkey sandwich."

"Yea, Oscar Mayer ain't got nothing on me." I said, turning on the tv, flipping through the channels. "What do you want to watch?"

"Oh, I don't care. You can pick something." Karla said. "What do you have planned for tomorrow?" she asked me between inhaling her sandwich. "Do you have to work tomorrow?"

"No, we're not having a class tomorrow. And by the looks of it we could use a day to recover. Why do you ask, are you working?"

"I have an email from a small shop in Durango wanting to do a New Year's campaign. I want to get started on it soon so that I don't have to take care of it at Christmas or during Lane and Molly's wedding. I don't know that I'll work on it tomorrow, but I will email her back and give her my thoughts. I also need to clean up the house from the weekend."

"How about we leave that to tomorrow afternoon; we can tackle it together?"

"Sounds good to me." Karla said, sitting her plate on the coffee table. "This isn't a really good show. I'm going to go take a shower."

"Are you coming back down?"

"I don't know, I'll decide when I get done showering. Thank you for the sandwich."

An hour or so later, Karla still had not come back down. I put our plates away and cleaned up the sandwich fixings and she still had not come down. I turned down the lights and went up to find her lying on the bed. *Wow, she is really wiped*, I thought, getting ready for bed. I laid down in our bed trying not to disturb her. I rolled over, moved her curly brown hair, and kissed the side of her neck. "Good night, honey." Karla did not even flutter an eyelid.

The next morning when I woke up, I turned over and noticed Karla looked like she did when I got into bed last night. I got up, dressed, and went downstairs to make some coffee and then went out to feed the calves and horses. I finished with the chores and stepped into the barn office with all the old rodeo pictures on the wall. They really were some incredible pictures. I never remembered Erving ever rodeoing. The boxes I had seen a couple of weeks ago, and the picture of the little girl were where I had left them. I should have brought Erving out here the other day. The young girl in the picture might very well be Katy or Ann; he might want these things.

I went back up to the house a while later to find that Karla had gotten up and was getting some breakfast ready.

"Hey hon, good morning. How are you?" I asked, hugging her. "What have you got going here?"

"I thought we'd have some waffles. You good with that?"

"Sounds good to me, you want some help?"

"Nah, I'm good." Karla said, waving the spatula in the air. "Grab some coffee and I'll be ready shortly. I got some bacon coming, too."

"Whoo hoo! It must be my lucky day. Look at you go." I said, looking over Karla's shoulder.

That evening I sat on the couch, propping my feet up, Owen not far behind since we had just finished putting supper in the oven. "Thanks for helping me clean up the house today, Owen."

"Did you get your emails checked?" Owen asked.

"Yea, I did. I sent a quick reply and told them I would be touch in a couple of days; I should be able to whip something out later this week or first of next week. Seems pretty straightforward." I said, yawning.

"You were pretty beat yesterday and now you're wore out again—what am I gonna do with you? Listen, why don't you stay here and rest; I'm gonna go out to the barn and do chores before supper."

"Are you sure you don't want some help?" I asked Owen.

"Nah, I'm good. See you in a bit."

"I'll have some coffee waiting for you," I called out to the porch. I could tell he was standing by the back door slipping his coat and boots on. I decided I better get up off the couch and get to making the coffee and getting the rest of the supper fixing going or I would not make good on the coffee promise to Owen.

"Hey there, how was feeding?" I asked Owen as he stepped up behind me while I stood at the sink, where I was washing my hands.

"It was good. Erving was here and helped, so it went quick." Owen said, grabbing some dishes from the cupboard. "Oh, dang it, I forgot." I heard Owen mutter snapping his fingers.

"What did you forget?"

"Oh, nothing. Something I was going to show Erving out in the barn. No big deal, just some stuff in the barn office. Is there any pie left? We haven't stayed up long enough the last couple nights to even think about dessert and now I want some."

"No, there's no pie left. We haven't even eaten yet and you're thinking about dessert. The pie was gone on Friday, anyways. There's some weird fluffy cake thing that somebody brought. Eide loved it—should have sent it home with her."

"Oh man, let me see this. Did Aunt Regina make her fluffernutter cake—how did I miss this? This stuff is the bomb." Owen said, taking it out of the fridge.

"Well honey, nothing against your aunt, but that stuff is not the bomb. You can have it all."

"What do you want to do this evening, beside finish the fluffernutter cake?" Owen asked, finally getting to his meal.

"Ugh, seriously. I'll pass on the fluffy cake and beyond that nothing."

"We're becoming worse than our parents." Owen said, mildly joking, although I think he really thought that.

"Morning, Ty." I said, stepping into the office where he was working on the computer.

"Hey, Owe. How was the rest of your weekend?"

"Yea, it was good. Glad we took yesterday off. Karla was wiped-out already Sunday night. We cleaned up the house a bit yesterday and took it easy. How's it going here? How about you and Rach?"

"Rach went with her sisters to her aunt's house for a couple days, she came back Saturday afternoon and then we went flying. I'm going over hours for this class; I'm a little worried."

"Yeah, I was thinking about that last night. Maybe we should put together an accelerated schedule."

"Wow, you must mean really accelerated. You realize that's only about three weeks away; and the next class is scheduled to start January tenth, not to mention the holidays."

"I think we can do it; maybe some longer days and throw in a couple Saturday mornings. Let's sit down at lunch tomorrow and hammer out a new schedule. How'd that battery compartment come out my dad was working on? I haven't had a chance to ask you or him."

"Oh, it's fine. He's already brought it back. Wasn't near as bad as it looked. I probably wouldn't have had to load it up, he probably could have come over here and taken care of it in less time."

"Well good, glad it's back together." I watched as students started filing into the shop and decided we shouldn't dally around any longer. "Don't forget we'll get a schedule put together at lunch tomorrow." I told Ty as we left the office.

"Morning." Ty hollered out to everyone. "Whoever's going flying first let's head out for pre-flight checks. The rest of you take a seat, Owen's ready to start.

"Owe, see you later." Ty said, flipping two fingers in the air and walking out of the hangar shop.

"Hey honey, I'm home." I said, coming in the back door. "Where you at?"

"Back here." Karla said. I could hear Karla's voice coming from her office.

"Hey, you." Karla said, looking up at me as I stood at the door of her office. "I didn't hear you pull in and apparently neither did Arnold. He probably would have met you at the door."

"I parked out by the barn. I picked up some mineral and oats from the Feed Store. Thought I'd come see you before I unloaded them, maybe get a cup of coffee, too."

"Yes, there's coffee and I'm just working on that New Year's campaign."

"Yea, how's that going?"

"It's great. Easy peasy. In another hour or so, I'll probably be finished." Karla said, smiling up at me.

"Ah, well, don't let me interrupt you any more than I already have, I'll grab my coffee and be in the barn taking care of things. Wait—is that a dancing penguin?" I asked, stepping closer to get a better look. Man, she smelled like flowers I noticed as I stepped closer to her.

"Yes, it's a penguin." Karla said, looking at her computer screen and then back at me."

"All right, cool." I said, heading out.

"There's fresh coffee in the pot." Karla said as I reached the kitchen. I poured myself a cup and hollered a thanks back to Karla and went outside.

When I finished in the barn, I was walking toward the porch and could see in the kitchen window. I decided Karla finished with her dancing penguin. I laughed to myself. Karla working with dancing penguins was working out so much better for the both of us than me dropping her off at the airport to go to some client's office each week. I thanked God all the time for that change. I could hear music blasting from the kitchen and decided Karla must be working on supper. I stepped into the kitchen, took Karla's hand, and twirled her around, dancing to the beat of the music. I take it you're done with your dancing penguin. What is this, Gangsta Rap?"

"No Gangsta Rap here and yes, I am done with the dancing penguin." Karla said, giggling over the dancing.

"How were things out in the barn, Cowboy?"

"Smelled like manure!" I said, laughing, nearly giggling myself. We continued dancing until the timer on the stove went off, interrupting us.

"How were things at work?" Karla asked, opening the oven door, and looking inside.

"Busy. Ty and I are going to rework the schedule to get this class finished a few days early."

"Really?" Karla said, shutting the music off. "Are you guys going to be able to pull that off?"

"Ty's a bit skeptical." I said, pulling some plates out of the cupboard to set the table. "I told Ty we'd need to put in some longer days and maybe a few Saturday mornings."

"You need to be careful working that many hours." Karla said with a warning look.

"We will. Things have gone much smoother now that Ty and I have been having classes together again, so we should be good. Supper smells great by the way; what are you making?"

"I was thinking of this recipe my mom used to make and I couldn't get ahold of her this afternoon, so I tried to Google it. Well, I came across this Coconut Chicken Curry recipe instead and felt adventurous. I hope it taste as good as it smells."

"Well, let's find out. Is it ready?"

"Yes, it is. Let's give it a go." Karla said as she set the pan on the table, and we sat down and filled our plates.

"Well, it's pretty good." I said after a few bites. "You can stumble across Google recipes anytime you like."

"Yea." Karla said. "I guess it pays to be adventurous."

"Owen, if you're going to be adding some hours the next few weeks; what do you have planned for this weekend?"

"What do I have planned for this weekend? Weren't you the one supposed to be deciding on a mini vacation? I haven't heard a word about that."

"Oh, yes, I forgot about that. I'll get back to you on that. This weekend I was thinking about decorating for Christmas, at least a tree and maybe some greenery on the porch. We don't have to go too crazy, but I would like a little."

"Yes, I'm all for decorating a tree, the porch; whatever you'd like hon." I spoke. "It'll be fun."

Early the next morning, I felt Karla rush from our bed. It was early, but I wasn't sure how early, my alarm hadn't gone off yet. I laid there a while, wondering if she had work to do this morning and forgot to tell me. I did not really think that was it, though. I got up and went to the bathroom and found Karla slumped over the toilet.

"Oh, goodness Karla. Are you okay?" I asked, leaning down beside her, moving her hair to the side.

"Ugh, next time I tell you I want to be adventurous with my cooking, tell me I'm crazy."

"Have you been sick all night?"

"No, just a little while, I'm going back to bed."

"You want me to stay home with you today?"

"No, no. Don't be silly. It's just a little stomach bug." Karla said, crawling into bed.

I quickly dressed, made some coffee, and went out to the barn. After I finished in the barn, I came back in the house and went upstairs to check on Karla. She seemed to be resting and didn't look up when I stepped just inside our bedroom. I walked over to her and kissed her cheek. I went back downstairs and grabbed another cup of coffee. I wrote Karla a note to call me when she got up and left it by the coffee pot. I left for work, hoping Karla would feel better later.

"Hey sweety, feeling better?" I asked, answering my phone. It was almost noon; I was getting a little worried she hadn't called me.

"Yes, I am." Karla said. "I'm just tired. Next time I tell you I'm being adventurous…"

"Yea, I know, you told me this morning." I said, cutting her off with a chuckle. "No more adventurous foods for you. You settle in on the couch this afternoon. I will see you in a few hours. Love you."

"Bye, Owen. Love you, too."

"Karla not feeling well?" Ty asked when I hung up the phone.

"No, she made this Coconut Chicken Curry thing last night. I thought it was good, but it didn't agree with her at all. She was losing it early this morning."

"Oh dang, hope she feels better." Ty said as I handed him the schedule I had put together.

"Here's a schedule I came up with—let me know what you think."

"Yea." Ty said, looking it over. "I think this will work. Given no one misses class or messes anything up."

"Well, we'll just have a visit with them this afternoon. Explain how important this schedule is to keep and that you and I are committed to following through. I think we're in the clear there."

"Be careful with the 'clear' talk—Matt and Ryan could still drop the ball. I've been worried about them two."

"They'll be fine." I said, waving my hand and brushing him off. "I think they've seen the error of their ways."

Chapter 17

The last two weeks, I had not felt well. Even today I still felt like I had a bug. I barely got out of bed earlier and now I had taken up residence on the couch. I was glad my clients did not have much going on right now. Owen and I hadn't even gotten a tree put up or decorated, I thought, lying on the couch when my phone rang.

"Hello." I said, answering my phone, not recognizing the number.

"May I speak with Karla Kaster."

"This is she." I said, vaguely recognizing the voice.

"Ah, yes. Karla, this is Bonnie with Elite Realty in Boulder. I'm sorry I haven't been in touch more."

"Yes, Bonnie. What can I do for you? How're things going with my house?" Owen and I listed our houses on the same day back in August and now it's December. I was thinking she must want to renew the contract.

"We'll actually quite well—that's why I'm calling."

"I've been talking with a young couple who's looked at your house a few times here recently and last night they put in an offer."

"Oh, wow. That's wonderful. How does it compare to the listing price?"

"Well, it's pretty low and they want to close in two weeks since no one's living in the house."

"Okay, well, how low?" I could deal with a two-week closing but didn't know how low to come down on the price.

"Twenty percent." Bonnie said hesitantly.

"Hmm, Owen's working some long hours right now, I don't know."

"How about the closing date?" Bonnie asked.

"That's ok with me. If we can meet the other deadlines. But, thinking about the price, I think I'm going to reject the offer."

"I kinda thought you might say that. Do you want to counteroffer?"

"Yea, I'll come down five-percent."

"Along with the two-week closing date?" Bonnie asked, verifying.

"Yes, that will be fine."

"Okay." Bonnie said. "I'll draw up the paperwork and send it over. I'll be in touch." I laid my head back on the couch and fell asleep.

Later that afternoon Bonnie returned my call.

"Hello, Bonnie." I said, recognizing the number this time.

"They were waiting for my call. But they rejected your counteroffer."

"Oh. Well, now what?" I asked Bonnie.

"Well, they counteroffered." Bonnie said.

"Oh, okay." I said, scratching my head and running my hand through my hair. *They must really want this house; and they must want to move in before Christmas. Who would want to move into a house just days before Christmas?* I thought listening to Bonnie discuss the counteroffer.

"They offered ten percent off the listing price this time and they still want the two-week closing date."

"Hmm." I thought briefly. "I'll go with it. Can you fax me the purchase agreement to sign?"

"I sure will, I can have it ready this afternoon and send it out. Let me know if you have any questions. Thanks, Karla."

"Yes, I will. Thanks, Bonnie." *Well, that was an interesting morning.*

"Karla, I'm home." I could hear Owen say as he came in the kitchen that evening.

"I'm in the living room, Owen. More precisely, on the couch."

"Hey, hon. Are you not feeling good again?" Owen asked, leaning up against the kitchen entryway.

"I'm fine." I said sitting up.

"You don't look fine." Owen said, looking at me skeptically as I stood up to meet him.

"Have you been to the barn?"

"Yea, Erving and I just finished up."

"You guys have been getting in later and later every night this week and now you're still going in tomorrow morning. You're probably exhausted."

"It's all right." Owen said. "I'm gonna catch a shower and then I'll be back to take care of supper."

"No need, Owen. I made a soup. I will heat it up while you're showering. You want some coffee?"

"I always want coffee." Owen said, leaving the kitchen. I turned the burner on under the pan of soup. *Owen sounded so exhausted just now when he made his coffee comment. These extended sessions seemed to be taking a toll on him.*

"Oh, this soup looks way better than the chicken and noodles I made you last week." Owen said, looking in the pan when he sat down at the table. We each took a ladle of the steaming soup.

"Sorry, I made this again, but the broth sounded good."

"No complaints here." Owen said. "So how was the rest of your day?"

"Well, I sorta did something today."

"Uh oh." Owen said, smiling. "Does this involve the sheriff? He didn't call me."

"I sold my house—or as Eide dubbed it, 'Garratt's rental.'"

"That's great."

"Yep. Signed the purchase agreement and we close in two weeks."

"Two weeks—that's pretty quick. We need to call Rachel and have her finish the paperwork and loan for this place so we can finally get Erving his money. I wish he'd have just let us finalize things when my house sold."

"Don't worry, Owen. I'll call Rachel in the morning." I said, yawning.

"I'll mention this to Erving the next time I see him, I suppose he'll make plans to take the herd to market now."

"Ah, really? I'm going to miss them."

"I'm not going to miss the cool, snowy days taking care of them. Erving's coming out less and less."

"Oh, but they're so cute, especially the horses. I can even get them to eat out of my hands." I said, looking back at Owen with a pudgy face. I finished my soup and put my bowl in the dishwasher and the leftover soup in the fridge and went to leave the kitchen.

"Where are you going?" Owen asked, finishing his soup.

"There's a Christmas music special coming on, I'm going to watch. You want to watch with me?"

"Yep, I'll be right there, do we have any cookies?" Owen asked.

"Oh, yea. I forgot. Your mom dropped some by earlier. I put a box in the cupboard."

"Ma was here?" Owen asked as he sat down on the couch next me.

"Yes, I'm sorry I forgot to tell you. I got so caught up in telling you about the house." I said, yawning again.

"Come here, you." Owen said, putting his arm around me and we both leaned into each other. "What else was Ma up to besides a cookie delivery?"

"Rosie and her Bible study group had a cookie exchange today and she said she wasn't taking all the cookies home to Joe. So, I guess we get the benefit." I said, taking a cookie out of the box.

"Well, I'm not complaining." Owen said. "Those ladies sure do know how to bake."

Karla and I had been lounging on the couch for a while watching the music special, I could hear her phone ringing.

Sounded like it was coming from the kitchen. She didn't seem to be making a move to get up to get it. I looked over, and she had fallen asleep. I slid out of our embrace; hopefully not disturbing her.

I went in the kitchen and found her phone.

"Hello."

"Owen, what's up? Why are you answering Karla's phone?"

"Eide, hi. She fell asleep on the couch."

"She did, is she all right? It's not even nine o'clock."

"Yea, I know. Did she tell you she's had a stomach bug off and on?"

"Yes, she told me. I thought she was feeling better."

"I think she is, just tired."

"Well, you better let her get some rest, Owen." Eide said. "Lane and Molly's wedding is coming up. That's actually why I called her."

"I'll let her rest, don't worry. She can tell you more about it later, but she sold her house today."

"Really? That's awesome!" Eide exclaimed. "I think."

"Eide, quiet down." Levi said, "You're going to wake Toby."

"Yes, it is awesome. Be sure and ask her about the details when you talk to her."

"I will, I'll let you go, Owen. Tell Karla I called."

"Okay, bye, Eide."

I went back in the living room and Karla was still sleeping on the couch. *Dang, Eide was right. It was not even nine o'clock and Karla was out cold.* I turned down the lights and shut off the tv. I woke Karla up. "Let's go to bed, Karla."

"Is the music over?" Karla asked, standing up.

"It is for us." I said, taking her hand. "We're turning into old fogies. I don't even think my parents go to bed this early."

I went to the bathroom and when I came back to the bedroom Karla had changed out of her clothes and was lying in bed. "You okay, hon?" I asked when I laid down beside her.

"Yea, why?" Karla asked, but I could tell she was nearly asleep again.

"Just wondering."

"Good night, Owen." Karla said, sleepily.

"Good night, Karla." I said, reaching over and kissing her.

The next morning, I woke up before the alarm went off; no wonder since Karla and I went to bed so early. Karla did not look like she had moved a muscle. I got up went down to the kitchen and made a pot of coffee on my way out to the barn.

I turned the horses out into the paddock and mucked the stalls out. *Well, guess you all get extra treatment when I go to bed earlier.* I finished after feeding the calves and moved into the barn office. I still had not told Erving about these boxes. *I needed to remember to do that*, I thought, looking at the rodeo pictures on the wall. These pictures are incredible. Most of them were somebody riding saddle broncs, a few team-roping pics. I heard the barn door open. I stepped out by the horse stalls and saw Erving coming in, brushing a light snow off his jacket. "Well, that's good timing. Morning, Erving."

"Hey, Kaster. You're up early." Erving said, looking at the freshly hayed horse stalls.

"I'm glad you came out this morning."

"Yea, why's that?"

"Karla signed a purchase agreement for her house yesterday. She's going to call Rachel and have her get things organized to close on this place."

"Oh, okay. No hurry. The holidays are coming, so whatever works for you two."

"Hey Erving, come in the barn office here. I have something to show you."

"Oh yea. What's that, Kaster?" Erving asked as we stepped back into the barn office.

"Did you know these boxes are here? These boxes must be yours, Erving. I dug through them a bit. At first, I thought, they might be Dad's from when he stored things over here when Karla and I got married. But after looking at a few items, I don't really think so. I found a picture of Katy or Ann, one or the other. She must be what, two?" I asked, Erving, holding up the picture.

"Hmm, Kaster. That's not Katy or Ann." Erving said, holding the picture, staring at it. Erving set the picture down in the box and looked a little more at the contents in it.

"Sorry, Kaster. Not my boxes. These are your ole man's."

"Hmm. Okay." I said, puzzled, looking up at the rodeo pictures. "I'll ask him about them. Tell me about these pictures, Erving." I said turning to the wall with the rodeo pictures. "You rodeoed back in the day?"

"Oh, heavens no, Kaster. That's my dad in all those pictures. He used to rodeo until he was oh, twenty, twenty-one—said he was tired of getting banged up. So, he and Mom moved out here. Dad started building fence and Mom started having kids. Not sure which was rougher, rodeoing, ranching or raising us kids." Erving said, pondering the pictures.

"Well, they're incredible pictures." I said, continuing to look at them. "You want me to wrap them up and bring them over to you?"

"No." Erving said, holding up his hand. "The pictures stay with the barn along with the herd."

"What herd?"

"These pictures have been hanging in this barn for nearly eighty years. We're not about to disrupt history." Erving said, ignoring my herd question.

"I'm not so sure I agree with that. What about Ann or Katy—won't they want some of these?"

"Kaster!" Erving said with a frown on his face. "These pictures are old and have been hanging in this smelly barn. They've got fly manure all over them. The girls probably wouldn't even touch them, just leave them as they hang."

"All right, Erving." I pondered for a moment looking at the pictures. "And don't think I didn't catch the comment about the herd. I thought you were taking them to market."

"I did, Kaster." Erving said, smirking. "Check your purchase agreement—I stated the price for the house, acreage, the herd, the horses and now some old rodeo pictures with fly poop on them. What you do with it all is up to you. But ah hey, don't take 'em to market just yet, I'm still a little fond of 'em —and besides that, the market is down a little right now."

"Ah geez, Ty was right." I said, shaking my head.

"Oh, don't worry about Ty." Erving said, patting my shoulder. "Give him a pitchfork and tell him to start shoveling manure."

"All right, Kaster. I better let you get to gettin'. I'll see you another day."

"Hey, Erving." I said, catching him before he went out the door.

"Yea." Erving asked, turning to face me.

"Thank you." I said, extending my hand to shake his.

"You're welcome, Kaster." Erving said, shaking my hand back.

"This means a lot to Karla and me. We'll take care of things."

"I know you will." Erving said as he went out the barn door.

I followed Erving out the barn door and watched him as he jumped in his pickup. He looked over at the horses that were out in the paddock.

I went back in the house to see if Karla had gotten up. She was not in the kitchen, and I peeked into her office and didn't find her there, either. I went upstairs to our bedroom.

There she laid in our bed, still sound asleep. I leaned over, kissed her cheek, and went back downstairs. I grabbed a pen and pad and left her a note, told her to call me when she got up. *This little flu bug was going on a little to long for my comfort, I should get her to go to the doctor.* I thought. I refilled my coffee and headed over to the Flight School.

Ty was pulling up beside me when I got there.

"Mornin,' Ty." I said, getting out of my pickup.

"Hey, Owe. I'll be glad when we get back to regular hours."

"Me too. At least this will be our last Saturday."

"We should go out next weekend and celebrate—you and Karla, Rach and I. Celebrate the fact we survived this class."

"I'd go along with that. We'll have to wait and see if Karla's up for it."

"Oh, yea?" Ty looked at me questioningly as we walked into the shop. "She still fighting that bug."

"Yea, something. I'll ask her about going out."

"Good morning, everyone, time to get started." Ty said as our students started showing up. "Anyone seen Matt this morning?"

No one responded.

"Oh great." Ty said, quietly picking up the paper from the tables. "Whoever's going flying for the first half let's go out for pre-flight checks."

A few hours into class, my phone rang. I called break and the climate of the room changed considerably. I took my phone and went to the office.

"Hey hon. How are ya?" I asked, answering my phone.

"Owen, how come you didn't wake me before you left?"

"Well, you fell asleep on the couch last night and you looked pretty snug when I left. I figured you needed the extra sleep."

"It felt great, but I shouldn't sleep until nine o'clock. That's ridiculous."

"I was beginning to think you were still fighting that bug."

"I'm fine." Karla said, brushing off my comment. "I gotta go. Eide's calling me."

"Yea, she called last night. I was supposed to tell you."

"Okay. Bye, love you."

"Love you too. Bye."

"Hey, Eide." I said, switching the call from Owen.

"What's up with you? I called last night—it wasn't even nine o'clock. Owen said you were out cold on the couch."

"Oh, pipe down, Eide."

"Just watch yourself." Eide said, sounding concerned.

"Yes, mother hen." I said in a mocking voice.

"Mock now." Eide said. "Owen told me you unloaded Garratt's rental yesterday."

"Yes, I did." I said triumphantly. "Signed the purchase agreement and we close in two weeks."

"Well, they must want it badly." Eide said.

"Maybe as badly as I wanted to 'unload it,' as you just coined it."

"When are you guys coming up for the wedding?" Eide asked.

"Probably around the twenty-second. We're finishing the paperwork for this house, first. Erving was kind enough with his plan to let us move in before our houses sold; we don't want him waiting any longer to close. Owen and I also talked about a little getaway right before the wedding."

"Oh, that sounds nice—where ya goin'?" Eide asked.

"I don't know. I was supposed to decide that, but so far all I've done is tell Owen I'd figure something out."

"Girl, what is wrong with you? Your husband offers to take you away on a romantic getaway and you put it on the back burner. There is something wrong with you."

"No, there isn't. I just finished a winter campaign for a boutique in Durango; so now I'll figure it out."

"I'm going to help you out once again. I saw this cute little chalet when Levi and I went out of town. I thought it would be cute at Christmastime. I'll look it up and send you an email but do yourself a favor, call them today and make a reservation."

"Hey, Eide. You keep getting fired up and you're going to wake up the little guy."

"Oh no, not a chance—he went with Granny Grainer this morning. I swear that woman does more kidnapping."

"Where'd they go?"

"Oh, I don't know. I quit asking. Laurel tells me it is so I can get some work done or Levi and I need an evening together or so I can catch a nap—who naps that much? Well, besides you." Eide said, laughing.

"I'm going to hang up now and do something productive. Conjure up supper for my hardworking husband."

"Um hmm." Eide said, sighing. "I should probably do the same thing. You be sure and video it so the next time you're caught napping we have proof."

"Bye, Eide."

"Bye, and hey, make that reservation."

Chapter 18

"What's going on behind those pretty little eyes?" Owen asked as he parked in front of the bank. We were able to meet with Rachel to finish at the bank when Owen's class was over. Owen's class was complete for this session: he and Ty had one more session tomorrow and then Owen and I were taking a trip to a cute little chalet up in the mountains for a few days.

"Oh nothing, really. Just thinking about having you all to myself in a couple days."

"Not having second thoughts about Erving's house, are ya?" Owen asked as we got out and headed for the door.

"Not a chance—got all the closets full." I said, laughing at my own joke.

Owen opened the bank door for me, and we went inside, and he followed me into Rachel's office.

"Hey, guys, how's it going?" Rachel asked as we walked into her office.

"Hi, Rachel, thanks for meeting with us this evening." Owen said.

"It's no problem. We all have a lot going on. I wished we'd have had the chance to get together before you guys were heading out." Rachel said excitedly.

"I know. For sure when we get back from the wedding."

"So, Ty says you guys just have tomorrow's class left."

"That's it." Owen said sounding excited and exhausted at the same time. He'll probably end up sleeping the entire time we're at the chalet.

"That's awesome. I know Ty's been worried about this class; he will be glad to have it finished. As you are too, I'm sure."

"Definitely." Owen said. "It's been a challenging one that's for sure. Do you know if Erving was coming in this evening?"

"No, he stopped by this afternoon and signed his paperwork." Rachel said. "He chuckled and said to tell you he'd be around later."

"Oh, geez. That guy." Owen said, laughing. "Well, I guess if Erving's coming around, we better get with it."

"Of course." Rachel said, sitting up in her chair, moving into business mode.

We finished the paperwork for the loan and thanked Rachel as we headed out of her office that evening. Karla and I walked out to the pickup.

"When I signed the papers on "Garratt's rental house," as Eide dubbed it, things just seemed odd. Well, now I know why. First off, I didn't know what Garratt had planned. Second, this is what it's supposed to feel like. It felt great signing with you, Owen; like we're on the verge of something great.

"That was great, wasn't it?" I told Karla hugging her. "I was thinking the same thing. I sure didn't have that feeling when I bought my house back in Silver City. It feels right because we did it together. Let's go grab some burgers at the Burger Barn and go home."

"Hey Erving, heard you were headed this way tonight." I said, pulling up beside the barn. "Did you have supper yet?"

"Not yet. I was over to the Kasters' up the road and decided to come over here and see how things were before going home."

"Well come inside, we got a burger for ya."

"Either of your daughters planning to make it back for the holidays?" Karla asked Erving as we sat down at the table and Karla started pulling burgers and fries out of the bag and passing them around the table. I went to the fridge to get ketchup and other condiments and set them on the table waiting to hear Erving's response.

"No." Erving said. "Ann and Katy both have weddings coming up the first part of the year. So, they're busy with details and such."

"Oh, sure, that's understandable. Are you going to visit them?" Karla asked.

"No, no. I'll just stick around here. Kaster up the road said you kids are leaving for a few days. Going to a wedding or something—gives me an excuse to come out and see the horses; take care of things for you."

"Well, you don't need an excuse to come out, Erving. Dad said he'd take care of things while we're gone."

"Hmm, excuse me." Karla said, sounding distressed and abruptly leaving the table, nearly knocking her chair over. Erving continued talking about his work back and forth with Dad over the years. I wasn't paying that much attention to him. I was wondering what was going on with Karla.

"Well, I suppose." Erving said, standing up. "Thanks for the burger and fries. Really hit the spot. I'm going to head out to the barn."

"Okay, Erving. I'm just going to check on Karla and I'll be right out."

"Hey, Karla." I said, tapping on the bathroom door. She didn't really answer so much as just a slight mumble. "You okay, hon?"

"Mmhmm." I heard Karla mumble from behind the door again.

"I'm going out to the barn with Erving. I'll try and hurry."

I heard Karla mumble again and then I could hear her getting sick. I didn't know whether I should go in and see to Karla or go help Erving in the barn. I went out to the porch and grabbed my coat and gave a second look back towards that bathroom. I ended up going out to the barn. *This wouldn't take long*, I thought, and I'd be back to see about Karla.

"Everything ok with Karla?" Erving asked when I opened the barn door.

"I'm not sure, I told her we'd hurry."

"I can take care of this, if you want to head back in."

I left the barn and returned to the house. This stomach bug Karla had, was going on for a couple of weeks now. I stepped into the porch and hung my coat up and took my boots off. Karla's mostly uneaten burger was still sitting on the table where she'd left it. I hope she wasn't still in the bathroom. I went to the bathroom and didn't find her there. I went upstairs to our bathroom and could hear the shower running. I stuck my head in the door and asked if she was ok.

"Yea, I'll be out shortly." Karla said.

She said she was okay, but she did not sound okay. She sounded dreadful.

I went back downstairs and cleaned up the kitchen. As I was putting things away, I glanced out the window and saw Erving drive out. *Hmm, seems like he's going to be all alone on Christmas. I need to remember to tell Ma and Dad—maybe they can have him over for dinner.*

I could feel my phone buzzing. I wonder if Rachel told Ty we were at the bank earlier and he's texting to razz me about it.

Just as I thought—looking at my phone, Ty did text.

"Hey, Owe, meet me early tomorrow. I want to look over the flight hours for this class. Make sure everything is covered before we finish. Don't want to miss anything."

"Sure, I'll be there." I replied to Ty.

I put my phone away and finished cleaning up the kitchen. Karla still had not come downstairs; surely, she's done with her shower. I popped upstairs and looked in our room and she was lying on the bed; she had barely gotten dressed before she lay down. She was facing away from me, her arms held around her stomach. I went around to her side of the bed and sat down beside her. "Hey, Karla. What's going on?" I realized after I had sat down that she had been dozing off.

"Just a little flu bug that's been going around." Karla said, sounding sleepy and very much out of energy.

"Hon, you've had this little bug off and on for a while. Maybe time to get it checked out."

"Just a couple times—I'll be fine." Karla said as she lowered her head back onto the pillow.

I leaned in and kissed her forehead after she'd gotten settled in. "Good night, Karla."

Karla barely whispered me a goodnight. I went and took a shower. After I showered, I made some coffee and sat down at the kitchen table for a while, reading my Bible before joining Karla in bed.

In the middle of the night, I felt Karla abruptly leave our bed. *Dang, she must not be feeling any better.* I got up and followed her to the bathroom. By the time I got there, she was slumped over the toilet. I could tell she felt and sounded miserable. I got her a towel to put under her knees and leaned down beside her and held her hair back. Karla would vomit and then she'd rest her head in my lap for a while. Then after a while something would hit her, and she would need to vomit some more. After a few hours of this back and forth she said she was ready to go back to bed.

I told her I was going to go out to feed the calves and then I would be back to check on her. I was supposed meet Ty early this morning, but now I was not sure If I should even go at all. When I got to the barn, Erving was just pulling up.

"Geez, Erving, you're up early."

"Yea, well sometimes I just wake up. Thought I'd come give you hand this morning. How're things with you?" Erving asked, nodding towards the house.

"Karla didn't have a very good night."

"Yea, kinda figured as much. Hope she gets to feeling better today," Erving said as he started pitching manure from the stall. I went to the next stall and started mucking it out. We had finished mucking the stalls and Erving said he would finish filling the water and put down fresh hay.

I went back to the house while Erving finished in the barn. I could hear Karla was back in the bathroom again as I ascended the stairs.

"I thought you went to work?" Karla asked as I stepped up to the bathroom door.

"No, I was just out doing morning chores. Erving's out there finishing. I think I will stay here with you today. We should get you a doctor's appointment; I don't want you like this through the weekend or Lane and Molly's wedding."

"I'm good." Karla said, wiping her face off before leaving the bathroom. "I'm just going to go lie down again. You can go to work."

"I don't know about that, Karla. Not two hours ago you were lying on the bathroom floor puking your guts out."

"I know, but I'm fine now." Karla said, lying down in the bed. "I appreciate you letting me use you as a pillow. But really, I am fine. And isn't today the last day of class? Won't Ty have a coronary if you're not there?"

"Ty'll understand."

"Well, not today. I'm going to back to sleep."

"You're the most stubborn woman I know. Where's your cell phone?"

"Hmm, might be downstairs in the kitchen."

I ran downstairs and grabbed her cell phone. I was not convinced I should leave her. I got back to our room and noticed Karla dozing off.

"Hey Karla." I said nudging her shoulder. I set her phone on the nightstand beside the bed.

"Owen. Go to work."

"I am." I said, reluctantly. "But will you let me take you to the doctor later?"

"I don't know, we'll see. I just want to sleep now."

"I brought your cell phone up, it's setting on the nightstand. You need to call me later or if you need something."

"Yes, nurse. Now go and let me go to sleep." Karla said, waving me off.

"Morning, Ty." I said, walking into the Flight School shop a little later than we had planned.

"Hey, Owe. How's it going?" Ty asked, looking up at me. "I guess it's written all over your face how it's going. What's up, man?"

"Karla had rough night and I sat up with her while she was sick."

"She still isn't feeling better?"

"Yesterday after work we met Rachel at the bank. We grabbed some burgers and took them home and she barely started eating and got sick. I tried to get her to let me take her to the doctor today, but she says she'll be fine. She thought you'd have a coronary if I missed the last class."

"Dang, hope she's feeling better soon. Did you finally get everything squared away with Ole Man Erving?"

"Yea. I figured Rachel'd tell you since she met us after class yesterday."

"No, she said she had a late meeting, but that was the end of it. We don't talk about her work. Erving finally sell you the herd?" Ty asked, chuckling.

"Oh geez, don't ask. Yes, I own the herd. I don't know how or why he wormed me into that one."

"Ah, ha-ha." Ty said, laughing. "I told you. So, what are we thinking here, you gonna expand?"

"Ty, it's barely six in the morning. I haven't had much coffee—or sleep, for that matter. I don't want to talk cattle with you." I said, shaking my head. "Let's just look these flight hours over."

"Okay." Ty said. "I made a spreadsheet of their hours last night and surprise, surprise: Ryan and Matt are the ones that fell short."

"Oh, it can't be that bad." I said, looking over his shoulder at the computer screen. "Did you look at the forecast for today, though? This afternoon doesn't look very good; I almost don't recommend flying this afternoon." I said, pulling out my phone.

"We don't need this." Ty said, rubbing his face.

"Don't worry about it, Ty. We'll do what we can before the weather moves in. Maybe we should both take flights out until the weather moves in. That will give us as much flight time as possible and then we can both work in the classroom this afternoon."

"Yea, okay." Ty said agreeing with me. "You look these flight times over and make sure I got everything good before we take off this morning. I'll go start pre-flight checks before everyone arrives."

"Okay. Sounds good. I'll be out in a bit."

That afternoon, Ty and I returned from flights. The weather didn't move in as I had thought so we were doing well. I went and checked my phone. Karla had called and left me a message. Said she was up and ok—nothing to worry about, Nurse Owen. *Well, that's good*, I thought, listening to her message.

Ty and I went in to set up for classroom time. He said everyone needs three hours classroom time to finish today, except for Matt and Ryan. "Matt needs an additional four hours including two hours flight time from the morning he missed. Ryan needs an hour." Ty said. "We could catch Ryan's this afternoon, but what about Matt?"

"I'll talk to him. I'll meet him here in the morning, we can knock it out right quick."

"What about Karla?" Ty asked.

"She called earlier and left me a message. Said she's okay. Must just be the flu bug like she said. I'll take this lesson and then Karla and I can take off tomorrow afternoon and you and Rachel can take off like you'd planned. It'll all work out."

"You sure about this, Owe? You better talk to Karla first and then text me tonight."

Chapter 19

"Ty is Owen with you?" Karla asked. "I tried calling him a few times and he hasn't answered."

"Karla? No, Owe's not with me. He was taking Matt on that final flight lesson this morning. Didn't he tell you? Are you okay?" Ty asked.

"Yes. he told me and I'm okay. I just thought he'd be back a while ago."

"He's not back. I would have thought those guys would've been done by now. I will do some checking. Rach and I are on our way back from Durango and we'll swing through the Flight School— I'll give you a call when we get there. If Owe gets home before I call you back, have him call me."

"Thanks, Ty."

"Karla, are you sure you're, okay?"

"Yes, I'm fine. I'll talk to you soon."

"Here, Rach." I said, handing her my phone, picking up speed. I could hear the concern in Karla's voice. *What happened to Owe? He should have been back hours ago.*

"Sorry, Rach, we might not get to spend the evening together like we'd planned. Will you call the Flight School hangar and see if someone answers?"

"Ty what's going on? Will you slow down, please? The roads are slick, this isn't a time to speed up," Rachel warned me.

"Just call the hangar, please."

Rach took my phone and started dialing and put the phone on speaker. It just rang and rang.

"Owe took Matt out this morning for a final flight lesson. They should have been back around noon, one o'clock at the latest. Now Karla calls and says he hasn't gotten home."

"Ty, it's after four. What's happened to him?"

"I don't know, I was hopeful that when you called the hangar those guys had just lost track of time and were just getting in. He doesn't do it a lot and I'd think not today, especially with Karla not feeling well."

"What's up with Karla?" Rach asked.

"I don't know, some flu bug. He wanted to take her to the doctor yesterday morning."

Just as I suspected, Owe's pickup still parked in the same place he always parks it, and I noticed Matt's car parked on the other side. I got out and walked into the hangar door.

The sound from opening the doors bounced off the walls. You could tell no one was around. Just for safety's sake, I hollered out, "Owe, you here?" There was no reply.

I went next door to the shop. All the while Rach followed me, not saying a word. We stepped into the shop; all the lights were off. I could tell no one had been in here since the day before.

We stepped back outside, and I looked up at the sky. I turned around to Rach, still hot on my tail. "Can you do me a favor?"

"Yes, name it. Anything."

"Can you go out, check on Karla?" I asked Rach, handing her my Jeep keys. "I'm going to radio Owe and the control tower and see if I can learn anything. I may possibly take a flight out, see if I see anything, maybe he's landed somewhere."

"Are you sure it's a good idea, taking a flight this close to dark, Ty?"

"I'll be fine, I won't be gone long."

I drove down Owe and Karla's drive a few hours later in Owe's pickup. I did not want to go in and face Karla. Little that I had learned in the last few hours wasn't enough to know where Owe was. I should have stopped off at Joe and Rosie's, brought them along. I decided to go in the barn and muck out the stalls, do the evening feeding. I could see Rach and Karla in the kitchen as I glanced up at the house before going into the barn. At least this would buy me a half hour or so. I started mucking out stalls; I could tell Owe had done morning chores this; he hung the pitchfork upside down on the far wall of the barn. Owe had hung his pitchfork in the same way, forever. The guy was notorious for putting things away in the barn in a particular spot, he must have learned it from Joe. I've helped Owe and his dad around Joe's farm nearly all my life. At least for me, I have never been good at these chores—and riding horses, you can forget it. I fell off so many times. Joe was always patient with me; he never gave up on me. And God bless Rosie, I think she did my laundry more than my own mom.

I walked up to the house, wondering where Owe and Matt were. It was a cold night and the weather Owe thought we'd get yesterday was likely going to move in tonight. I clasped the doorknob to the house, pausing a moment before walking in.

I finally opened the door and walked into the kitchen, getting the look from Karla and Rach I knew was coming and the dreaded question.

"Where's Owen?" Karla asked before I could say anything.

"Ty, where's Owen?" I asked him as he stood in the door all alone.

"Well, I don't know where he is." Ty said, looking down at his boots. "I do know a little more than I did a few hours ago. Maybe we should call Joe and Rosie."

"Ty, just tell me." I said, annoyed, as my phone started ringing.

"Is that Owe calling?" Ty asked looking at me hopeful.

"No, it's Eide." I said, answering the call. "Eide, I can't talk right now."

"Karla?" I could hear Eide calling out to me before I hung up. I clicked the end button on my phone and tried to focus my attention back to Ty.

"Why did you ask if that was Owen?"

"I radioed for Owe and Matt several times, but I didn't get an answer."

"They never responded?"

"No, they didn't. I radioed the control tower, too. I wanted to see about their communications and flight activity. They had communication with the control tower around eight this morning, requesting permission for takeoff. They were detected on the radar up until ten this morning, but there's been no communication since."

"Ty, did they crash?"

"I didn't say that; let's not get ahead of ourselves."

"What plane did they take?"

"The Cessna, the one he bought before your wedding. Why does that matter?"

"Oh God." I put my face into my hands. I could feel tears well up. "That's the same plane."

I was thinking about the start to our honeymoon when Rachel handed me some tissues. I looked up to find Ty and Rachel staring at me.

"Same plane as what?" Ty asked, looking back at me, concerned.

"Ty? Did Owen tell you about what happened to that plane on our honeymoon?"

"No, I don't think so. What happened?"

Ty asked me what happened, but I couldn't sit there any longer and I certainly couldn't answer him.

Karla did not answer me before she hurriedly moved from her chair and ran toward the bathroom.

"What happened on their honeymoon?" Rach asked, looking at me, concerned.

"I don't know." I said, shaking my head. "I hope she's not sick." I said, nodding my head toward the bathroom.

"Sorry Rach. Not how we planned to spend the evening. Will you go check on her? I'm going to call Joe and Rosie. I don't really know what to do about all this." I said, running my hand across my head.

"Please don't call Joe and Rosie, not yet anyways." Karla said before either Rach, or I had moved from the table.

"Karla? Are you okay?" Rach asked.

"Yes." Karla said, wiping the tears from her eyes.

"I'll hold off on calling Joe and Rosie for a bit. But first I would like to know what you are talking about. What happened to that plane on your honeymoon?"

"I don't know exactly what happened; Owen tried to explain it to me. Some kind of failure, he said. We were near Kalispell and the plane started shaking. It was terrible, we suddenly descended several times, it seemed like Owen was having a tough time controlling the plane. Things just did not seem right. Owen quickly made adjustments and then radioed into the control tower requesting permission to land. His request was not exactly how I had heard him before. He was cleared for landing and instructed to contact ground control at the Kalispell Airport for further instructions."

"Did he have engine failure?" Ty asked.

"I think so. The ground traffic controller and another gentleman came over to the plane as Owen finished shutting down. They thought they had the wrong plane at first. They said they knew Owen was having a rough landing but to be in engine failure and to land a plane that well, takes skill."

"Owe's had engine failure before. He knows how to handle it. It's a precision between glide and speed. Did Owe say what the failure was?"

"Something about some pistons and rings, maybe. I don't know about these things." I wiped the tears out of my eyes that had welled up before they started streaming down my face. My phone started ringing again, I quickly grabbed it before looking at the screen hoping this time it was Owen.

"Hello." I said soon realizing it was Eide, again. "Look Eide, I'm not talking to you right now." I said loudly, interrupting her ramblings. "Owen's not home and I don't know if he's coming home tonight." I started sobbing, I clicked the phone off and set it back on the table. After a moment of silence, I stood up and started to walk toward the door. "I don't know when Owen will be home, so I need to go to the barn and take care of the evening feeding."

Before I'd had a chance to tell Karla I'd done the evening feeding, she turned heel and ran off to the bathroom, again.

"I'm going to call Joe and Rosie. Somebody needs to call Eide back and tell her about Owen."

"You call Joe and Rosie, I'll call Eide." Rachel said, picking up Karla's phone.

"Thanks for the call, Ty." Joe said as he and Rosie came walking into the kitchen a short time later. "I thought it was odd that Owen and Karla didn't stop by on their way out of town or at least call."

"Ty, what's going on?" Rosie asked as Karla came back into the kitchen. "Oh, Karla, honey." Rosie said, meeting her, opening her arms for a hug. "How are you?"

"I've had a few times that I didn't feel well, Rosie, but it's okay I'm fine. I didn't realize Ty called you, we talked about waiting." Karla said giving me a glance. "I need to go out to the barn and do evening feeding."

"Oh, honey. Let Joe and Ty go out and do that." Rosie said, guiding Karla to a chair. "You sit down here and tell me what's going on."

"I haven't had a chance to tell you, Karla—I took care of things out in the barn before I came in earlier."

"So, what's going on?" Joe asked. "Where's Owen?"

"That's why I called. He took a class out this morning; they should have been back hours ago."

"Oh dear." Rosie said, looking at me for more information.

"There's been no word from any of them?" Joe asked.

"I talked to the control tower earlier and their radar detected them about ten miles south of Telluride. I flew out but didn't see much before it got too dark. I rounded up a couple guys to go out early in the morning. We are heading out at first light to look again. Karla told me something after I got here that drives home what I was thinking. They had trouble with that plane on their honeymoon. I'm wondering if there was trouble again today and they had to land, and the control tower hasn't detected it."

"Ty, did you let any of Matt's family know about this?" Karla asked.

"Yea, I called whoever he had listed on his registration form to contact in the event of an emergency and left a message."

"Maybe we should call your family." Rosie said. "You and Owen are not going to get into town tonight and they're probably expecting you guys."

"We weren't meeting up with my family today. Oh goodness, Eide."

"It's okay, Karla." Rach said. "I called Eide back for you. I explained to her about Owen. She's going to call you later; she understands. Actually, she thought you and Owen were having a blowup—her words not mine." Rachel said, holding her hands in the air.

"That would be Eide." Karla said, chuckling through her tears. "I wish Owen were here to have a blowup with me."

We all sat around the kitchen table, not really saying much of anything. I don't think any of us knew what to say. I think we all secretly hoping that Owen would land at the Flight School and call one of us and say, "Hey, where's my pickup?" But that never happened, and it grew colder and windier outside. At nearly one in the morning, Ty stood from the table and said, "I'm going to the couch to take a nap."

"Take one of the bedrooms upstairs, Ty, you'll sleep better."

"We should all take a bed or couch." Joe said. "It's not doing any of us any good staring at each other like this."

I went upstairs to the bed I shared with Owen. For weeks, I had been feeling crappy and not able to stay awake when Owen was home in the evenings. Now he was—well, I did not know where he was, just that he was not here with me. Just a few nights ago, he sat on the bathroom floor most of the night when I was sick, either holding my hair or my head, whichever I needed. It's a wonder he made it through work the next day on as little of sleep as he got that night. He even wanted to change plans and take me to the doctor the next morning. I should have let him. My mind just would not close—where are you, Owen?

This kind of reminds me of the day Owen's team was called out and I took his pickup home from the Mountain Rescue hangar. He did not return for over twenty-four hours; I didn't sleep much that night either. Tonight, I laid in our bed holding Owen's pillow, so lost without Owen by my side. I must have dozed off because I did not hear my phone right away. When I finally woke up enough, the ringing had stopped.

I moved the blankets around enough to find my phone. *Please, Lord, let this be Owen*, I thought and prayed, getting to the missed call list.

Pulling up the missed call, it said "Dad." I quickly redialed and realized it was just after four a.m., still no word from Owen.

"Hey kiddo. You, okay?" Dad asked when he answered the call.

"No, Dad." I said, nearly crying again. "Owen left yesterday morning for class, and he hasn't gotten back."

"I know. Eide left us a message and I just now got it. So, what's the plan? Is there something I can do?"

"I don't know, I don't know what to do. Ty and some others are going back out in a few hours to look for him. We think they had engine trouble and they have no cell service."

"That's understandable. You lay back down, kiddo, keep us posted. Love you."

"Love you too, Dad."

Owen and I were supposed to be on a getaway these next few days, and then head on to Lane and Molly's wedding after that. Their Christmas Eve wedding. I decided not to lie there dwelling on this. We still had time, Owen would get home today, and we could still take off after that. I got up and dressed. I went downstairs, made some coffee, and put on my barn boots and coat and went out to the barn. I let the horses out into the paddock and started mucking out the first stall.

I don't know how Owen mucks these stalls so quickly. I think it took me almost an hour and I was just finishing the first one when I heard the barn door open.

"I thought I saw the lights on out here." Ty said. "Karla, what are you doing out here?"

"My dad called, and I couldn't get back to sleep; so, I decided to come out here."

"Joe or I will take care of this."

"I know." I said, heaving a forkful in the wagon. I want you to go look for Owen. Should I go along and help you?"

"No, Karla. You need to stay here. Besides, I don't want any puke in my plane." Ty said, leaning against the horse stall.

"Very funny, Ty."

"How do you feel this morning?"

"I'm fine." I said, continuing to muck the stall. "Do you want something to eat before you take off?"

"No, stop worrying about me, I'll be fine. Why don't you let Joe finish this?"

"Let Joe finish what? Karla?" Erving said, looking surprised to see me.

"Better yet, let Ole Man Erving finish it." Ty said, patting Erving's shoulder.

"Ty, just go." I said becoming more irritated with him the longer he stood there.

"Yes, I'm going. I'll call you later." Ty said, hugging me, and then turned to Erving.

"Morning, Erving." Ty said as he went past him out the barn door. "Take care of the rest of this for her, she's sick."

"Of course, see ya, Ty." Erving said, looking puzzled.

"Morning, Karla." Erving said after Ty'd left. "I thought you and Owen were going out of town yesterday."

"We were planning to." I said, wiping a few stray tears away. "Owen didn't make it back from his flight class yesterday."

"Oh, dear." Erving said, taking the pitchfork from me.

"Ty's going out to look for him."

"Ty'll take care of things. Go back in the house, get yourself warmed up."

"I will, but you stop up before you leave and get some coffee, please."

"Yes, I will, Karla." Erving said, throwing manure in the cart, picking up where I had left off.

I left the barn and started walking towards the house. As I walked to the house, I looked up at the sky; it would be light in a little while. It was always coldest at this time of day; *I hope Owen was able to stay warm last night.* My phone started ringing, interrupting my thoughts. I reached into my pocket, hoping against all hope that it was Owen. Looking at the screen, it said it was my dad, again.

"Dad?" I said, answering the phone, stepping up onto the porch. Joe was just coming out of the house and stopped, then gave me a puzzled look.

"Hey, kiddo. I was thinking about all this. Did Ty call Mountain Rescue for help? The place Owen used to work for?"

"I don't think so, I don't know. He just said he and some other guys were going out."

"I think he should call them; it wouldn't hurt. I bet they'd be glad to help out."

"Why don't you call and ask Ty about it? I doubt they have taken off, yet. They are probably still doing pre-flight checks. I'll text you his number and then you guys can come up with a plan."

"Everything okay?" Joe asked when I ended the call.

"My dad wanted to know if someone called Colorado Mountain Rescue to help?"

"That's a good idea, what did you tell him?"

"I sent him Ty's number and said they should come up with a plan."

Erving came walking up towards the steps, looking up at Joe and me.

"Morning, Erving." Joe said.

"Erving, I'm sorry I haven't gotten to your coffee yet. Come inside, I'll get a pot started."

"Rosie's making a pot." Joe said as we all stepped into the kitchen.

"Colorado Mountain Rescue, Shane speaking."

"Yes, ah hi. My name is Darren Grainer I'd like to request your services or report a missing person or something."

"Yes, I can help you with that. Can I get some information from you? How many people are involved?"

"Two, I think"

"Names of the missing individuals?"

"Owen Kaster, uh, he used to work there."

"Well, I'm new here, but that's okay. Next name?"

"Yes, a Mike or Matt; I don't know his last name."

"Do you know the intended area of travel?"

"Their plane was last detected ten miles south of Telluride yesterday around ten a.m."

"Can I have your contact information so the crew can be in contact with you?"

"Yes, it's Darren Grainer. Phone number 970-219-8005. You should also have Ty Anders's cell phone number, 970-719-2020; he's coordinating the flight efforts out of West Creek."

"So, that's Darren at 970-219-8005 and Ty at 970-719-2020." Shane repeated.

"Yes, that's correct."

"Okay, I'll dispatch the crew and we'll be in touch."

"Thank you." Darren said.

"Hey, Aaron."

"What's up, Shane?"

"We just got this call."

"Yes, I know, I just got the page."

"Well, I took the call."

"Okay, so what's the problem?" Aaron asked.

"Well, the guy that called in," Shane said, looking at his notes. "Darren Grainer."

"Darren Grainer." Aaron said, testing the name out. "That name sounds familiar."

"Darren said the guy he called about, Owen—" Shane said, looking at his notes.

"Owen Kaster?" Aaron said. "We're going after Owen Kaster. What happened?"

"This Darren doesn't know much. Their plane was detected about ten miles south of Telluride about ten a.m. yesterday morning."

"Did you get any contact information?" Aaron asked.

"Yes, this Darren's and a guy named Ty." Shane said, handing the note to Aaron.

"Oh yea, Ty. The ring pop guy." Aaron said, looking at the contact sheet.

"The what guy?" Shane asked, looking perplexed.

"Never mind, not important. Just tell the other guys when they come in that we are going after Owen Kaster, especially Todd. I'm going to my office to see if I can get ahold of Ty."

"What about Owen?" Todd asked as Aaron headed to his office.

"I'm going to my office to get more details; but it looks like we got paged about Owen Kaster."

"What happened to him?" Todd asked.

"Not sure, I'm going to try and get some more information. You want to let the rest of the team know?" Aaron asked. Todd went off to meet the rest of the team and load their gear.

Chapter 20

This was the second night that Owen's pillow had laid empty. There were many people that had darkened our door today, but none of them was Owen. I prayed to God that he was safe and warm. Tears streaked down my face, and I started to wipe them away. I did not know what to do without him. Ty returned earlier this evening and was talking about the territory he and the Mountain Rescue crew had covered. I missed most of what Ty said. I was thinking back to Owen and my wedding. Owen and Ty collaborated a dance together to the oldie's song "Shout." They were dancing, shaking, and throwing their hands in the air, it was a hoot! They had all our friends and family clapping their hands and dancing right along. Those two are a crazy pair.

My phone buzzed and I quickly rolled over and grabbed it, hoping it was Owen. It was a text from Eide. My phone said it was nearly five in the morning—*where had the night gone?* I thought, looking at Eide's message. *"Hey you up?"* Eide asked.

"Yes." I replied

"Can I call you?" Eide quickly replied.

"Yes."

"Hey, what's up?" I asked, answering my phone when it rang.

"You, okay?" Eide asked.

"No, I've been laying here wondering where the night went. I was hoping that was Owen when my phone buzzed."

"I'm sorry I got your hopes up. You know we'd come down there." Eide said.

"I know, but I'm hoping by the time you get here Ty, and the crews will figure everything out and bring Owen home. I pray to God that he's safe and warm."

"He is. Gods got this. You know Owen would tell you that."

"This isn't about buying a house, Eide, it's my husband" I said with tears slipping further down my cheek. I could feel my stomach churning.

"No, I know it's not about buying a house. Owen was not talking about buying a house when he said that. He was talking about having faith; have some faith, girl."

"I have faith, I'm just scared."

"We all get scared and lose faith occasionally, but we get back up, dust ourselves off and keep on trucking. I gotta get Toby, he needs another diaper change. I'll call you later, okay?"

"Okay, bye, Eide."

I laid there a little bit longer, thinking about Owen and my stomach. Soon I decided I had had enough laying here thinking about things. I got up and decided to make some coffee. I poured myself a cup and did not see Erving's pickup out by the barn, so I decided to go out and start mucking the stalls. These animals were not Erving's responsibility anymore.

I hated thinking how cold it was as I trudged across the yard to get down to the barn.

I let the horses out into the paddock and pulled the manure cart up to the first stall and started pitching manure into the cart. I had been very queasy to my stomach, and it seem to be getting worse, I knew what was coming. *Owen, where are you?* I thought, stamping my foot on the barn floor as I leaned over the cart. I went back to mucking out the stalls, but it was not long before I needed to vomit again.

I was slumped over the manure cart, vomiting, when I heard the barn door open, and someone walk in.

"Karla, what's going on? Are you okay?" Erving asked. "Oh dear, this isn't good." he said, coming up beside me, placing his hand on my shoulder.

"Uh, well, no, not really." I said when I was able to speak, wiping my mouth off with the sleeve of my coat.

"You shouldn't be out here; I said I'd take care of things." Erving said.

"I know." I said before my stomach rumbled again. I knew what was coming. *Poor Erving having to witness this*, I thought, with my head bent over into the manure cart.

Erving grabbed a towel from the bench and handed it to me, taking my arm, guiding me away from the cart. "Here, sit down in the office while I finish up and then I'll take you back to the house."

I sat in the chair next to the desk. I didn't even know what was really in here. I think once, Owen left his coat in here and I stepped in to grab it for him—*oh God, please let Owen have a good coat with him*.

I sat by the desk, I noticed there were boxes sitting beside the desk. *Hmm, I wonder whose pictures these are*. I picked up a few and looked through them. After flipping through several of them, I stopped at a picture of a very cute young girl, a year or two—she looked an awful lot like Owen. *Does Owen have a daughter? No, he would have told me; my mind's just playing tricks on me*, I thought as I looked at the picture again. She does look an awful lot like Owen, though.

I heard the outside barn door open. I slipped the other picture back in the box and put the picture of the young girl in my pocket.

I could hear Joe talking to Erving out by the stalls and then they both came into the barn office.

"Karla, you, okay?" Joe asked, looking me over.

"Yes, I'm fine."

"Erving said you weren't feeling well."

"I had a moment where things were a little rough, but it's passed." *I am not so sure this was just a moment any longer*. I thought.

"Okay, well. I'm going to drive you up to the house and then I'll come back and help Erving finish." Joe said, looking concerned.

"Thank you. When you guys are finished come get some coffee."

I sat at the kitchen table late that afternoon drinking coffee; I pulled the picture out of my pocket I had found in a box in the barn this morning. I was waiting for Ty to come and tell me yet again they were still looking for Owen. Ty's said the same thing the last few days—they were getting closer, yet they still had not brought him home. *Was Owen ever going to come home?* I thought, drinking my coffee in silence. Owen and I always drank coffee together—if he had a daughter, how come he had never talked about it? Owen and I spent a lot of time dating over a cup of coffee; we talked about a lot of things—how come this never came up? Where was this little girl that looked so much like Owen? There was a light tap at the door, I did not get up to meet Ty. I just put the picture in my pocket and went to the fridge to get him a Dr. Pepper. Only when I turned from the fridge, it was not Ty. I saw Joe was getting ready to take a chair at the kitchen table.

"Joe." I said, surprised. "I was expecting Ty. Do you want some coffee?"

"I know, he'll be along anytime."

"Where's Rosie?" I asked, getting the coffee ready to brew.

"She stayed home. Church was pretty hard on you both."

"Yes, I know. I didn't think Pastor Jacobs was going ask for prayers and explain Owen's situation right off the bat." I said, sitting down beside Joe. "I just, I'm sorry. I didn't mean to cry so much and then get up and leave."

"No need to be sorry." Joe said, waving his hand. "How are you feeling today? You really should let Rosie or me take you to the doctor."

"I'm fine, Joe." I said, wiping tears from my face. "I just need Owen to come home." I told Joe as more tears built.

"Hey, Karla." Joe said, extending his arm across the table, taking my hand. "Owen will be home, I know this, just believe it. Wherever Owen's at he is praying to get back here; to get back to you. He's praying and fighting with all his might to do what he can to get out of whatever situation he's in."

"Joe, it's been four days." I said tearfully as Ty came in the kitchen.

"Ty, good to see you, how are you doing?" Joe asked when Ty came in the back door. "Any news?"

"I'm okay." Ty said, although he looked far from it. I could see dark rings under his eyes and about a five-day shadow highlighting his face.

"Yes, I do have some news. One of the Mountain Rescue guys thinks they spotted something; but it is too dark and dangerous to head out on foot tonight. We are going out at first light again. The Mountain Rescue team is putting together a plan to hike in."

"I talked to Max, he and Elaine and Rachel are coming along. Do you want to go, Joe?"

"I'm going." I said, interrupting Ty's question.

"Karla, no. I think I'd be remiss to let you go." Ty said. "I think you and Rosie should stay here with the kids."

"I think he's right, Karla." Joe said, agreeing with Ty.

"I'm sorry, guys, but I'm going. I need to get out of this house and do something; are we meeting at the Flight School, what time?"

"I'll pick you up, Karla." Joe said reluctantly. "You can come with me. Just don't make us regret this and don't forget to bundle up."

"You won't." I told Joe. I'd had enough of this just sitting around and waiting game, I wanted to go out and help. "Ty, have you eaten today, do you want some soup?"

"No thanks, Karla. I just came to tell you about this. I'll see you in the morning."

Chapter 21

The next morning, we all met at the Flight School. The last time Ty gathered us all up and took us off somewhere—Owen included—was to move us. He acted like a drill sergeant, getting everyone organized to pack up Owen's house. At the time, and even after the fact, I had made fun of Ty for the way he had gotten everyone organized. Now I was grateful for Ty's organization and all he had done to help Owen and me. I could hear Ty radio the control tower for permission for his flight to take off. I sat in my seat and stared out into the darkness.

We landed about an hour later in a remote, wooded, mountain terrain area. I presumed we were somewhere near Telluride. I saw that there were a few pickups and trailers, and the Mountain Rescue crew was unloading four-wheelers from the trailers. Somebody had set up a tent and tables. I feel like the Mountain Rescue crew must have worked all night putting this together.

"Ty, where'd all this come from?"

"Local law enforcement officers, contacts and connections. Aaron and Todd put a plan together last night to zero in on the site. We can't get close enough with the planes so we're splitting up and each taking a section of coordinates."

I noticed Aaron and Todd were walking toward us as we were discussing the plan for the day. Everyone exchanged morning greetings.

"Karla, hi." Aaron said. "I didn't know you'd be joining us. We usually don't—"

"—I'm coming along." I said, cutting Aaron off. "Ty, Joe and I already had this discussion last night. So, just tell me what to do."

"Just stick with me." Joe said. "Max has instructions, were going to take this pickup." He said, pointing to one parked along the road. "We can let Aaron, Todd and Ty get going with the others."

"Thanks, Joe." Ty said, looking at me concerned. "Rach's going to group up with you guys. Be careful and radio in if you need anything."

"Thanks, Ty." Max said as Ty headed off. "Are we ready?" Max asked after Ty left us to meet up with Aaron and Todd.

Ty, Aaron, and Todd and the two other Mountain Rescue crews headed off in different directions.

We all jumped in the pickup that Joe had just referenced earlier, Max drove down a smaller trail that was probably closed this time of year. I saw lots of animal trails but otherwise the trail looked untouched.

"Give us the details on this plan, Max. How long do we travel by vehicle? And then where do we go once, we're on foot?" Elaine asked.

"They gave me a map; the county guys came out and drove this trail last night but then it snowed right away so we can't follow their tracks. They said we can't take this trail as far as the map shows, only about twenty miles and then we need to get out and start walking southeast about four miles. It's pretty rugged and jagged terrain across there; not exactly great hiking in good conditions, let alone this time of year."

"We only go four miles?" I asked.

"Yea, all the other groups are coming in from different directions and we'll all end up hiking in about four miles surrounding the coordinates that Mike had the sighting from yesterday. So, this way they're hoping they cover everything." Max said.

We reached the end of the twenty miles that Max talked about earlier; he could only travel about forty miles an hour, seemed forever to get to this point. Max parked the pickup. He and Joe turned around from the front seat and looked at Rachel, Elaine, and me. I looked out the window. I could not believe we were about to go hiking out here, in the cold looking for—well, I didn't know what we were going to find. *Was Owen even still alive? Several days in this cold would make me want to give up.* Joe asked if everyone was ready.

There was not an overwhelming desire to jump out; we were not sure what we were about to find, if anything. Max was the first to start opening his door.

"Ah, hold on there a minute." Joe said. "If you don't mind. I would like to take a minute and say a few words. Can we join hands?" We all joined hands as Joe started speaking. "Our heavenly Father, we call upon you today as we head out. We look to you for strength and comfort as we embark on this mission into the cold to find and bring Owen home today. Lord, we look to you for guidance in this challenging time; we know that in the end everything will be to your will. We pray to you to see us through this. In your name we pray, amen."

A resounding amen echoed through the cab of the pickup before Max and Joe embarked out into the frosty morning air. I stepped out of the pickup behind Joe. "Thank you for your kind words, Joe."

"I meant every word of 'em. Are you doing okay, Karla?" Joe asked, eyeing my suspiciously.

"So far so good." I said, tightening the scarf around my neck.

"Okay." Max said. "We're taking this trail; stay near someone at all times."

We had been walking awhile that morning, everyone seemed content to just walk in silence. The only sounds I heard were the snow crunching under our feet or an occasional small animal that nearly scared the wits out of me. The last rabbit that jumped through the trees I thought was going to give me a heart attack.

Owen, if I get to tell you any of this, you are going to laugh at all of us. Especially me vomiting in the manure cart in the barn and Erving witnessing it. My stomach had been churning most of the time we had been gone this morning and it was not surprising when I bent over and nearly vomited across my shoes.

"Karla, my goodness. Are you okay?" Elaine asked.

"Yes, I am." I managed to say between vomiting bouts. Elaine came over and rubbed my shoulder as I was slumped over with my hands holding my knees.

I was finally able to stand up and reached for a nearby tree to lean against. "You good?" Elaine asked.

"Yea, just some kinda bug or stress."

"Uh huh." Elaine said, chuckling.

"I had that bug once, called it the 'Kaster Curse' for a while. Eventually named them Luke and Caity."

"I know." I said, moving away from the tree. "Let's not discuss this anymore. At least not in mixed company." I said, hunching over and vomiting again.

"Do you want to go back to the pickup?" Elaine asked.

"No." I said, continuing, following Joe and Max up ahead on the trail. It was almost noon, and we hadn't seen anything. I was beginning to think Mike did not realize what he saw or one of us had already seen whatever he saw and dismissed it. This was getting frustrating. Was all this walking even doing any good? I stopped where I was. I looked up at the sky, nearly crying, and shouted. "PLEASE, GOD. JUST TELL ME WHERE OWEN IS. PLEASE." Joe and Max turned back and hurried over to me.

"Maybe it's time for a break." Joe said looking over at Max. "Come on, Karla, let's go find a log to sit on."

"No." I said. "I'm fine." Tears streaming down my face.

"Here's some water." Max offered.

"Come over here." Rachel said. "There's a good-sized log we can sit on."

"Guys, I'm sorry for the outburst. I don't want to stop."

"Don't be sorry." Joe said.

"Who stands out here and shouts to God?" I asked crying. "I'm sorry."

"Maybe we should all give a shout out to God." Max said, chuckling. "It might work."

"We're getting closer." Joe said. "We have to have faith. Let's have a seat and have one of Rosie's sandwiches."

God bless that woman. With all she has been through as well and she still sends us a sandwich. We all sat on the log a little while, resting, and eating.

Joe got up from his log and started cleaning up the sandwich items before starting out again.

"Why don't you gals stay here." Joe said. "Max and I will continue the rest of the way and we'll pick you up on our way back out?"

"No, I can keep going." I said, putting my gloves back on.

"I know you can keep going, I have no doubt about that." Joe said. "I'm just giving you the chance to take a break."

"Yea." Max said. "You can sit here and talk about—well, I don't know what you're going to talk about. Elaine can tell you some horror stories about me. Just sit tight and Dad and I'll be back."

"Max's right." Elaine said. "Let's just stay here and let them go ahead."

Against my better judgment, I sat back on the log with Elaine and Rachel while Max and Joe continued.

Before Max and Joe got far down the trail, I could hear the radio go off. Ty was radioing in. I got up and nearly ran down the trail to hear what he was saying.

I heard the end of Ty's message, he said they were sending four-wheelers out to pick us up.

"What'd they say, Max?" I asked.

"Ty's just across the way, not too far. They're coming to pick us up on the four-wheelers."

"Why?" I asked.

"We're going back." Max said.

"We haven't finished. Ty, what's up?" I asked him when he pulled up beside up on his four-wheeler.

"We found what Mike saw yesterday, it's Owen's plane."

"Is Owen in it?" I asked.

"Yes, Owen and Matt are both in it."

"Take me to him, Ty." I said, getting on the back of his ATV.

"You can't, Karla." Ty said, looking back at me.

"Is he alive?" I asked, hesitantly. Not sure if I wanted to know the answer to that question.

"Aaron and Todd are going to assess their injuries and take them to Denver for treatment."

"What injuries—how bad are they? Is Owen, okay?"

"I haven't seen him. I will take you back to the pickup and we can fly into Denver and meet him when he arrives. It's better this way."

I turned around and vomited off the back of the four-wheeler. *Owen, you seriously better be okay.*

"You need anything?" Elaine asked. I shook my head, tears falling down my face.

"Come on, Karla." Ty said. "Owe's going to be the same ole pain in the butt he's always been and he's gonna be pretty ticked off when he finds out we let you come out here in the shape you're in."

"You let me take care of that—let's go." I said, coaxing Ty.

We all crowded on the four-wheelers that Ty and the others came back with and got back to the pickup. We still had the twenty miles of trail road to travel back to the plane.

"Ty, what are the extent of the Owen's injuries?" I asked again after we had reached the pickup and were traveling back to the plane.

"I don't know, Karla." Ty said, shaking his head.

"You should have let me go see him."

"Those guys are the experts, so it's best that we just stay out of their way."

"Did they say anything about Matt?" Joe asked.

"He was trying to explain what happened to Todd and Aaron, so I'm guessing he's in better shape than Owe, but I'm still going to—man, I knew something was going to go wrong with that clown. If only he would have made it to class on time or had not been messing around so much, none of this would have happened."

"Ty, you can't go blaming Matt." Joe said. "This could have happened any day; it's all part of God's plan."

"Before we got back to the plane, Aaron radioed Ty and said they were loaded and cleared for take-off. Both Owen and Matt were stable, and they were headed for Denver."

"Thanks for the update, we'll see you there." Ty said.

I started sobbing in my hands, I laid my head between my knees.

Chapter 22

An hour later we landed in Denver. I had texted my dad before our plane took off to see if he would pick us up at the airport. I did not know if I would even have enough cell service and I didn't get a reply, so I didn't know if he would be there waiting or not. After we passed through security and made our way out front, I saw Dad and Levi parked out front, waiting with two vehicles for us.

"Hi, Dad." I said as he held his arms out to hug me. "Thanks for coming."

"Hi, kiddo, glad you texted. How's Owen?" Dad asked, still holding me.

"I don't know, we don't know anything. None of us has seen him. The Mountain Rescue crew brought him in. Last we heard when their flight took off, he was stable."

Dad released me from his hug and said hello to the others and shook Joe's hand before we jumped into his and Levi's vehicles and they took us to the hospital.

We found Aaron and Todd at the hospital shortly after we arrived.

"Hey guys, how was your trip?" Aaron asked, standing up from the chair he had been occupying in the waiting room.

"How's Owen?" I asked. "Can I see him?"

"No, I don't think you can. They just took him back to surgery," Aaron said, placing his hand on my shoulder.

"Surgery, why? What's wrong with him, Aaron?"

"Why don't you all have a seat and I'll fill you in as best as I can." Aaron said. "It might be a while before a doctor can give you an update."

"Is he going to be alright?" I asked, sitting next to Aaron.

"I think so." Aaron said. "It's just going to take some time. They were both trapped in their seats. I could tell they had both tried to get out—Owen was worse, there was something impaling him from the seat through his back. We ended up removing the seat from the plane to prevent further damage to his back. They both have severe facial lacerations, but those should be easily cleaned up and possibly some internal injuries."

"Okay, okay. I think I've heard enough." I said, standing up and walking away.

I walked down the hall, looking for the nearest bathroom. I had been crying and walking in a huff and not really watching where I was going, I bumped into someone. I briefly looked up and said, "Excuse me," and kept on walking. I found a bathroom right after that and managed to make it into a stall and close the door before I vomited. As I was leaned over, vomiting, I could not help but feel a familiar vibe for the person I had run into. I had barely seen their face and could not even recall it now, but I just couldn't shake the feeling that I knew that person. I was leaning over vomiting again when heard the bathroom door opened. I could hear two women come into the bathroom; it was not long, and I realized that one of them was Eide. She was checking under the stalls for me. Finally, I was able to talk. "Yes, I'm in here."

"Oh, good, Darren thought you'd gone to the bathroom, but we didn't know which one."

"Are you still sick?" Mom asked.

I could not answer; I was vomiting again.

"Take that as a yes." Eide said. "We'll wait for you. Do you need anything?"

Seriously, I thought. *I'm slumped over this nasty toilet. The only thing I want, is to see Owen.*

I got up and went out of the stall feeling like this wave had passed. Tears were streaking down my face; and I felt as though I have not slept in several days.

"Guys, I'm fine. Don't look at me that way."

"You're not fine and you don't look fine." Eide said.

"I know." I said, throwing away the paper towels I had used to dry my hands. "Owen's in surgery, I haven't seen him in five days, and I don't know if he's going to be okay."

"I know all that." Eide said. "What about that?" Eide asked, referencing the stall from which I had just come.

"Let's go back out and see if there's any word about Owen." I said, ignoring Eide's questioning.

When we got back to the waiting room all the guys seated as I had left them, talking in murmured voices. When they noticed I had returned they fell silent and looked up at me.

"How ya doing, kiddo?" Dad asked, looking at me intently.

"I'm fine, any word on Owen?"

"No." Dad said, shaking his head. "They'll be out soon."

"It's okay." Eide said, picking Toby up from Levi. "Come over here and take a seat."

I turned away and started to feel tears welling in my eyes. I went and sat in the row of chairs Eide pointed out. I watched her play with Toby and leaned my head back against the wall.

As I sat there, I noticed Joe come back into the waiting room he slipped his cell phone into his pocket. I hope he had been talking to Rosie. Poor woman, at home all day with no word. It was bad enough being out in the field. But then, they finally found Owen, and everything moved so fast and there was no cell service until we got to Denver. I finally decided to get up and talk to Joe; I wanted to see how Rosie was doing.

"Where ya going?" Eide asked. I ignored her and kept on walking.

"Joe." I said, walking up to him. "How's Rosie? I figured you just got done talking to her."

"I did, she's relieved to hear that Owen's been found, obviously. She'd like to be here with everyone, especially when he gets out of surgery, but she knows it's best that she be home with the grandkids."

"Oh, Joe, this is awful." I said, tearfully.

"I know." Joe said, putting his arm around me. "Rene and Riley have been there with her today; they baked Christmas cookies with the grandkids. Luke attempted to eat about every ingredient they added to the bowl. Erving stopped in a few times to see if there was any word."

"Oh goodness—Luke, you're a character." I sat there beside Joe awhile longer visiting with him. This man was as strong as Owen, I took comfort in the wisdom he's shared with me. I got up, returning to the other side of the waiting room with Eide and Mom.

"What was that all about?" Eide asked after I had returned from talking with Joe.

"I noticed that Joe had been on the phone, and I got to thinking about Rosie. I figured Joe just got off the phone with her."

"How is Rosie?" Mom asked. "I should go call her."

"Well, I think she's doing okay. She would like to be here with us. I do not think anyone ever thought we would end up here when we left this morning. It all just happened so fast, today. But really, I mean, what was I thinking being stuck out there for five days. What were we going to do—go home and get ready for Lane and Molly's wedding? Oh no." I stopped mid-sentence. "We need to be helping them get ready, I nearly forgot." I said, crying again.

Chapter 23

"Lane, can we talk somewhere?" Molly was shouting when he answered the phone.

"Woah, calm down there, Molls. Put the water works away. Of course, we can always talk. Where you at?"

"I'm outside. Where you at?"

"Your brother and I are getting some tables."

"Can you come out here?" Molly asked.

"Yes, I'm headed that way. Are you out front or—"

"No." Molly fired back, cutting him off mid-sentence. "I'm out back by my car. Trying to decide if I want to stay here or get in my car and drive off."

"If you're driving off, wait for me." Lane said and he took off running, leaving her brother standing at the other end of a table. "Just hang on, I'll be right there."

"Molls, what's going on?" I asked as I approached her. She was standing beside her car, looking terribly upset.

"This is not what I signed up for. This has turned into such a gala affair. My mother has not listened to a single thing I have told her we wanted. And now, she just snapped at some waiter because the water glasses didn't shine enough—is that not ridiculous? Why didn't I listen to you every time you joked about eloping? I have had this picture of a simple Christmas Eve wedding with our families. Now she has half of Denver coming, including the mayor; for all I know she may be getting the queen to come, too."

"Oh, no, I draw the line there. I'm not fancy enough for the queen." Lane said, dramatically.

"Lane, can we get out of here?" Molly asked, smiling at my joke.

"You mean you want to leave campus? This sounds illegal. Do you intend to tell the house mother?"

"No. Let's just go see your family. At least they're normal."

"My family, normal?" Lane asked laughing, hysterically. "Have you met Levi?"

"Oh, stop it," Molly said chuckling, slapping his chest playfully. "Come on, get in the car."

I ran around to the other side of Molly's car and jumped in the passenger seat beside her as she started it. We should have met your sister at the hospital as soon she landed." Molly said as she pulled out of the parking lot. "We should also re-think this whole wedding business, anyways."

"Whoa, hold the phone there, Molls."

"No, no I'm not talking about calling it quits on you. I am talking about the wedding my mother is trying to put together back there; we should just elope and not tell her until we are married. Do you think we still have time?" Molly asked.

"Your mother would kill us."

"What about the sweet, simple Christmas Eve wedding we talked about? I'm sure we can find a church on Christmas Eve that has lights."

"You know that's tomorrow, Molly."

"We'll figure something out, let's go to the hospital now. Has Levi texted you recently?"

"Just a couple times, said Owen's still in surgery and Karla's been sick."

While Molly was parking in the hospital parking garage, she missed a call. "I'm guessing she's figured out we left." Molly said as we got out of the car.

I could hear Molly's mom, and the phone wasn't even on speaker, when Molly returned the call. "Is she really mad?" Lane whispered to Molly.

"Yes, we left." Molly told her mom.

"We're walking into the hospital, now." Molly said, shaking her head towards me.

"No, we don't have an update yet."

"Well, we don't know what we're doing about the wedding; we were talking about changing our plans on the drive over."

"Well, yes. I know it's short notice, but the way things are going with this wedding, can we just talk about this later?"

"Well, Mom."

"Mom." Molly was trying to get a word in edgewise, but her mom just kept at her about the wedding.

"Mom, I need to go. Mom, I'm hanging up now. Thanks for calling. Bye, Mom." Molly said and then clicked the off button on the phone.

"Did you just hang up on your mom?" Lane asked.

"Well, kinda. I did tell her I needed to go, and I thanked her for calling. This is what it's been like for weeks. Every time we discuss something I end up feeling like I'm doing something wrong planning our wedding."

"Now she's telling me we can't very well change things around at this short of notice. The reception halls paid for, the caterer is all paid, a whole litany. I really don't care about all that. Do you even know where we're going?" Molly asked as we walked down the hall towards the elevator.

"Yea, I texted Levi while you were getting the litany riot from your mom."

"Oh, sure, mock now." Molly said as we exited the elevator and looked down the hall to see everyone sitting in a large waiting room.

"Hello, everyone." Lane said, surprising us all, then he leaned down in front of me and hugged me. "Hey, Kar. Are you okay?"

"Lane, Molly. What are you guys doing here? I just asked these guys if we needed to be helping you with the wedding details."

"We sort of just put our wedding on simmer." Molly said.

"No." I said. "You guys can't change your wedding plans for Owen, he wouldn't want that."

"Well, you've heard of a bridezilla, well we got us a motherzilla-of-the-bride production going on across town." Lane said, joking. "We took us a little break and talked about some things on the drive over."

"Lane!" Mom scolded. "Don't say that. Molly's mother's wonderful."

"She is wonderful." Molly said. "She's just gone a little overboard with our wedding and Lane and I've decided to take a different route. But we can discuss that later; is there any word on Owen?"

"No." I said. "He's been in surgery going on five hours. Molly, can you use your pull and find anything out, please?"

"Sorry, hon, this isn't my hospital." Molly said, patting my shoulder. "I don't even know anybody here. I'm sure they'll be out with an update soon."

"What do you guys need done for the wedding?" Dad asked.

"Hey, Dad." Lane said. "We were just telling Mom, we've kinda put the wedding on simmer for now. Molly just had a visit with her mom after we left the reception hall unexpectedly."

"Uh oh." Dad said, lifting his eyebrows with a surprised look. "Is there still a wedding tomorrow night?"

"Yes. Somewhere." Molly said. "We just need to figure it out and then keep the news from motherzilla of the bride, as Lane just dubbed her."

"Molly, you guys, it can't be that bad." Mom said.

"About an hour ago she snapped at a waiter because he didn't have the water glasses shinning enough. So, yes, it's bad." Molly said, getting interrupted when someone called for the Owen Kaster family.

Chapter 24

"Excuse me, is this the Owen Kaster family?" a tall man in a white jacket asked again as he came further into the waiting room.

"Yes, yes." I said, standing up, nearly tripping over Lane. "I'm his wife. Is he all right?"

"Hi, I'm Dr. Vark. I'm the primary on his case. I see you've got quite a gathering going on out here." The doctor said, looking around.

"We're all family. How's Owen?" I asked impatiently.

"Well, he's had multiple injuries we've needed to tend to, the number one being he sustained a crushed pelvis. Once we removed the plane seat and piece of iron that had impaled his back; he went into hemorrhagic shock and then we found an unstable right hip and a tibial fracture, so we had to place him in a pelvic binder. He is going to need a lot of rehab and possibly another surgery to repair some internal pelvic injuries. We won't know if that's needed for a month or two; probably after he goes through some rehab and starts the process of walking again. We had to remove his spleen, make a repair to his liver. His face has many contusions and lacerations. Does anyone have any questions? I know I just threw a lot at you."

"Walking?" I asked. "Is he going to be able to walk?"

"Yes." Dr. Vark said. "We'll have him up and walking soon; it will be imperative to his recovery process. This will be a lengthy recovery process, ma'am, I'm sorry to say."

"Oh gosh." I said, holding my head. "I'm not going to pretend to understand anything you just said. I just want to know when I can see him?" I asked.

"He's going to be heavily sedated for quite a while, possibly through tomorrow. I would suggest going home get some sleep tonight and come back tomorrow. But even then, I gotta tell ya, I cannot allow you all to visit him, yet"

"I can't see him tonight?"

"No, ma'am. I'm afraid not, we are keeping him in the ICU for observation. I will have someone update you later. You can leave your name and number at the desk." The doctor disappeared behind a door as quickly as he had appeared moments before.

"This just keeps getting worse." I said, sitting back in my chair and putting my head between my legs.

"Hey." Eide said, rubbing my back. "Everything going to be fine."

"You tell me how you'd feel if you hadn't seen or heard from your husband in five days." I snapped back at Eide, before getting up and rushing away.

I'd been in the bathroom for a while and was feeling a little better when Mom came in. "I was just about to wash up." I said coming out of the stall, meeting her.

"How are you feeling?"

"I'm fine, Mom."

"Joe and Ty and the others are flying back to West Creek tonight and returning tomorrow."

"What? Well, they can, I'm not going anywhere." I said, walking towards the row of sinks. "This is the closest I've been to Owen in a week; I'm not leaving him."

"I understand that I really do, but I think you should go with them."

Mom and I stepped out of the bathroom; everyone was standing there waiting for us. Joe told me about their plans to fly home.

"No, thanks anyways. I want to stay here."

"Karla, you're going." Ty said abruptly. I have never heard Ty talk like that to me or anyone else, for that matter. He was not rude; he was just getting his point across. I think we were all a little stunned.

"Okay, Ty."

"Ty's right, go home and regroup. Your mom and I will stay here; we'll stay here all night if you want us to." Dad said, hugging me. I could not speak anymore, tears were coming down my face in a wet, sloppy mess.

"Come on." Ty said.

Chapter 25

"Hey Mags, Magpie. Where you at? Come in here—you gotta see this."

Oh please, Ollie, I wish you would really give up these nicknames, I thought. You know my name but refuse to use it.

"What Ollie, I'm trying to get ready for work, I have a night shift; what are you watching?"

"The news; they found that plane that went down several days ago. You've gotta see this guy."

"Oh Ollie, please stop. I know where you're going with this, but you've got to stop this." I said, sitting on the couch next to him to tie my shoes.

"I'm serious." Ollie said, gesturing to the TV. "Look at the older gentleman standing by the white pickup."

"This guy isn't my family." I said, pointing to the television, "And neither are the 400 other people you've shown me."

"But, Mags, look—" Ollie took my hand, caressing my fingers. "You share the same jawline as the older gentleman. And if the camera would just move down a bit, I would venture to say the younger guy also has the same jawline."

"Aarrgh! Knock it off, Ollie. I'm going to be late for work. There's a load of towels in the dryer; you want to help me out, why don't you fold them for me." I mentioned as I grabbed my jacket before heading out the door.

"Mags, I'm sorry, I just care." Ollie said, rushing over to meet me at the door.

"I know you're sorry; just give it up finally. I'm going to church tomorrow evening for the Christmas Eve services. Do you think you can make it?"

"Yes, I'm going to try." Ollie said. "It's our big Christmas day at the stables tomorrow afternoon; you know all the kids come out; but yeah, we should be done in time, I'll meet you there." Ollie leaned in for a brief kiss before I left. "Goodbye, have a good night."

"Good night, Ollie."

That evening, Ty was taxiing us into the Flight School hangar. I had yet to see Owen; it had been five whole days. *But at least now I knew where he was,* I thought, looking out the window I saw two women standing around the vehicles parked out front. It looked like a strange situation; one looked like an older lady and the other lady was quite a bit younger, way younger. Younger than me and extremely pregnant. Ty did his final shutdown and told us we were all able to disembark the plane when he quickly left before the rest of us stepped down from the plane. Ty must have seen the odd situation as he taxied into the airfield behind the Flight School.

"Hello, can I help you?" Ty asked.

"Hi, I'm Chelsea. I talked to a Ty that works here a few nights ago."

"Yea, I'm Ty. How can I help you?"

"Everything okay, Ty?" Joe asked as he and I walked up beside him.

"Well, I'm not sure." Ty said. "You were saying, ma'am."

"We're looking for my boyfriend, Matt. I've been trying to call here but nobody answers."

"Oh, no." Ty said. "I'm sorry I never called you back. We have been looking and today we found them outside Telluride. They were flown to Denver, but I do not know about Matt's condition. We're all headed back tomorrow; you can fly back with us, if you like."

"Really?" Chelsea said. "Thank you—the only car we have is Matt's and it's been down here."

"Sure." Ty said. "We hadn't discussed a time to meet, yet."

"Six a.m." I said, interrupting Ty.

"You heard the lady." Ty said. "Be here at six."

"We'll be here, thank you." Chelsea said as she and the older lady got in Matt's car and left.

"Thank you, Ty." I said hugging him.

"Karla, you can stay with Rosie and me tonight, if you'd like." Joe offered as he drove away from the Flight School.

"No, really. I'm good. I do have things to get ready. When I get back, I'm staying with Owen for the long haul."

"I know you will, just be sure and take care of yourself, too." Joe said.

Joe pulled into the driveway at Owen and my home, and I felt deflated again. I left home this morning, which felt like a hundred hours ago; I think a little piece of me thought we would be bringing Owen home with us. I do not know why I really thought that would be a likely scenario, for as long as he'd been gone. Joe put his pickup in park and turned to look at me.

"Owen is going to be okay, and he will get home again. God will bring us through this." Joe said, taking my hand. "Heavenly Father, I pray for this special young woman sitting here. Speak to her tonight, give her comfort and peace tonight and in the days ahead. Help her to keep looking to you through prayer and your word. Cover her with your grace and be near her as she and Owen go through this challenging season. In your name we pray. Amen."

"Joe, that was wonderful. Thank you." I said, hugging him.

"Don't thank me, thank our Holy Father, our guiding light. Rosie and I'll pick you up about five-thirty; unless you decided you want to stay with us?"

"No, I'll be fine. I'll see you in the morning. Thanks for the ride." I said, sliding out of Joe's pickup.

I walked up on the porch and watched Joe drive down the driveway. I looked up at the crisp, cold dark skies. At least Owen was out of the cold tonight. I came in the kitchen, setting my things on the table. There was a small box with a note there waiting for me.

I stopped to look at it. The card said, "To Aunt Karla, to cheer you up. Love, Luke and Caity," written in the reddest crayon around. *Oh, Rosie*, I thought as I looked in the box to find several decorated Christmas cookies. *Rosie, with all you have going on and watching two little ones; you still bring me a box of cookies.* I sat down and looked at the card the kids had drawn for me. *Oh, Owen you're going to love this.* I got up and made some coffee. I poured my coffee and slipped on the jacket I had left hanging on the chair. I sat down and continued looking at the card that Luke and Caity drew. I picked out a cookie and started eating it.

I sat there eating the cookie and put my feet up on the chair, thinking about the last few days. This was not how Owen and I had planned to spend them. I pulled the jacket around me, hugging myself after I had finished the cookie. I grabbed my coffee and decided to go take a hot shower. I slipped my hand in the jacket pocket and noticed the picture I had found a few days ago.

I pulled the picture out, looking at it. *Why did she look so much like Owen?*

I set the picture on my dresser and headed for the shower.

I was sitting at the table early the next morning, drinking a cup of coffee, studying the picture I had come across in the barn. Joe lightly tapped at the kitchen door and came in.

"Joe, good morning." I said, surprised. "I'm sorry, I didn't hear you drive up, I was going to meet you out front." Standing up from the table, I dropped the photo in my purse and moved toward the door to gather my things.

"That's okay. Can I get your bags for you?"

"Sure. I have the two by the door. I didn't really know what to take."

"Yea, I know, Rosie said the same thing. Are you ready to go?" Joe asked.

"I am. Do you and Rosie want some coffee? I have some left."

"No, that's okay." Joe said, picking up my bags. "She made some."

I turned out the lights and closed the door behind us and we went out to the pickup.

I opened the backseat to find Luke and Caity sitting half-asleep in the backseat as I slid in beside them. I don't think they even realized I got in. "Good morning, Rosie." I whispered as I leaned up beside her.

"Hi honey, how are you?"

"I'm fine, how are you?"

"Oh, okay." Rosie sighed.

"You all settled?" Joe asked when he got in from putting my bags in the back.

"Good to go. Thanks, Joe."

"I didn't think about it, but it makes sense that Luke and Caity would have stayed the night with you last night."

"Yes, it was a joy to have them around yesterday, kept me busy all day. Luke and his many antics—Caity, too. Rene and Riley are going to drive up later today and lend a hand; they enjoy spending time with the kids and then we can all be together. They stayed with us all day yesterday—Luke and Riley, those two. I think Riley had just as much fun."

I could see that Ty had the plane out and was working on preflight checks when Joe parked at the Flight School. Max and Elaine pulled in beside us and went around and looked in on Luke and Caity, who looked to be completely zonked-out.

"Maybe we can get them on the plane without waking them." Max said, picking Caity up.

"I'll get Luke." Joe said. "We'll make it quick; looks like Ty has it all warmed-up."

"It is all warmed-up." Ty said. "Do you want help with luggage or, uh, little people?"

"We got these two." Max said.

"Okay." Ty said. "I'll see about your luggage."

"Good morning, ladies." Ty said he joined us the at back of the vehicles. "Let me get the luggage, you can go join Rach on the plane."

"Thanks, Ty." Elaine said. "I've got these bags, they're particularly important for tomorrow tonight. I can't lose track of them, if you catch my drift."

"I read you loud and clear. Just put them in the overhead compartment."

"You need help, Karla?"

"No, thanks, Ty. I just have these two. I can get them."

"Are you feeling alright?"

"Yea," I said, brushing the hair out of my face. "Did Matt's family get here?"

"No. Chelsea called last night and left a message in the office, she said she didn't want to wait until this morning; they decided to drive up last night."

"They drove all night, in her condition?"

"I guess." Ty said motioning for us to board the plane.

When we returned to the hospital that morning, we found my parents sleeping in the same waiting room as we had left them last night.

"Mom, Dad." I said, shaking their shoulders. "Has there been any word on Owen?"

"Yes." Mom said. "Another doctor, a Dr. Carviour, I think. He came out a few hours ago and said Owen was stable and they were going to start decreasing the sedation. He said he'd give another update before the end of his shift."

"We might have missed him." Dad said, looking at his watch. "I'm guessing shift turnover has already occurred."

"Well, I'm going to find someone; I don't want to just sit here idly by like I did yesterday. I want to see Owen." I said, walking off.

"Hold on, Karla." Ty said.

"I don't want to hold on." I said, in tears, and kept on walking down the hall. Ty caught up to me and grabbed my arm.

"Karla, wait a minute." Ty said.

"What, Ty. I just want to see Owen. Is that so much to ask?"

"No, I just don't want you going in alone. If they let you in."

"What do you mean if they let me?"

"Come on." Ty said. "Let's find someone to talk to."

We walked up to the nurse's station and Ty said we'd like an update on Owen Kaster.

The nurse at the desk flipped through some paperwork and made some clicks on her computer.

"Are you family?" she asked.

"I'm his wife."

"Okay, I'll see if Dr. Carviour has time to speak with you before he leaves. If you want to have a seat in the waiting room …"

"Can I see him?" I asked interrupting the nurse before she left the desk.

"You'll have to ask the doctor that, the patient's in restricted ICU."

"Do you know how long it's been since I've seen my husband?" I said, holding my head, leaning my elbows on the counter. I could feel tears welling up in the corners of my eyes and making an escape.

"Come on." Ty said, putting his arm on my shoulder guiding me away from the desk.

Ty and I started walking away from the nurse's station. "Ty, I need a restroom. I'll be back." I took off, nearly running down the hall.

I could tell Ty was trying to keep up with me but did not follow me when we got to the bathroom door.

When I came out, I was surprised to see Ty waiting for me at the door.

"You didn't have to wait for me" I said to a stunned-looking Ty.

"Sure, I did. I could tell before we boarded the plane you didn't feel well. Owen told me awhile back you didn't feel well—is there anything I can do?"

"No, Ty, it's nothing. I'm sorry to be a bother."

"Karla, you're not a bother. Let me know if there's anything I can do, okay?"

We walked down the hallway to find a man in a white coat heading towards the waiting room; *oh, please, God, let him tell us something about Owen.*

"I'm looking for Mrs. Kaster." The man announced.

"Yes," I said, walking up beside him. "That's me."

"Hi, I'm Dr. Carviour. I'm sorry I have not been out with an update before now. It's been busy in the unit and I'm the only doc back there, so take pity on me." The doctor said chuckling. "Owen is stable, we're continuing to decrease the sedation. We've been having some trouble with his blood pressure, though."

"Can I see him?" I asked. interrupting the doctor.

"Well—"

"Look, doctor." I said, interrupting him again. "I haven't seen him, well, for six days now."

"You have to understand he doesn't look good, probably not like your husband at all, and he's still slightly sedated."

"That's fine, I just want to see him, be near him." I said, getting teary-eyed again.

"Okay, I'll tell the nurse. I'm allowing you five minutes now."

"Doctor." Ty said, catching the him before he left. "I'd like someone to go with her. She's been through a lot, and I don't want her to see Owe alone; so, either Joe, Darren or I go with her."

"That'll be fine, I'll update the nurse." The doctor said, leaving the waiting room.

"Ty, I'd like to go with Karla, if you don't mind." Joe mentioned as we all stood there in the doctor's wake.

"Of course, Joe. I just think it's best for her not to be alone."

"Ty, I'm right here and certainly not a child."

Joe and I went down the hall to the nurse's station where I once again met up with the same woman I had snapped at a while ago. "Hi," I said meekly. "I was told we could see Owen Kaster."

"Yes, follow me."

The nurse escorted us to a small room and gave us both a microfiber suit to put on. Joe and I quickly put them on and followed the nurse through large double doors. This was getting scarier by the minute; six days without Owen and now I had to dress up like the chief of the local hazmat crew. *Owen, we have so much to discuss when you join the real world again. Seriously, a hazmat suit, like I was going to contaminate my husband.* Joe and I walked along past several ICU rooms, each one looking worse than the other, until the nurse stopped and turned back to Joe and me.

"The doctor has permitted you five minutes." The nurse slid the large glass door open. "I'll be back then." She closed the door behind us as we stepped inside Owen's room.

I looked at the person lying in the bed. "This was supposed to be Owen." I cried. This did not even look like him, just like the doctor had said. I walked up closer to the bed.

"Karla, you, okay?" Joe whispered to me.

"Yes." I said, crying as I picked up Owen's hand. I looked at his hand, studying each finger. I stopped at his ring finger. Owen was so badly hurt; I could not recognize him besides the ring I had given him just three short months ago. *It was a beautiful ceremony with you and Arnold standing by my side.* "Oh, Owen." I pleaded. "Please be okay." I whispered.

Joe took Owen's other hand and reached across his lap, holding out his hand for me to take.

"Our Father, Lord in heaven." Joe said. "We need you to strengthen our faith and help at this very moment. Care for Owen as you have cared for us all; see him through this season and heal his body, soul, and spirit so that we may rejoice in your grace and blessings and enjoy the fullness of your presence in life to come. Amid our frustrations, give us patience to see your wisdom. In your name we pray. Amen."

"Amen." I brushed a light kiss across his hand before replacing it along his side. I noticed the nurse had returned, but she had not said anything, yet. I leaned down beside Owen's ear and whispered to him. "I love you, Owen, please be okay. I'll be back to visit later."

Joe and I turned and noticed the nurse still watching us as we started moving away from Owen's bed. We followed her out of the unit to the changing room to remove the hazmat suits.

"Thank you." I told her when we left the changing room.

"Of course. Dr. Carviour is off duty now. But he left a note for Dr. Vark that if this visit went well and your husband continued to do well you could have another visit later."

"Thank you so much." I said, giddily. "Should I come to the desk, or when can I see him again?"

"I'll come out and get you when it's a suitable time."

We barely got to the front counter where we originally met the nurse, and I felt nauseous again. "Joe, I'm going to the restroom." I said, quickly taking off and holding my mouth.

As I hurried down the hall, I saw Lane and Molly along with Levi and Eide carrying Toby coming from the opposite direction. I just waved and kept on going.

"You don't look good, Kar." Lane said as I passed him.

I finished in the restroom and came out to find them all standing in the hallway waiting for me.

"Hi," I said as I stepped out of the door.

"Hey yourself." Lane said. "Come sit down, we're going to talk. You need a doctor yourself."

"No, I don't, I'm fine."

"Kar, you're doing no one any good, now come on."

"Lane, no. I don't want to leave again, I left last night, and I just got to see Owen and I get to see him again later. I don't want to leave."

"And you don't want to be in the bathroom throwing up, either." Lane said. "Molly made you an appointment."

"Molly! You don't even know the doctor I want to see."

"Actually, yes, I do. So, let's go." Molly said.

"Come on, Kar, I'll take you." Lane said. "We'll be back in an hour."

"Oh fine, I need my purse." I said, about to walk away.

"Here you go, I got it for you." Eide said, hugging me.

"Tell—never mind. You probably already told them what you're doing." I said, grumbling, walking down the hall.

I had finished with the doctor Molly made an appointment with and was checking out. I could see Lane and Molly sitting in the waiting room; Lane looked up expectantly when he heard me thank the receptionist.

"How's everything?" Lane asked when I stepped out into the waiting room.

"Everything's fine. Just as I told you before."

"What'd the doctor say?" Lane asked, looking perplexed.

"Just gave me some information and some prescriptions—can we stop at the pharmacy?"

"That's it? Are you okay?" Lane asked.

"That's it." I said, walking out the door, putting my coat on. "I'd like to hurry."

We got back to the hospital and Eide caught up to me before I had a chance to sit down; she was about as annoying as Lane was. "How was it? How are you?"

"It was fine. I'm fine. I told you I was fine." I sat down, laying my head against the wall, closing my eyes.

"Yea, and you look just fine." Eide said sarcastically.

"Eide, please." I wanted to tell her she needed to mind her own business but was interrupted when Dr. Vark asked for Mrs. Kaster again.

"Yes." I said, standing up to be ready to follow him since the nurse had said I could see Owen again later. I figured this was my chance. "How's Owen?"

"Ah yes, Mrs. Kaster." The doctor said. "Owen is doing well, considering. I am pleased with his progress. We have completely weaned him off the sedation. It can vary for some patients to wake up from prolonged sedation."

"Does anyone have any questions?" the doctor asked, looking around, holding his hands out in a welcoming gesture.

"Yes, I do. Is that tube still down his throat?"

"Yes." the doctor said. "To protect his airway."

"Any other questions?" the doctor asked.

"Yea." Ty spoke up. "It was mentioned earlier there was trouble with his blood pressure. Have you taken care of that?"

"Well, funny thing." The doctor said, chuckling. "We thought it was. Mrs. Kaster and the patient's father visited earlier. I'm told for a while following the visit Owen's blood pressure stabilized."

"Yes, I was told I could visit again later, can I?" I asked, interrupting the doctor.

"Yes, I'll take you back shortly. The nurses noted before I came out here that Owen's blood pressure is starting to elevate again. So yes, apparently your visit did him some good."

"Thank you, God." I whispered. The doctor and I started walking away, I stopped and turned back. "Joe, did you want to come too?"

"No, that's okay, Karla. I think you are okay this time. I'll go next time." Joe said.

I followed the doctor back to the same room to get a hazmat suit like Joe and I used this morning. I quickly suited up again. I had so much to tell Owen, I knew he was not awake to talk to me about it, but still I just wanted to tell him. The doctor and I walked back through the patient area to Owen's room, seeing all the patients and their conditions again. It was just a grim scene walking through here.

We finally came to Owen's room; he did not look that much different. His face looked terrible; I suppose from all the glass hitting on impact and shattering against him. I walked up and took his hand again. The only part of him that I recognized was his hand and his wedding ring. I liked twirling his ring and remembering our wedding day. It was a wonderful day, our day held in the barn at his parents' farm. I noticed the doctor slip in behind me and place a chair beside me.

"Mrs. Kaster." He whispered. "You can stay about ten minutes, okay?"

"Thank you," I said. I felt a few stray tears falling down my cheek. *At least the visits are getting longer.*

"Owen." I whispered to him. "You scare me, come back to me. I have something I want to tell you and it's almost Christmas." I whispered. "This isn't how we intended to spend Christmas. I spent five days wondering what happened to you, wondering if you'd make it back home." I could feel the tears increase their stream down my cheeks. "Our families are here, even Luke and Caity. They are having adventures with Rene and Riley. Your mom was trying to make cookies with them, and Luke was eating the ingredients. She said, 'What one doesn't think of the other does.' They made me the sweetest card. Oh Owen, I love you." I said, kissing his hand as I noticed a nurse waiting near the door.

"I know." I told the nurse.

"I'm sorry." the nurse said. "I'll be back to get you before visiting hours are over."

"Can I bring his mom? She hasn't been back to see him," I asked the nurse as she led me to the changing room.

"Yes, that will be fine, miss. I'll make a note."

I came out of the changing room and immediately needed a bathroom, again. I hustled down the hallway to the bathroom and hit the stall door just in time. I nearly vomited down the side of the toilet bowl. I was hopeful the medicine the doctor prescribed would start working soon. He also said to get some fresh air. The closest thing to fresh air in here was me imagining it when I looked out the window. *Oh, well, I could live with the vomiting a while longer,* I thought as I got up, wiping my mouth with a piece of toilet paper. I went out and rinsed my mouth out and wiped my face off.

I came out of the bathroom and stopped there at the door frame; I could not believe it. I could not believe he was here. What was he doing here? He was the one I had bumped into yesterday; I had forgotten all about that.

He just stared at me, and I stared back in disbelief.

"Garratt." I said when I could actually speak.

"Karla." Garratt said. He looked about as stunned as I felt; his eyes got about as big as tires before he turned and went the opposite direction.

I stood at the door for a moment and stared after him. *What in the world. Did I just imagine him? No way.* I could feel my heart pounding. I walked back to the waiting room and sat off to the side where no one was sitting and thought about this. I leaned my head back and closed my eyes, *no way that was Garratt—what are the odds?*

"Hey, you alright?" Eide asked, nudging my knee. "You look like you've just seen a ghost. How's Owen?"

"Well, I guess it's Owen. I can tell by his wedding ring. It's just something else."

"You feel, okay? You want to talk?"

"No, I'd rather not discuss any of this."

Chapter 26

"Ty, wake up. Ty," I said, shaking his shoulder.
"Hmm. You, okay?"
"Yes. I am fine. Everyone has got to quit asking me that."
"Karla, face it, you're sick and you don't look the best." Ty said. He had not opened his eyes, just sat there with his feet up in another chair, his head resting on the wall behind him.
"Never mind that, just wake up."
"Where's Rach?" Ty asked once he sat up, looking around. "And everyone else for that matter." Ty just sat there rubbing his eyes.
"Rachel, Joe and Rosie, Max and Elaine and the kids went to Rachel's sister's last night. Rachel didn't have the heart to wake you. You looked terribly uncomfortable, but we left you. Rachel said you probably haven't have more than five hours of sleep in the last week. All my family went home. Owen's nurse was out here a little while ago, they are going to change some bandages and when they finish, she is going to come back, and I can see him. I told her you were going with me."
"Really?" Ty asked.
"Yea, so get yourself together, she'll be coming."
"I'll go to the bathroom and wash up and meet you back here in a minute." Ty said, getting up and stretching and walking toward the bathroom. "You sure you're alright?" Ty asked after he was about mid-way across the waiting room.
"Ty, go." I said, frustrated.

"What's up with the zoot suits?" Ty asked after the nurse left the changing room before we could enter the ICU.

"I've decided I'm currently the chief of the local hazmat unit; but anything to see Owen. I don't care. You know the only thing I recognize right now is his hand and his wedding ring."

"Yea, I know, you told us." Ty said as we stepped out of the changing room to wait for the nurse to escort us to Owen's station.

"Geez!" Ty was looking around the unit. "This is depressing. How have you been doing this; coming back here and sometimes alone?" Ty asked when we reached Owen's unit.

"I just go in, take his hand and start talking. It's hard, but I just tell him random things."

"Hey Owen, I'm back. I brought someone new to visit today. Ty's here. Ty, take his hand."

"I'm not taking his hand—Owe and I have never held hands." Ty said, standing back and looking shocked.

"It's Christmas Eve morning, Owen. We were supposed to go to Lane and Molly's wedding tonight. I don't know what they are doing about that; they said yesterday they were changing things up a bit. Remember when Lane kept telling Molly they should just elope. I think Molly wishes she would have taken more stock in that now. I will tell you more about it when you wake up, it's a funny story. Lane actually called Molly's mom, motherzilla of the bride."

"Wait, wait did you just negotiate with him?" Ty spoke up.

"No, why?" I asked confused by Ty's question.

"It sounds like you just withheld a portion of the story, and said you'd tell him the rest when he wakes up. I feel like you are negotiating with him. Hey, no judgment. Whatever it takes."

Ty and I had been sitting with Owen for an hour and the nurse hadn't come back to scoot us out. I was surprised. I wondered if the nurse had lost track of time or if we were just supposed to leave and I didn't realize it. I looked out of the curtain and did not see the doctor or any of the nurses. I sat back down, picking up Owen's hand again, looking at his ring.

I started twirling it, I was probably going to wear the inscription "Faithfully Yours" off.

"Everything all right?" Ty asked, breaking into my thoughts.

"Yes, I guess. Usually, they boot me out of here after about fifteen minutes or so. We have been here about an hour. You know, Ty, I just thought of something."

"What's that?" Ty asked, looking at Owen's battered face.

"Owen hasn't had any coffee in over a week."

"Coffee? Seriously, Karla. You're worried about his coffee intake—Owe, are you listening to this? I'll be sure and notify the waiter on the way out get you a refill."

"I'm serious."

A short while later Dr. Vark came into Owen's station to check on him. Ty and I had stayed there, watching the doctor review the machines connected to Owen. He made a few adjustments and turned to talk to Ty and me. I figured he would tell us we needed to return to the waiting room.

"Good morning, do we need to leave?" I asked the doctor.

"Yes, well, not yet. I told the nurse you could stay longer this morning. Owen's doing well, his blood pressure is stabilizing."

"How are things from his surgery?"

"Well, it'd be good to have him up and moving around at this point following surgery, but I guess he's not quite ready for that." Dr. Vark said. "These things take time; I plan to call for a neuro consult later today, for precaution. Otherwise, he really is doing well, considering."

"You can stay a few more minutes and then I'll send you back out. You can visit again this afternoon. Sound like a plan?" Dr. Vark asked.

"Yes, thank you, doctor. I appreciate the time."

I prayed with Owen and shared some more random, useless information. But I still did not get a reply or any movement from Owen. I would even take a finger movement at this point.

"Owen, we're going to leave now. I will be back later. You could at least move a finger to acknowledge this random useless information I've been feeding you."

Owen laid there, stone still.

"He will." Ty said, reassuring me putting his arm around my back escorting me from Owen's room.

Ty and I returned to the waiting room to find most everyone had returned this morning to wait with us.

"Did you get to see Owen?" Rosie asked. "How's he doing?"

"Yes, Ty and I got to sit with him for over an hour; I was incredibly surprised they didn't kick us out. The doctor said he is doing well; his blood pressure is stabilizing. They're going to call for a neuro consult today."

"What did the doctor say about him not waking up?" Joe asked.

"That's why they're calling for a neuro consult later; but these things take time. In the meantime, I keep feeding him random information when I go back there."

"Yea." Ty said, chuckling. "Like letting everyone know when he'd had his last cup of coffee."

"Well, she's right." Joe said thoughtfully. "Owen's had more cups in a day than I can count since he was a teenager, you know his body's probably in some sort of detox state."

Lane and Molly came in just then overly excited, interrupting our conversation. "Hey guys," Lane said excitedly.

"Woah." Dad said. "What flew up your skirt?"

"We're getting married, at St. Andrew's Cathedral at 47th and Vine at nine o'clock tonight between their evening Mass services." Lane said, still excited. "Molly gets her Christmas Eve wedding with all the lights like she wanted.

"And our reception is at Doc Eye Diner, the one two blocks from here—oddly enough, it's where Lane and I met. We're having cheeseburgers and milkshakes." Molly said just as excitedly as Lane.

"Ohh, neat, a diner." Eide said. "Never been to a wedding reception in a diner before."

"What about your mom, Molly? Everything she did."

"It's okay, Laurel." Molly said, cutting Mom off. "Lane and I talked to her and Dad last night. My dad said most of the people coming will be happy they don't have to be at this shindig anyway. He kept telling her all along not to go to such extravagances."

"So, you're both good?" Mom asked, looking from Molly to Lane and back to Molly.

"Yes. We are fine. Lane even takes back the motherzilla comments. So, you'll all come?" Molly said, looking around. "This includes you, too, Joe and Rosie; you guys have become family."

"Oh, we couldn't impose." Rosie said, brushing her hand away. "Besides, it'll be later."

"We insist." Dad said, patting Rosie on the shoulder. "We're all in this together. You too, Ty, Rachel."

I sat in the church that night looking at all the lights; it truly was beautiful with the lights Molly wanted. *It may be Christmas Eve, but it sure did not feel like it*, I thought, sitting there staring at the lights, listening to "O Holy Night" playing lightly in the distance.

"Hey, kiddo, how are you doing?" Dad asked, sitting in the pew beside me, interrupting my thoughts.

"I'm fine. How are you?"

"Hey, I'm great—this was an easy wedding for me. No long travel days and didn't have to set up a barn. Seriously, though, how are you? I was afraid you weren't going to come. Did you get talk to the doctor after the neuro consult today?"

"Yes, they say Owen is doing well considering all that he's been through and there's no brain damage. Really, no reason for any prolonged comatose. They just keep telling me that these things take time. I can't believe Lane and Molly changed all their wedding plans in less than twenty-four hours; that's crazy."

"This is Lane we're talking about." Dad said. "This doesn't surprise me one bit; and it just tells me that if Molly goes along with this, she's perfect for him."

"Hi Mom." I said when she came up and stood behind Dad.

"What are you two doing seating yourselves?" Mom asked.

"This is an informal wedding. Haven't you figured that out? No escorts. Dad and I were just discussing that. What become of all the plans Molly's mom made for the more extravagant wedding?"

"They called the reception hall and called it all off, told them the groom's side of the family had an emergency we were working through, and the couple was not going to have the wedding there tonight. Her dad told me the staff was probably so relieved they'll probably give them a full refund."

The rest of our families came in and sat in the church and Lane joined the minister at the altar.

I noticed that Joe and Rosie had not come in. I wished they had; Max and Elaine were going to take the kids to a show. But that left Joe and Elaine alone for the evening.

Molly made her way down the aisle. She had such a stunning dress; the beadwork shone off the lights. I think this really was the way she envisioned her wedding: a small, elegant church wedding. Molly and Lane didn't even know most of the people invited to the wedding her mom was planning. There were small trees at the front of the church decorated with little white lights. When she reached Lane, he held out his hand. Made me think of Owen and me getting married in the barn; it was such a wonderful day. *I miss you being by my side, Owen*, I thought as tears streamed down my face.

The minister was talking about cherishing and loving one another. A song played about being nearer, bringing peace. Lane told Molly they were two souls lost without each other, but complete as one. It was a lovely ceremony; I was only getting pieces of it, though. My mind kept wandering, all I could think about was Owen, lying in that hospital bed. *We were supposed to be doing life together. I cannot even recognize you Owen, and you are going to hurt something awful, this is going to be so tough for you. I will be there for you, always.* I thought as the minister continued speaking.

The minister said: "I now pronounce you husband and wife; you may kiss the bride." Lane turned to Molly and dipped her in a steamy, heartfelt kiss. *Owen's kissed me several times like that, holy cow. He's knocked me off my feet,* I thought as I closed my eyes thinking back. I was sitting there, thinking back when Dad nudged my arm. "Come on, kiddo, there's a chocolate milkshake in my future." We walked out of the church as "Angels we Have Heard on High" played. The energy level was high all around.

We stepped out on the sidewalk to get cabs to the diner only to find it snowing. It was a calm, peaceful snow, perfect for Christmas Eve. Everyone was delighted with the snow. I was thinking about the next time I would get to see Owen. But now, I would not get to see him until tomorrow. I looked up into the snow, up at the sky and saw the stars shining bright and almost twinkling. *God, please let Owen be okay. I love him so much.*

The cabs arrived and everyone jumped in to get out of the cold. Ty and I grabbed a cab with my parents. Once we settled into the cab, I called Rosie. "Rosie, we missed you and Joe at the wedding," I said as she answered the phone.

"How was the wedding?"

"It was beautiful, would you come join us at the diner?"

"No, honey. Joe and I are content. We bought some terrible things to eat and Joe's reading from the Bible. You enjoy yourselves and we'll see you tomorrow."

"Are you sure, Rosie? It'd be nice to have you join us."

"We're good, Karla. We'll talk tomorrow, you all have a good night."

"Okay, goodbye Rosie. Tell Joe good night."

"I take it Joe and Rosie's not joining us?" Dad asked when I hit the end button on my phone.

"No, I think they just want to be alone."

As we continued through the streets of Denver, the snow continued falling peacefully over the city, lightly hitting the cab windows. I was looking out the window, seeing some cute Christmas lights and displays.

"I'm really looking forward to this milkshake," Dad said before the taxi arrived at the diner. "I was much more impressed with this ceremony than the big gala affair that Lane kept talking about."

The taxi driver parked in front of the diner, and we all stepped out into the snow again, looking at the diner in its festive state. "Remember the pancakes we used to eat here, Laur?"

"Oh my, I forgot about those pancakes." Mom said. "We might have to come back and get some sometime."

"Well, maybe they're open in the morning." Dad said.

We all walked into the diner and there were tables arranged in the back with little trees decorated in the center. It was cute. As soon as we took our seats, Lane went to the counter and told the guy we were here. The guy at the counter cranked up the Christmas music and the waiters came out and asked what flavor of milkshakes we all wanted. Trays of cheeseburgers and fries started coming out of the kitchen.

We all started talking about the wedding and how nice it was. *"All I Want for Christmas is You"* started playing and Lane got up, taking Molly's hand. Lane escorted her down the center aisle of the diner. I think he was even singing along to the song in karaoke style. Our family had a long-standing tradition of crazy dances at weddings, and I was sad that Owen would be missing this one. The song ended and everyone clapped for them, another song began. Lane and Molly continued dancing in the center of the diner. I think Lane and Molly must have arranged some song selections with the diner; they were perfect for these two.

I sat there watching Lane and Molly dancing, I felt my phone buzzing in my pocket. I looked at the display on my phone, it was almost ten-thirty. I wondered who would be calling me now, I didn't even recognize the number. I decided to step outside and take the call.

"Hello." I said skeptically.
"Hello, is this Mrs. Kaster?" I recognized the voice but was not sure where I knew it from.
"Yes."
"Mrs. Kaster, this is Dr. Carviour. Are you still at the hospital tonight?"
"No, I'm over at the Doc Eye Diner; is something wrong?"
"Could you come back to the hospital tonight?"
"Yes, of course. I'll be right over." I click the end button on my phone. I looked up to see Ty had joined me outside. I stood on the sidewalk in front of the diner in the snow. I was numb, I did not know what to think. *Why did the hospital want me back there now? What was going on with Owen?*

"Karla, you, okay?"
"Ty." I said surprised to see him. "I need to leave."
"Okay, where are we going'?"
"The hospital." I said, stunned. "Owen's doctor asked me to come back."
"Let me get our coats, and we'll go." Ty came back out of the diner and handed me my coat and purse. "I told your dad we were leaving."
"Oh, Ty, you shouldn't have done that." I said as we bolted down the sidewalk.

"Someone needs to know where we went. Did the doctor say what is up—is Owen okay? Is he awake?"

"Ty, I don't know, don't get my hopes up. He just asked if I could come back tonight. I didn't want to take time to ask questions, I just wanted to get going." I said taking off in a slight jog as best as I could in the dress shoes I was wearing, and the sidewalk dusted in snow.

Ty and I rushed down the hall, through the hospital corridors to the elevator bank. We got into the elevator and Ty punched the button for the fourth floor. Ty and I rode up in silence.

The elevator doors finally opened and there he was again. Was I imagining him? I stood there, stunned. Ty turned and looked at me.

"Karla, are you okay?" Ty asked, skeptically looking at Garratt and back at me.

Garratt turned around at the sound of the elevator doors opening and looked at Ty and me.

"Karla, hi." Garratt said nervously. "Can we talk?"

Ty looked at me confused. "No, I can't." I said, getting out the elevator, stepping around Garratt as Ty followed me.

"Karla, what was that all about?" Ty asked while we were waiting to talk to someone at the nurses' station.

"Long story, I'll tell you about it later." I said running my hands through my hair.

"Can I help you?" The nurse asked.

"Yes, I just got a call from Dr. Carviour about Owen Kaster."

"Oh, yes. Are you Mrs. Kaster?" The nurse asked smiling back.

"Yes, and this is Ty."

"Very well, let me get the doctor; he'll be out to speak with you shortly."

Ty and I stood at the desk waiting for the doctor. We seemed to be waiting forever. "What's taking them so long, Ty?" Ty did not answer me nor was I really expecting him to.

"Mrs. Kaster, hello. Sorry for the wait. How are you this evening? I hope I wasn't interrupting anything when I called."

"How's Owen?" I asked, ignoring the doctor's questions.

"Everything's fine. There has been a bit of a change and I thought you'd like to see him again tonight." The doctor said, smiling.

"Yes, of course, what's the change?"

"What kind of change?" Ty asked after no response from the doctor.

"Here's some drapes." the doctor said, handing us our hazmat suits. "We'll discuss it when we get to Owen's room."

Ty and I quickly donned our hazmat gear and followed Dr. Carviour past the stations in the ICU. The doctor had been good to let me see Owen, even letting me stay longer than usual, but this was unusual, almost frightening for him to call me back so late at night. Something must have gone terribly wrong. I felt myself starting to tear up and my heart pounding in my ears. We walked into Owen's station and the doctor pulled the curtain aside for Ty and me to enter.

"Hello again, Owen." The doctor said after we had gotten into his room. He had not done that before.

"Did you take the breathing tube out?" Ty asked.

"Yes." The doctor answered.

"Owen, I brought some people with me this time." Dr. Carviour announced.

"Hmm, what?" Owen said, holding his head. *Was Owen awake?*

"Owen." I said taking his hand, the same hand I had been holding and twirling his ring the last two days. "Owen, it's me, Karla." I said with tears streaming down my face.

"Karla, you need to go to the doctor." Owen said in a raspy voice.

"Oh, Owen." I said through heavy, happy tears. "Thank God." I said, lifting Owen's hand to my heart.

The doctor slid a chair in behind me and I took a seat. "Thank you, how is he?"

"He's very groggy right now; but that will slowly fade over time. We'll keep talking to him and keep his mind active. If things go well the rest of the night, we'll move him out of the ICU and upgrade his status. Do you hear that, Owen? You're moving on from here." The doctor said. "Were kicking you outta here."

"Hmm. Where's here?'" Owen asked, sounding distressed.

"The hospital." I whispered, wiping my tears away.

"Owen." I said, caressing his hand. "I went to Lane and Molly's wedding tonight."

"Wedding." Owen sounded confused.

"Lane and Molly's. They're all still at the reception—they had the reception at a diner with cheeseburgers and milkshakes."

"The Burger Barn?" Owen asked, lying there looking half-asleep.

"I know, we'll get back to the Burger Barn. Hey, Owen, Ty's here."

"Ty."

"Hey, Owe, good to have you back."

"Hmm."

I laid my head beside Owen's shoulder, still holding his hand, looking at his ring, still the only recognizable part of Owen, even his voice was different because of the tube that had been down his throat.

"Karla." Ty leaned down and whispered near my ear. "I'm going to give you guys some time. I'll go out, give Joe and Rosie a call."

Before I could say anything, Owen weakly spoke up. "Thanks, Ty." Ty and I both looked at each other and then back at Owen in shock.

"Yes, Owe. Of course, see you after a bit." Ty said, stepping out of the unit.

"Oh, Owen, Merry Christmas, honey." I said, squeezing hid hand.

Early the next morning, Owen was awake some, sleeping off and on. It scared me when Owen went to sleep the first few times for a lengthy period, but the doctor assured me it was okay, it was imperative to his recovery. I was afraid he was not going wake up again. Owen still was not engaging in much conversation. His doctors had him moved to another floor later that morning. They changed his condition status from serious to critical that he had been in the ICU. To me they still both sounded terrible; but at least I got to see him, and I was not required to don a hazmat suit.

Joe came in and told him about things at home. Ty tried to ask him about what happened that day. Rosie came in and went on and on about how glad she was that he was okay. Max came in and talked about the kids; Rene and Riley were such an immense help keeping the kids occupied. Owen had not been involved in much of the conversations until Max brought up Luke and Caity. Then he came alive and wanted to talk about them.

"Where's Luke and Caity?" Owen asked.

"We've all been camping out at Rachel's sister's apartment." Max told Owen. "We had a small Christmas morning there. It was nice."

"Christmas?" Owen asked. He had not realized it was even Christmas.

"They've been asking about you and now I can tell them you really are okay."

"They made you some drawings." Max said, pointing to the table, picking them up and handing them to Owen.

Owen took the pictures and looked them over. I could see tears streaming down his cheek.

"Do you want me to—"

"No, I'll just keep them." Owen said, interrupting Max's attempt to retrieve the pictures from Owen's lap.

Later that night after Owen's visitors left, I told the doctor I'd only seen him in spurts and fits the last few days, and I was staying by his side. *I had been sleeping in chairs anyway.* I just wanted to be near him. The doctor agreed and the nurse brought me a pillow and blanket. I sat in the chair staring at Owen. I thanked God he had come this far.

It was late at night; I could hear some hospital noises out in the hall. The hall lights spilled under the door to Owen's room. I could hear the machines helping Owen with his injuries. *I hope he's resting comfortably,* I thought as I drifted off to sleep.

I woke up later to hear Owen rustling. I stood up out of the chair and looked at him but since it was dark in the room, I could not really tell whether he was awake or not and certainly did not want to turn on a light, so I just stared at him. I stood there watching him, not sure what to do—until he startled me.

"Karla?" Owen said, distressed.

I still stood there and stared at him in the dark, wondering, *did he just call out to me?*

"Karla?" he said again.

"Yes." I whispered. "Are you okay?"

"I'm just trying to move. Are you staring at me?"

"Well, yes." I said, chuckling. "I heard you and wondered if you were okay. Do you need a light on?"

"Yeah, a little light might help, maybe you can help me, too."

I turned the night light on, which produced a small glow in the room and saw that Owen had twisted himself in the blankets.

"Oh, goodness, honey, no wonder you need to move, this blanket is a mess. Are you cold? Are you in pain?"

"Well, it hurts some to move." Owen said, wincing a little as he turned, and we readjusted his blankets. He relaxed some. "Why don't you lay down here beside me? And talk to me."

"The talking thing I can handle, but I'll sit over here."

"I know you can handle the talking thing but come here. You're not going to hurt me. I managed that on my own."

"Oh, Owen." I said, sitting on the side of his bed and taking his hand. "I've missed you so much."

We were both crying and saddened by my comment.

Chapter 27

We were approaching the new year; Owen was making progress. His doctor had him up walking and he started physical therapy as the doctor told me early on. I could tell that it was rough on him and wearing him out. I was not allowed to go to any physical therapy sessions with him, so I went to get a snack in the cafeteria. It gave me an hour to gather my thoughts. According to my doctor, it would help with the nausea and vomiting. I sat down with my snack and opened the book I had brought down and started reading. Just as I had bit down on the apple, someone tapped my shoulder.

"Excuse me, can I join you?" I looked up from my book, there stood Garratt, staring at me as I stared back. He circled the table, taking a seat across from me.

I followed his moves as he took a seat. I was speechless—*What was this all about?*

"Garratt, uh, hello. What are you doing here?" I asked, finding my voice.

"I'm visiting a friend in the hospital, well was. Are you sick, Karla? I've seen you here a couple times and thought something was wrong. I wanted to talk to you, but then you sort of ran away from me."

"Well, I didn't really run away from you. Well, I did that one night—I was trying to get back to Owen. Garratt, where have you been? You rented my house out to people and I came home and—"

"I know, Karla. I know." Garratt said, interrupting me and looking shameful. "I wanted to tell you why and how sorry I am."

"You wanted to tell me you were sorry." I said as I started to get up. "There were people in my house, Garratt. Someone came in my house one night after I had gone to bed and left before I got up. That could have been dangerous."

"I know. I know, Karla. Please sit down and hear me out."

I stood there looking at Garratt for a moment and then sat back down.

"Thank you, Karla. Remember when we were in Mexico for Levi and Eide's wedding?"

"Yeah, one of your renters kept setting my security alarm off."

"Okay, well not that part." Garratt said. "Levi and Lane were convinced I had a girlfriend. Well, they were partially right. I had met this girl. Only after we met, I learned she was in trouble with drugs, alcohol who knows what else. I was trying to help her, only I didn't know how. She nearly made me go broke. I knew you were out of town all the time, so I thought I'd try an Airbnb thing a few times, just to get caught up."

"Garratt, how could you!"

"I know, I know. It was stupid. Then it got worse."

"I know it got worse—I came home really sick and found a whole family had moved into my house. It was scary." I said nearly yelling at Garratt.

"I'm sorry about that." Garratt said. "The girl found out she was pregnant and after Eide confronted me and then attacked me. I really didn't know what to do. I ended up taking the girl and we left for a while."

"Garratt, why didn't you come talk to us—talk to me? You were always like family to us; we would have helped you. Even from the beginning, we would have helped you get this girl some proper care."

"Where's the girl and the baby now?"

"We had a car accident a couple days ago, and the baby was delivered prematurely. The mother didn't make it."

"Oh, Garratt. I am sorry. The baby? A boy or girl? Are you okay?"

"It's a girl. And yes, I'm fine."

"Garratt, congratulations, you have a little girl."

"No," Garratt said as he fidgeted in his seat. "No, I can't be a father."

"What do you mean, you can't be a father? You are a father." I said raising my voice.

"Karla, you see what I've done with my life. I cannot stay, I just wanted to tell you I am sorry. Really Karla, I am so sorry. Goodbye."

"Garratt, wait, come back," I said as he jumped up from his seat and left the cafeteria. I grabbed my things and tried to follow him, but he was gone.

Did I just have that conversation or am I just exhausted? He can't abandon his baby.

Lost in thought going back to Owen's room. I did not even realize when the elevator stopped on Owen's floor. Finally, the doors opened, and I realized I needed to get off the elevator. Levi and Eide and Lane and Molly were waiting in the hall outside Owen's room when I came down the hallway. I did not see them, and Edie called out to me, but I didn't respond to them.

"Earth to Karla, you look like you just saw a ghost." I looked up and saw them all standing there looking like they were planning another intervention.

"Hey you okay, Kar?" Lane asked. "Owen, okay?"

"He's at PT."

"What's up with you?" Edie asked. "You look like you saw a ghost."

"I might have." I said, sitting down in the waiting room.

"Why, what's up?" Levi asked, sitting beside me.

"Hey all." Ty said, walking up. "Is Owe back from PT? I wanted to talk to him. Woah, Karla, you don't look so good, you all right?"

"That's what we just asked her." Edie said. "She was about to tell us what's up."

"I just had a conversation with Garratt—I think I did. He said he's seen me a few times around here this week and wanted to talk to me."

"Is this the guy we saw the night Owe woke up and you just blew him off?" Ty asked.

"Yes. I forgot about that. I did just blow him off. I was on my way to see Owen."

"You saw that weasel?" Eide asked.

"I think one of you guys should call him."

"No way, he put my wife in danger. He put you in danger, too." Levi said.

"Lane, would you call him?"

"Kar, I don't know. I think Levi's right, maybe we should just leave well enough alone."

"He has a baby upstairs and he's going to abandon her. He was trying to help this girl and that's why he rented my house out. He got this girl pregnant, and they had an accident of some sort, and the girl died and now Garratt's abandoning his baby. He was your best friend, guys. You can't let him do this."

"Woah, woah, Kar. You better rein it in or somebody's gonna put you in a hospital gown. You're exhausted and ranting. You should think about taking a nap."

"Are you sleeping at all?" Molly asked.

"Yes, some. That's not the point."

"Well, I don't think it's enough. You're coming home with one of us tonight." Eide said sternly.

"Guys, I'll be fine. I'm not leaving Owen."

"Would you stop worrying about this guy, Garratt and decide where you're staying tonight? I'll stay with Owe. I want to talk to him anyways." Ty declared.

When Owen returned from PT, I told him I was going home with Eide and Levi for the night and would be back in the morning. I hugged and kissed him as best I could. I could tell it was uncomfortable for him, but he said it was all right. We all said goodbye and Levi drove us back to town to meet Mom and Dad.

After leaving the hospital, we met Mom and Dad for supper. It was nice getting out for a while, but I was still worried about Owen. I called Ty after supper to check on Owen, which helped some. Eide and Levi brought me home with them and Eide suggested a nice hot bath. After the bath, I came out and sat on the guest bed; I grabbed my bag and was about to get my book out but the picture I had found in the barn office fell out. I had forgotten I had thrown it in my bag. I sat there staring at it; this girl looked so much like Owen. *It really made me wonder if Owen had a daughter.* Tears were falling down my cheeks. I wiped them away and laid the picture on my chest. I leaned my head back on the pillow, falling asleep. Later in the night I woke up and heard Toby across the hallway chattering to himself. I got up and went to his room. I picked him up from his crib, sat down in the rocking chair and laid him against my chest and started rocking him. I hummed to him; it was soothing. I could not believe Owen and I were going to be parents soon. I was excited to tell him but just had not found the right time.

"Hey Karla, what are you doing in here?" Eide whispered as she sat down on the floor beside Toby and me.

"Oh, I heard this little guy talking to himself, so I thought I'd come visit with him."

"Yeah, he likes to start talking to himself about this time every morning, we've been just letting him talk it out. Did you get some sleep?"

"Yeah. Actually, I did."

"Good, I'm glad—you needed it. Whatcha got in your hand?"

"What? Oh, this? You'll think it's silly. The other day I was out in the barn and found these old boxes and they had a bunch of stuff in them, some old newspapers, pictures, other stuff. Well, I found this picture of a little girl, and she looks so much like Owen it's almost like it's his daughter."

"What, no way." Eide said sounding flabbergasted. "Owen doesn't have a daughter. He would have told you."

"That's what I keep thinking but look at this picture. Owen and I had so many dates over coffee and had so many chats. Chats about kids, friends, and family. If he had a daughter, where is she?" I said, handing Eide the picture.

"Ah, she's cute." Eide said as she looked at the picture. "You look pretty good holding this little guy. You better hurry up and add to the Grainer grandkid crop or you'll get behind."

"What do you mean 'get behind'? I'm already behind."

"Well further behind." Eide said, looking sly.

"Eide, are you?" I whispered widening my eyes.

"Umm-hmm. We are."

"No way. What are you, a fertile myrtle? Well, at least Toby'll have someone to talk to now."

"Oh Lord, help us now." Eide said laughing.

"Hey Dad, Ma. When did you guys get here?" I asked them after waking up and seeing Ty and them sitting in my hospital room.

"Hey Owen, we've been here an hour or so." Dad said. "Looks like Ty, here's been keeping you company."

"Yeah, Karla went home with Levi or Lane tonight, she hasn't been feeling too well."

"We know. How are you feeling, honey?" Ma asked, taking my hand.

"Oh, it is what it is, Ma." I said, trying to sit up.

"You don't have to sit up if it bothers you."

"It's good for me. I can't lay around forever; the sooner I get up and about the faster I get out of here."

"Well that a good attitude, Owe. Just don't overdo it."

"Have you seen Matt since we got here? How's he doing?"

"Yeah, talked to him a couple days ago. He's okay. He was actually discharged yesterday, I think he's got some, just a sec—" Ty pulled his phone from his pocket. "Seriously, Karla. Yes, he is fine, you haven't even been gone two hours. Okay, I will tell him, see you tomorrow.

"Was that Karla? Is she okay?" I asked Ty when he got off the phone.

"Yea, she's worried about you. Can't say that I blame her beings that you look like you've been through Armageddon. But I told her she needs a night off; she didn't have a particularly good day."

"What do you mean 'She didn't have a very good day'?"

"She's exhausted and needs to sleep in a real bed." Ty said.

"I know, she doesn't look very good."

"You're one to talk. Besides, I wanted to talk to you, so I said I'd stay with you."

"You do, about what?"

"I'm going to leave for a few days."

"Oh, yea, of course. I don't need you sitting around babysitting me, holding my hand."

"Trust me, there's no hand-holding, Karla tried. I'm going to go see Rach tomorrow for New Year's Eve. She went with her sisters to their aunts on Christmas Eve. I want to see her before she goes back to work next week."

"It's probably getting boring around here for you, anyways."

"Well, not so much that; I've had some time to think about things and I've decided—I've decided—" Ty said, stuttering. "I'm going to propose."

"Ty, that's wonderful."

"Thanks, Rosie."

"Yeah, man, that's great. What are you waiting for? Get going."

"Don't worry, you're stuck with me until tomorrow. I told Karla I'd babysit your sorry butt tonight, remember?"

"I always knew you'd cash in at the bank, Ty. It's about time."

"Yep, there's the Owe we all know and love, you must be getting better. That's the most joking I've seen from you in over a week."

Chapter 28

"Good morning, Ty."

"Hey, Karla. Did you have a good night?" Ty asked, sitting up and rubbing his eyes.

"Actually, yes I did. How's was Owen's night?" I asked, sitting down beside Ty in the waiting room.

"You shouldn't sleep in these chairs anymore, they suck." Ty said. "I think Owe had an okay night."

"I know, they're terrible. I'm glad Owen had a good night. Is he still sleeping?"

"I think so, I looked in on him a little while ago and he was."

"That's good, he needs it. Ty, can I ask you something?"

"Sure, anything, what do you need?" Ty asked, turning to look at me and still wiping his eyes.

"Well," I said, digging in my bag. "I just have a question. I don't know, just something niggling in my mind. A few days ago, before we found Owen. I was trying to muck out the stalls and I kept getting sick. Erving came in and had me sit in the barn office; well, there's a couple boxes of miscellaneous items in there. Anyways, I found this picture and the more I look at it, the more I think she looks like Owen," I said, showing the picture to Ty. "Does Owen have a daughter?"

"What? No!" Ty said, almost laughing, looking the picture over. "No."

"But look at the girl, Ty. She looks just like Owen."

"Owe and I are like brothers; I know these things—just ask him."

"What, ask him about the picture?"

"Of course, he'll tell you the same thing I'm telling you now. He doesn't know that girl. If Owe knew that girl I would know that girl. Owe and I have been through everything together; that's why I wanted to talk to Owe when you left yesterday. I'm leaving this morning."

"You are?"

"Yep, I'm going to see Rach. I'm proposing to her tonight."

"Ty. That's awesome. Do you think she suspects anything?"

"Well maybe, we had a romantic night planned the night Owe didn't make it back. I was going to propose in front of the fireplace after we got back from Durango, but we didn't get that far. Thinking back, I think Owe kinda saved me from a lame proposal. She knew I had something planned and I told her I was sorry we didn't get to it."

"Ty this is exciting! So, what do you have planned now that it's New Year's Eve?"

"Hmm, I don't. Nothing definite, anyways. I'm not Owe when it comes to this sort of thing to run out and get $300 worth of sparklers."

"That was pretty awesome, wasn't it—I loved it." Joe and Rosie along with Max and Elaine came walking down the hall with the kids. "I didn't realize they'd be here this early."

"Yeah, they're heading back with me this morning. I'm flying home before I go see Rach. Max and Elaine are wanting to get back for school and Joe and Rosie are going to go home for a few days. They're all just here to say goodbye to Owe this morning before we all take off."

"Yeah, I suppose that makes sense. Ty, we can't thank you enough for everything."

Chapter 29

"Hey, I thought I heard a party going on out here." I said, taking slow, cautious steps toward the waiting room.

"Did we wake you?"

"No, Ma. I've been awake for a little bit."

"How are ya, honey?" Karla asked, standing beside me, hugging me the best we could.

"I'm great. I think this is the earliest I've been up all week. But I am going to take this chair over here and talk to these little people. Luke, Caity you got a hug for me?"

"Um, Dad?" Luke asked looking cautiously at Max.

"Give your uncle a hug, he's missed you." Max said, coaching Luke.

"But what's on his face?"

"He has lots of owies. Just like you got when you wrecked your bike, so just be careful."

"That's my boy." I said as Luke came up to hug me.

"How did you get hurt?" Luke asked timidly.

"I was in an accident. But I'm getting better. I will be home soon, and you can come see Karla and me again and we can play games. How's that sound?"

"Good. I love you, Uncle Owen."

"I love you too, buddy."

"How about you, Caity—you want to hug Uncle Owen before we leave?" Max asked her.

"No." Caity said, shaking her head standing behind Elaine.

"It's okay, Caity. I don't really feel like myself either. How about a high five and a see you later?"

Caity gave me a high five but did not really say anything when I told her I would see her soon and then she went back and stood beside Elaine.

"All right, Kasters, sorry for the rush." Ty said. "But I'm kind of in a hurry today."

"Hey, Ty. Take it easy. She's going to say yes."

"Yes, Owe. I know. But unlike you I don't have an elaborate scene all planned out."

"Hey, I didn't have an elaborate scene, either." I said, taking Karla's hand. "I just sat her down in the back of my pickup and we had a nice talk. Just sit down with Rachel and have a nice chat."

"You don't call $300 worth of sparklers, elaborate?" Ty asked me.

"No, that's just the Fourth of July. You'll be fine, Ty. Call us when you're finally engaged."

"Okay, see you in a couple days," Ty said as they all started walking to the elevator.

"So, what's a couple crazy kids like you two doing for New Year's Eve?"

"Hi, Nurse Adi. You drew the short straw working tonight?"

"Yes, Owen. I'm not really a New Year's Eve celebrator—haven't been in eons. That's a young people's holiday, such as yourselves. I would just fall asleep in my chair anyway. What would you all be doing tonight if you weren't here?"

"Hmm, not sure." Karla said, looking at me with a smirk on her face.

"Oh, I do. I'd have her out on the town—we'd be celebrating, for sure."

"Can I get either of you anything? Owen, do you need any pain medication?"

"No, I'm good, thank you, Nurse Adi."

"Okay, you two kids enjoy your night and holler if you need anything."

"Good night." Karla and I said in unison.

"Come here, you." I said to Karla, holding out my hand.

"I'm good sitting in the chair." Karla said.

"For you, but I can't hold your hand clear over there. So, come over here."

Karla sat on the edge of the bed next to me. "You need something, Owen? Are you sure you don't need some pain medication? I don't remember you getting any after physical therapy today, either."

"Would you just lay down beside me? I'm okay. I just want you near me. What do you mean you do not know what we would be doing if we were not here? We're not a couple of old fogies?"

"No, we're not." Karla said, taking my hand and placing it over her belly. "I've been wanting to tell you something, but it never seemed to be the right time. Now seems to be about the best. Owen, we're about to be parents."

"What? Say that again," I said, looking shocked.

"You know all that time before your accident that I was tired and didn't feel good?"

"Yes, how have you felt now? Ty said you didn't have a very good day yesterday."

"It's okay. Lane and Molly took me to a doctor friend of Molly's a few days ago to confirm my suspicions. We're going to have a baby."

"I knew it. When?"

"Next summer."

"Molly and Elaine recognized what was going on. I think everyone else did too. I have just kept putting them off and said I did not want to talk about it. I wanted to talk to you about it first."

Karla gently kissed me, and I winced.

"Oh goodness, I'm so sorry, Owen," Karla said when she felt me wince. "I shouldn't have done that. There's plenty of time for celebrating."

"No, no." I said, weakly. "I'm glad you did. I will be fine. This is great news. I don't know what to say."

"It's okay, I didn't either, I've been trying to ward off some comments when I was vomiting. It was hilarious. We were out in the field looking for you the other day and I was vomiting, and Elaine caught on. She dubbed hers 'The Kaster Curse.' Then, one morning you were gone I was out in the barn mucking out the stalls, I kept vomiting in the manure cart until Erving came in and made me sit in the barn office. I figured that must have been an awful sight for him."

"Oh, honey, I'm sorry I wasn't there, but the manure cart—that is kinda funny. What were you doing out there, anyway? You should have let my dad do it, or even Erving—he'd want to do it."

"I know, Erving had me go sit in the barn office. There are a couple boxes of odds and ends, like old newspapers, pictures. Owen, do you have a daughter?"

"Well not yet," I said, rubbing Karla's stomach.

"No, I'm serious. I found this picture and every time I look at it, the more I think she looks like you, Owen," Karla said, getting up off the bed.

"Where are you going?"

"I'm just getting my bag. I want to show you this picture." Karla brought her bag back to the bed and pulled out a picture I had seen awhile back. I took the picture from Karla and started studying it. I had completely forgotten about seeing this picture or the fact those boxes were still in the barn office.

"I saw this picture; I don't know who this girl is. I'm sorry you found this picture and thought she was my daughter. You must have been agonizing over it."

"Doesn't she look like you, Owen?"

"Well yes, I guess to some degree. Karla, I would have told you if I had a daughter."

"That's what I kept telling myself. Ty and Eide told me the same thing. But I kept looking at the picture and could not get the thought out of my head. Ty said if you knew this girl, he would know the girl."

"That's absolutely true—and another thing: This girl is like two years old. The style of the picture is not from two years ago; it's more like when we were two years old."

"Oh, my goodness, you're right." Karla said, sounding relieved. "The style of her clothing is almost identical to the style of clothing I had at that age. I don't know why I did not realize that. I can't believe I thought you had a daughter."

"Like I said, not yet honey." I rubbed her belly as we both continued looking at the picture.

"Hey, there could be a Kaster boy in there, as much grief as he's caused me. It tends to run in the family." Karla said, slightly nudging me.

"I'd take that, too."

"What about 'Owen Jr.'?" Karla asked.

"And what, call him 'OJ'? I don't think so, not after a breakfast drink. Come here, you, lay close. We have nine months to figure out names." I said, turning on the tv.

"Oh, honey, look, they're playing *It's a Wonderful Life*. That is such a good movie," Karla said as we lay together.

Made in the USA
Monee, IL
10 March 2023

29340162R00154